Praise for
Straight Up

"Like an expert barista, Lisa Samson takes bits and pieces of her characters' lives and fixes them into a story that is fascinating and profound. Loss can lift you up…or destroy you. *Straight Up* shows both options and then lets you decide. Which will it be? This is one good book!"

—ROXANNE HENKE, author of *After Anne; With Love, Libby;* and other books in the Coming Home to Brewster series

"What if we chose differently in life? *Straight Up* is pure Lisa Samson—original, raw, and laced with grace. As always, Lisa's characters came to life in my imagination, becoming my friends. This book made me cry and also allowed me hope. What a treasure."

—ROBIN LEE HATCHER, best-selling author of *A Carol for Christmas*

"Lisa Samson's writing is an extravagant gift to her readers. I am eternally amazed at the benevolence that spills so generously from her pen. She is not only a compassionate writer but a young poet with an old soul, a woman that uses her writing as a dance in which her readers can revel."

—PATRICIA HICKMAN, author of *Earthly Vows* and *Whisper Town*

"In *Straight Up,* Lisa Samson draws us into the joys and consequences of this free-will thing called choice. It is a story that is at once both tough and tender, with Samson exhibiting unusually keen insight into human nature—the longings of the heart, the failings of the flesh, the need for redemption. A powerful read, too important to miss."

—ANN TATLOCK, awarding-winning author
of *Things We Once Held Dear*

"Lisa Samson is one of my favorite authors. Her characterization is always brilliant, and *Straight Up* is no exception. Samson just keeps getting better and better."

—COLLEEN COBLE, author of *Fire Dancer*

Straight Up

OTHER BOOKS
BY LISA SAMSON

Apples of Gold
Club Sandwich
Tiger Lillie
The Living End
Songbird
Women's Intuition
The Church Ladies
Indigo Waters
Fields of Gold
Crimson Skies

a novel

Straight Up

Lisa Samson

Best-selling author of *The Church Ladies*

WATERBROOK

STRAIGHT UP
PUBLISHED BY WATERBROOK PRESS
12265 Oracle Boulevard, Suite 200
Colorado Springs, Colorado 80921
A division of Random House Inc.

All Scripture quotations or paraphrases are taken from the King James Version.

The characters and events in this book are fictional, and any resemblance to actual persons or events is coincidental.

10-Digit ISBN 1-57856-886-2
13-Digit ISBN 978-1-57856-886-4

Library of Congress Cataloging-in-Publication Data
Samson, Lisa, 1964–
Straight up : a novel / Lisa Samson. — 1st ed.
p. cm.
ISBN-13: 978-1-57856-886-4
ISBN-10: 1-57856-886-2
1. Cousins—Fiction. I. Title.
PS3569.A46673S77 2006
813'.54—dc22

2006013436

Printed in the United States of America
2006—First Edition

10 9 8 7 6 5 4 3 2 1

for Heather
true blue

Acknowledgments

I've never had a book come out of me with greater frustration. So thank-yous abound:

To Claudia Cross, Dudley Delffs, Shannon Hill, Laura Wright, Jeane Wynn, and always, my partner in crime, Erin Healy, who simply makes it so much better!

To my family: Lori, Will, Ty, Jake, and Gwyn.

To my friends: the Carrington Road girls, Leigh, Marty, Claudia B., and B.J.

And to my blog buddies: too many to mention.

Finally, to my readers!

Find me at www.lisasamson.com. I love being in contact with my readers.

Summer 1980

Georgia Ella Bishop sways her narrow, squeaky little hips in time to the jazz music emanating from her mother's piano, carnival spins and whirls of sound twirling in her ears, around her brain, and down to the toes of her red rubber sandals.

Polly Bishop plays without looking, timing her music to her daughter's movements, swaying and smiling, kindred of angels.

Part I

Blue

Georgia

Why are wine velvet curtains, soft carpets, and mellow lighting reserved for the dead? Why do we whisper around them, these people who are the least likely to hear anything we have to say? Even less likely than when they lived and we tried to communicate—dire, quiet pleadings somehow lost in our throats and the airwaves.

He looks good, strangely so, considering his passing.

Odd to say that about a corpse, yes, but my dad is handsome, even in death. His hair shifted years ago to colorless darkness rivered with silver. I watched the transition happen on the cable news channel to which he gave his life, if not his frequent-flyer miles. I have no idea who received those.

Not the gals assembled here.

These women knew him best years and years ago, high-school friends now aging, some of them grandmothers with suedelike skin and clothing ironed into angles. They stand in respectful pumps, feet comfortable in their cocoons of suntan nylon. They skinned their knees with him, failed geometry tests, understood when he became famous and forgot them.

But they're with him in this small funeral home that's buried more people than can be found right now in these humble blocks of Highlandtown. Conkling Street's claim to fame will soon be covered by the earth. Brave, good-looking Gaylen Bishop, intimate with the whole world, come home to Baltimore, back to the neighborhood to end the final journey.

Charm City calling.

They wind their rosaries around knobby hands, fleshy hands, callused hands, and scarred hands, and pray, "Hail, Mary, full of grace, the Lord is with thee: blessed art thou amongst women, and blessed is the fruit of thy womb, Jesus."

They've gone to the beauty parlor for the occasion.

Some men pray as well. Not as many of them, and not with the same gusto, and I wonder how they knew my father. Dad didn't seem like the type of man to carry friendships from decade to decade like that school picture your first child gave you during kindergarten. No. Dad wasn't the type to value childhood friends. Truthfully, he's fortunate any of them came at all. That's what I say. He would have been put off by their plaid pants, clip-on ties, and inexpensive sport coats.

It's a private viewing today. No network bigwigs I haven't the foggiest notion about. And I'm the queen of foggy notions.

The media highly publicized his death. I suppose when you're decapitated in some obscure Iraqi town, you're going to show up on the news. The sutures around his neck hide beneath the collar and tie. I can't bring myself to lower the collar and take a look. The resulting lifelong haunting isn't worth the firsthand knowledge. I have enough hauntings. Like the day my husband, Sean, left.

Dad didn't beg for his life. He knew that culture as well as his own, both equally unbending, and so he appeared on the television screen, blindfolded and sitting more stiffly than a suicide bomber on a crowded bus. He knew he would die. I'm certain of that.

Gaylen's emotions suffered at the hand of his brilliance, though. But then again, do we ever really know our fathers?

The floor lamps guarding the casket shine through opaque, tulip-shaped bowls. Their pinkened light illuminates the mellowing faces of these forgiving souls who came anyway, not so much because they wanted one last brush with Gaylen's fame, but because they never stopped remembering the days when they ate fried codfish cakes at the summer carnival at church and tended the altar at Sacred Heart of Jesus Church. "Holy Mary, Mother of God, pray for us sinners, now, and at the hour of our death. Amen."

Oh, Dad. All those letters. All those cards. Sealed up tight.

"Hail, Mary, full of grace—"

I kept promising I'd read them. How many nights I stared at the box under the bedroom chair…stared and sipped…stared and sipped…hoping somehow that your ink would bleed through onto the cardboard of the white storage box, or that whispers of your contained words would seep into my heart. But they never did.

"Blessed is the fruit of thy—"

I hate the smell of gladiolus and spider mums.

Tomorrow. I just have to make it through to tomorrow.

"Now, and at the hour of our death."

A hand grasps my shoulder, and I know before he speaks who it is. "Uncle Geoffrey."

I turn and melt into my uncle's arms. Mom's baby brother. All the way back from business in Pakistan.

"Georgia, Georgia."

I can't cry. I guess I really didn't know my dad well enough to cry. "Yeah. Unbelievable, huh?"

He smells like journeys and spices and wind. He smells like warmth and tears and sadness. He smells like lonesomeness and smiles. Like goodness and strength. I settle inside his circle. I smell his neck, the crude wooden cross underneath his shirt poking into my cheek.

"You're too young to be an orphan," he says in a whiff of wintergreen.

"I'm thirty-two."

"As I said."

I close my eyes.

The wake ends. The women and the husbands who brought them file out of Lilly & Zeiler's. And the carpet stays clean, and the lighting stays pink, and Gaylen Bishop stays quiet and still, and I hope and pray that my mother was right when she said "We really do go to a better place, Georgia" just before she died.

"Believe that if it makes you feel better," Dad said to me the night after we buried her and he left on assignment for Bangladesh.

"Let's get a cup of coffee, Georgie." Uncle Geoffrey tugs my ponytail.

I tug his. "Right."

Georgia Ella could stare into her mother's eyes for hours if the days were full enough. They snuggle under the puffy quilt for a few minutes more. The bus will be by soon, but there's time to gather the shiny new folders and pencils, pack the lunchbox, and begin a whole new way of life.

"You're a big first grader today," Polly says. "I'm so proud of you!"

"Let's snuggle some more."

So Polly draws her daughter close, enfolding her in sunshine.

Fairly

My mother held her hand up to her mouth as the smoke and ash poured into the sky. The fascinating image that filled up the screen of our television cast my third birthday into the backseat like the coat you needed in the morning but found unnecessary in the warmth of the afternoon. For some reason, I didn't mind this. I watched the news coverage from my miniature rocker, and we ate all our meals that day in the living room off TV trays bearing stylistic pictures of cats.

Mount St. Helens lay in peace for generations, but beneath the quiet crust, another world vibrated and bubbled and eventually swam its way up to the surface only to burst forth like a red-spangled lady from the top of a bachelor-party cake. Without the smile.

That's how I see it, anyway.

Something about volcanoes has fascinated me since that day, which is my earliest memory. Even as a little girl, when my mother and father rigged up one of those curious baking-soda volcanoes in the kitchen, I wished to stand on the edge of one. I wouldn't be frightened. I wouldn't care to jump. I'd simply stand there, feet planted, or sit with my feet dangling over the edge, and I'd think about everything going on beneath my feet. About how I'm a quarter breath away from death, how there're always ten more explosions hidden from the eye, how in one second an eruption can change a person for good.

When they completed Hort's diagnosis, I stood in a flow of lava, desiring total engulfment. Twenty-six years old and widowhood looming ahead of me? And now here I sit at his bedside in our apartment.

I don't blame him for refusing treatment any longer. Enough is most definitely enough, the poor man. How beautiful he is, my older man, my lovely man. I'm only twenty-six, wondering if my life is over, wondering if when he dies I'll ever feel alive again.

He may seem aged compared to me, but fifty-two years old is young to die by anybody's account.

It's a good thing he's asleep. If I voiced these thoughts, he'd probably tell me to hike myself down to ABC and sign on as a writer for *General Hospital.*

My cell phone rings in my handbag, and I swirl my hand down into the contents, feeling for the plastic. I pull it out, scope the number, and press the button. "Uncle Geoffrey?"

"Hi, Fairly. How's our man?"

"Not good."

"I'm sorry. I've got some terrible news to tell you. Are you sitting down?"

"Yes, right here by Hort's bed."

"Your Uncle Gaylen died a couple of days ago."

"Give me just a second."

I can handle only a few seconds of grief. I'm already drowning under Hort's illness. But where to cast some sort of blame for my inadequacies?

"Georgia never called me."

"No. Georgie's in bad shape, Fairly. You can imagine."

Still. I mean, people die all the time, and their families make rounds and rounds of phone calls. "When's the funeral?"

"Tomorrow. I just got in from Pakistan."

"Oh, so she called you."

He chuckles a little. "Fair—"

"Okay, I suppose you're right. It's not like I can leave Hort anyway."

"I know. I'll come up to New York and see you two after I'm done here in Baltimore with your cousin."

"What funeral home?"

"Lilly & Zeiler at Foster and Conkling."

"I know it."

We ring off. I'll have to call the florist. I think about waking Hort, but he sleeps so peacefully without any wires and tubes attached. The crisp sheets smell like mountains and glow golden in the small bedlamp that rests on the nightstand. Outside, somewhere above the lights of the city, stars shine down on us. We just can't see them right now.

Solo stands in the doorway of the bedroom. "I'm about to leave for home, miss. Anything else for tonight?"

"No, Solo, but thanks."

Solo has worked with Hort for ten years on a publication that will never come to fruition now. Something about world literature and God. He came over as a young Congolese refugee, a widower with two small children, and asked for work one day after Hort came home from school. Right there on the steps of the apartment building. Solo's going to school now, and he takes care of us in between his research for Hort. Not for long, though. Once he finishes his master of divinity, he'll be off to much greener pastures than this apartment overlooking the park.

Maybe someday I'll be as wise as this gleaming man.

"I made up some fresh pili-pili for you. There's some leftover chicken in the icebox."

Solo's food somehow waters any bit of hope you have left.

"How is he?" Solo asks.

"Come on in. He's sleeping."

Solo lays a dark hand atop Hort's head. "Yes. Won't be long now."

Solo can tell truth in a way you don't mind.

"Yes." I lift my face toward his. "You'll stay when he goes? Won't you?"

"I will not leave you to be alone, miss."

"Thank you."

"Must go pick up my kids. I'll be here as usual tomorrow. Nine o'clock. Hort must see the work going on."

I cannot hear Solo leave the house, though I try. He moves so quietly and never by accident.

Mary-Margaret
1991

Mary-Margaret cuddled the baby girl, not daring to attach her to her breast. She'd tried to keep from conceiving. They couldn't afford the six already at home.

She had only herself to blame

Frank made himself clear the day their previous child, Barbra, screamed her way into the world. "If you get pregnant again, MM, we'll have no choice but to give the baby up for adoption."

"But Frank, I can't help it. We can't stop making love, you know."

"You're the devout one, not me. I'll use protection anytime you say so."

"You don't love the kids?"

"Of course I do." He sat down at the kitchen table with her as she nursed Barbra, and ran a tender hand over the baby's head. He'd have a million children with MM if he could afford them. He'd made that clear too. "I'm a mechanic."

"I'll get a job."

"How can you with all these kids?"

"They're beautiful, Frank. We make beautiful children."

Frank knew that, of course. With their dark hair and with eyes a color you couldn't put a finger on, the Salatin children threw the everyday features of the neighborhood kids into sharp relief.

Who'd have thought a mechanic and a waitress could create such beauty?

"This has got to be it, MM. We're done."

And that was final.

But now she lay in the hospital bed again, and this time the little baby in her arms wouldn't be coming home.

Georgia

The briny smell of the harbor, usually humid and thick, rarely reaches me up here on the eighteenth floor of my building. My father gave me the condo after Sean left and Dad moved to New York. From my balcony I cannot focus clearly on the foam cups, shoes, bits of paper, plastic drink bottles, or storm debris that accumulate around the edges of the Baltimore Harbor.

But I stand here at my window almost every morning no matter how late I've fallen asleep the night before, and I grasp my mug, holding it against my chest while watching the harbor waters begin to glisten in the city's awakening. Somehow Baltimore is bold enough and tough enough not only to take everything in stride, but to somehow grasp it all to her sagging bosom. The strains of Beethoven's Sonata *Pathetique,* the second movement of course, play inside me…softly at first, then gathering almost enough strength to carry me along in its current.

And then—when the commuter traffic condenses; when the crosswalks resemble swollen, rushing arteries; when I've dry heaved my way into a horrible headache, held down the resulting painkiller while lying under a cool rag; when I can finally face the acidity of the coffee—I retreat to my piano. I sit before the keys, praying that this day, something will come. When nothing does, I turn on a little Ella Fitzgerald, and she comforts me. Godmother of soul. My jazz lady.

Like my mother, I became a musician. She played piano frequently at the Ten O'Clock Club, a place she and her best friend Drea owned together. Artists flowed through that place in a steady stream like warmed butterscotch over ice cream. My father was on assignment most of the time, and Mom liked it that way. "A little Gaylen goes a long way," she always said, and she'd laugh at her own joke, tossing back her dark waves and winking at me.

The cool factor of life growing up in a jazz club exceeded anything else I could imagine. I didn't miss swim lessons or cookouts on the patio. I was relieved not to have sleepovers or large birthday parties at the bowling alleys: bulky groups of children, strident voices shrieking, feet pounding the carpet, and mayhem spattering the air with discordant drops of sound created a rhythm in which I found no place to sway. Marching-band stuff.

For sitting atop the big Steinway at the club, I grew, pressing my ear to the cool surface, feeling the shiny black lacquer heat up beneath my head as I listened to the inner soul of Mom's playing. It went down inside of me somehow, and when I started to press the keys myself, it wasn't long before my progress was noted as something approaching exceptional.

Not my words, there.

"Georgie, come on down from there and sit beside me," Mom would say after a while. And we'd park on that bench as though sewn together by two invisible threads, hip to hip, shoulder to shoulder, while she taught me chords, simple chords at first. "Start with the root." She touched a note. C.

I played the C an octave higher.

"Now, count four keys up." She touched her index finger on each key, black and white, and ended on an E. "And five keys down." She landed on a G. "Now play all three together and that, my dear, is a C chord."

"How about a D?" I asked. I think I was five.

"Same principle, four up and five down. See if you can figure it out."

After about ten minutes, I was off. Finding simple chords all over the place. She taught me how to find minors and sevens and nines and elevens and wonderful progressions that utilized them all.

Polly Bishop gave me my life in more ways than one.

The musicians at the club picked up where Mom left off, eagerly imparting their secrets after she died. I was young, posed no threat, and perhaps in me their genius might live on in some measure of obscurity incapable of eclipsing their singular glories, their whimsical, powerful styles. I am an amalgam, an assemblage of other people, a winsome Frankenstein capable of groove, of cool, and while those who heard my jazz back in my high-school days said I had a style all my own, I knew down inside I'd never come up with anything truly original even if I lived three lifetimes. Not if I compared myself to my mother.

I adopted Ella Fitzgerald as my replacement mother later that year. She could take a rainy day, roll it around her vocal cords, and sing out sunshine anytime she wanted.

I chose to study classical music in college, the organ my preferred instrument. Who can compete with the likes of the jazz greats? My uncle Geoffrey suggested it when I played Bach on the piano at the club the day after my high-school graduation. I was seventeen.

He sucked in his breath. "Oh, Georgia. Why didn't we ever see this coming?"

I shrugged.

"Let's get you started at Peabody right away."

And my mother was too dead to protest, I guess.

I didn't get accepted to Peabody, wasn't good enough at that point. But Uncle Geoffrey knew an old man who gave organ lessons, who played Carnegie Hall in the thirties. We took to each other right away. Robert Darling and I loved each other. We knew it the moment our eyes sparkled into each other's with that telling familiarity: *I have found a soul like me.* Robert Darling wore plaid suits with tattersall shirts and striped ties. Robert Darling made goulash. Robert Darling lived alone in a little apartment complex off of Loch Raven Boulevard except for twenty-two tropical fish that tinseled up the tank, their colors shimmering under the fluorescent light overhead.

Robert Darling made the musical switch feel okay.

Robert Darling moved off to Tucson to live with a niece a few years ago.

And now, because somehow I believed that if God gave me musical talent the only place to use it for Him was in church, I'm stuck.

The Grotto, the church where I minister as music director, sent a nice bouquet of flowers here to the condo—lots of crabbed yet somehow beautiful twiggery, some Queen Anne's lace, and bells of Ireland. I've never connected with anyone there at that church, and I doubt I'll go back. I feel something bleeding inside of me, from that dark, sealed container somewhere deep in my cells. I feel it bleeding into the light spaces, wetting them down, drowning them. I never really liked the music at that church anyway—all those predictable praise-music chord progressions. It's pretty hard to get excited about D, G, A, B-minor, E-minor chords over and over again. And when I tried to throw in something a little bit offbeat, well, forget it. "Too jazzy, not garage enough, Georgia," the hip pastor would say. I did like Robbie though. He had a good heart. Just didn't know music for squat.

Now Grove Church where I ministered before—hardly better. Nothing but Bach and, to mix things up in a crazy way, some Fanny Crosby. At least I used my classical training there. I thought maybe I could maneuver the Grotto in a jazzy direction, but they were too steeped in the pop culture to sip anything truly edgy.

Oh, I don't want to play another song again.

I'm sorry, Mom. I'm so sorry.

This morning I hate music. I don't even like Ella very much. I stand up from the piano and trudge into my bedroom. I have to get dressed. And I have to brush my hair. Brushing my teeth will require heroics.

Usually I turn on the radio. Not today.

No music at my dad's funeral later on this morning. He didn't like it much after Mom died.

I pass the little mahogany cabinet in the living room, the door swung open, inviting. Maybe just a smidge, just a tiny tip to get me through all this.

And the smell of these people. These TV people. Perfume and coffee and gasoline and rubber. I don't even know who they are. Producers he worked with? Who? One woman wearing something with a fox collar weeps with large, silent-screen movements. She pushed past me several minutes ago and won't leave the casket, closed now before we head out to the grave site.

I'm relieved the viewings have ended.

When my mother died, her viewing felt like a party. I almost expected her to sit up, call for a piano, and instigate a jam session with all her musician friends who had gathered right here at this same funeral home.

And the bells of the church across the street bonged as we left from her final viewing. But no casket descended those steps into a waiting hearse. Instead, a bride emerged, veil flying in the breeze like a joyful song behind her, and she and her groom floated down through handfuls of Minute Rice into a horse and buggy.

I was twelve.

But today, the only breeze that blows slices me clean down to the soul. And brides always turn into old women.

Mary-Margaret

Mary-Margaret stares down into the smooth face of her nameless newborn, heart rent to rags by the stripping mouth of fate. She hands the child over to the social worker and wonders what the world will hold for the beautiful child she'll always call Miranda.

Frank helps her climb into the old Econoline; all the kids yell her name and are happy to see her. She smiles and greets them like always.

That night at home Frank says, "See, MM? We still have each other and these kids."

"Who does Miranda have?"

"You just need time, babe."

But who can forget her child, no matter how long she climbs out of bed, throws on her robe, makes breakfast, buys thread, reads Golden Books, joins a diet club, plans weddings, organizes forty years' worth of photos, and adds to a soon-coming grandchild's layette?

"It's not just this baby, Frank. We're not just giving away a child, we're giving away a life. We're giving away her relationship with Barbra, and her relationship with Greg, and her relationship with Heather, and her relationships with Abbey and with Erin and with Meg."

"I can't do this anymore, MM. We can't afford it."

"Then fix it. Call the urologist, and may it be on your head." She turns her back to him in the bed, and he waits for her to cry. But she doesn't. And her silence fills him with fear.

On his own, he tries to get the baby back, but it isn't possible. And he can't tell MM. Best to keep the break as clean as possible.

Georgia

Whenever I feel sorry for myself I remember guitarist Charlie Christian. Charlie Christian was born in 1916 and died in 1942. Poor baby.

The son of a blind guitarist-singer, with siblings who played as well, Charlie was engaged by Benny Goodman to play as a frequent guest on Benny's radio show. Charlie gained respect as a nationally renowned jazz soloist and died of tuberculosis before the first year ended.

Wonder what he would have done had he lived?

He sure as thunder wouldn't be tying one on in a darkened apartment in Baltimore, Maryland. I can sure as thunder tell you that.

My little cat, Miles Davis, looks at me with those large green eyes as if to say, "I'm a cat, for cryin' out loud, and *I* know better!"

And he'd be right. He always is.

I have good reason, though.

He came to the funeral this morning. Sean did. The man who is, yet isn't, my husband. And he looked so handsome, his mahogany skin gleaming and supple, his long dreadlocks infused with chestnut and gold. The product of an African American father and an Irish mother, Sean holds the world inside of him. I've never seen a more gorgeous human being who's less aware of his physical blessings.

I hope he's happy at that monastery place in Richmond. I hope it's worth it.

I don't know how he heard about Dad's death, and I don't want to, really. Probably UG called him, because Uncle Geoffrey sticks his nose into everybody's business and somehow does it so gracefully you can't be angry at him for long.

Sean knew better than to put his arms around me, but he walked me to my car and suggested a time to get together. He's coming over at seven tonight.

I'm not going to let him in.

I grab some Wild Turkey. It was on sale.

He left me years ago. Seven years ago. And he made his choice. I can't go back to the old days.

Why can't I be more like Herbie Hancock? Mom took me to see him in the eighties. While purist Polly Bishop only played acoustic, Herbie obviously never met a keyboard he didn't like. He began playing the piano at only seven years old and played concertos with the Chicago Symphony Orchestra at eleven.

So whenever I feel down and depressed, I try not to think of him.

I'm not going to think of him right now either.

Move over, Miles, I think I want to pass out now. Or at least try.

But until I do, I'll slip back into my red rubber sandals and dance around while my mother plays something. Let's think about what she'll play. I can't remember her music, so maybe I'll just make something up inside my head.

Yes, there's a nice theme.

I'll just go with that.

Fairly

My father loved color. Not on himself—he wore only black. He was an artist; Mom was a social worker. He searched for meaning and expressed it; she gave it. They were inhabited by gentle spirits: kind, generous, big-hearted, curious. I never once heard my father utter a cruel word about anybody. And Mom, sometimes furious at the evil in the world, somehow never lost the compassion inside her eyes, even though at times her profession bowed her back and left her numb.

And on those evenings when the storms of the world flooded over the banks of her soul, Dad would rub her crazy-tiny feet and tell her stories about places where the rivers flowed with wine, the mountains were made of cheese, and grapes were always in season. She'd fall asleep to his soothing voice, and he'd stay there on the couch, legs falling fast asleep, not daring to wake her from the healing sleep she needed so desperately.

They weren't good looking. Cool looking, yes. But not beautiful or winsome. Rather horsy in a slightly beatnik fashion, they laughed and drew people to them with something so lovely inside, the honey fell like rain all around them on whoever happened to be nearby.

I missed them so overwhelmingly, at times I was forced to take long walks no matter the weather. And in the cold of winter, I'd feel my mother's warm hands inside my gloves. In the onslaught of a dense rainfall, I'd feel the dry softness of my father's shirt as he held me against him when I cried because I got made fun of at school for my old-fashioned shoes, or the fact that my lunches were mostly bread and butter and a piece of fruit.

But they did the best they could with who they were.

Hort looks so dried out now. He hasn't spoken for two days.

I know I will miss him every bit as overwhelmingly as I miss my parents.

I love him. I love Hort.

I rarely see the wrinkles on his face or the way his chest has started to droop a bit. I love Hort because he is Hort: kind, giving, smart, funny, and embarrassed about his stutter. Inside, there still lives the young man who ran track in college, loved to go to festivals and eat ethnic food, the guy who stood in line for hours to get front-row seats to the Rolling Stones concert, who wore Adidas sneakers because they felt good and looked cool all at the same time and failed to notice when Nike came to the forefront.

I love Hort because he is shy. I mean, a bachelor till forty-eight?

He carried me through his English comp class, helping me at least once a week. It was during his class I was called out to the hallway by my uncle, who lived in New York at the time. Hort stood next to me when I heard the bad news.

"Fairly, your parents were, well, honey…," and Uncle Geoffrey looked down. "They were in an accident. Your father was killed instantly, and your mom was flown to Shock Trauma."

And it was to Hort that I turned then, burrowing my face into his chest as his arms closed around me and I wailed.

I've spent more than anyone's fair share of time in waiting rooms this year, and more time now by Hort's bedside, so I read a lot of books. Funny books. Books with happy endings about big families or two aged sisters who solve murder mysteries in small towns; books that lift their characters out of the gutter. I reject books that examine people pore by pore with a dispassionate magnifying glass and then end, leaving me in the midst of their sufferings without one speck of hope, as if I can begin to cope or deal with that kind of literary correctness from my husband's deathbed. I want books with talking animals and sometimes even flying cars and wizardry schools. Too much time to think depresses me because I always stare at Hort and start likening myself to a volcano that's been dormant just a little too long.

And don't you wish places like Narnia and Hogwarts really existed?

Memories that were so gorgeous in the making—sunsets in Key West or even on the balcony of the apartment overlooking Central Park, strolls through museums, ice-cream eating contests—are now so hideous in the recalling. I am twenty-six and will most likely be widowed by year's end. I've experienced the one, all-consuming love of my life, and he's all but dead.

Yes, we must have a detached Creator who set the top aspinning and watches in fascination as it bumps around from corner to corner, sometimes crashing into a table leg, sometimes getting stuck in one of the cracks between the floor tiles.

It's very late and I cannot sleep. So I wander this apartment that Hort inherited from his well-heeled parents. Too bad they couldn't have taken these hideous antiques with them. Rococo. And who in her right mind thought more was, well, more?

I see the foot of his bed from the hallway and cannot help but wander inside our room.

I tuck the blanket further beneath his chin, the flesh still smooth from the shave I gave him earlier.

He is ageless inside, clear spirited. Always curious and bright. Before he was sick, when I was with him, I felt like I'd been dropped into a book about me where the author knew exactly what I needed, exactly what I loved, exactly who I was; who didn't expect me to be fully developed and capable of great wisdom and perfection at the outset of the story.

I lied to him about my age, told him I just looked young but was really in my early thirties. I've always acted rather mature or, as my college roommate said, "stuffy and snobby." Hort wasn't angry so much as relieved when he found out after he'd closely examined our marriage certificate.

"I couldn't get over how much older I looked and felt than you, Fairly."

"I'm sorry."

"Well, at least you weren't underage. And at least the romance was whirlwind and you stuck to your principles. Egads, how appalling it would have been otherwise."

We lived inside a happy little novella for three years until the diagnosis. Him the loving mentor, me the protagonist with far to go.

I click on the light by the couch, grab my book, and sit down.

So my little books allow me an escape, but between the death of my parents, the illness of my husband, and, wouldn't you know it, my old cat dying four weeks ago, you can just keep your hideous memoirs. I'm living one. It's hard enough to forget even on the best of days.

What will I do when he's gone? I've already quit my job, and with what he leaves behind, I'll have enough money to do whatever I want. But the heart has gone out of me. I couldn't design a beautiful room for myself these days, let alone anybody else. And I was so good at it once. Really, really good.

Hort told me so all the time.

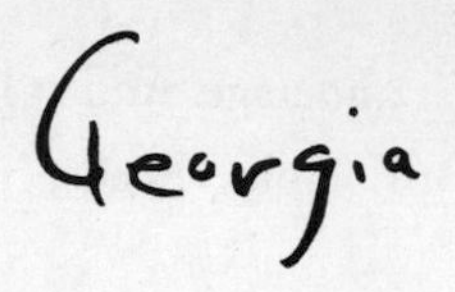

I don't know if I can visit her grave again. But I'm sitting here on the little stone bench nearby, and though she's gone, something about being close to her remains comforts me. My mother was like that. Her presence was a delight, like finding yourself in the middle of the forest with your favorite food spread out on the softest blanket imaginable. And there were no ants, no rain, a perfect breeze, and nothing but time.

Perhaps I'll come back again and again with both of them here.

Or perhaps I'll finally move forward with both of them here.

The dirt on Gaylen Bishop's grave is still fresh, and the aroma of the newly turned earth works its way into my nostrils. Maybe I'll get along better with him now that he's dead.

Part II

Purple

Two Years Later

Fairly

The alarm rang five minutes ago, and already I sit on the sofa in my apartment office, anticipating my espresso, sketching in my new journal, a sweet one covered in lime-green silk with a ribbon bookmark beaded with amber. Oh, this client, when they see the 1924 Gerrit Rietveld chair I located for their salon, well, they'll kiss my feet. Forty thousand pounds opening bid at Christie's! I am a miracle worker.

Solo knocked on the lintel and peeked around.

"Fairly?"

"Come on in, Solo."

"That machine gave me much trouble again today. I say we schedule an exorcism." He laughed, the bald spot at the back of his head reflecting the morning sun.

"You didn't have to make me my coffee, Solo."

"I was making myself one. Would be bad form not to fix one for you, too."

He hands me the demitasse cup, and I sip. Oh my, yes.

"Good?"

"Oh yes, Solo. Perfect, devilish machine or not. How's the book coming?"

"Good. Still on Gilgamesh. Your husband uncovered too much for me to do on Gilgamesh."

I laugh. Not because I understand what he's talking about, but because in Solo I still get a little bit of Hort.

With the money Hort left, I've kept Solo on the project. More for my sake than the project's, truthfully.

I stand up. "I'm going to toast my bagel. Want one?"

"Oh no. Ate at home at break of day."

"How were the boys this morning?"

The smile consumes his ebony face. "Aw, Fairly. Andrew come home from school yesterday with a...what do you call them?" He circled his eye with his finger.

"A black eye?"

"Yes, that's it."

"Oh, my heavens. What happened?"

Solo laughed. "Some big boy picking on a little boy. Andrew decided to balance the scales." He leaned forward. "My religious tradition tells me that violence isn't the way. But my father's heart rejoices that he took up for the lesser."

"You have good boys."

"Yes. I'm very blessed. Must commence the day!"

He left the room then. Hard to believe he was almost done with his MDiv and then some lucky church would get him. Probably a Wesleyan church or a Methodist church, as Solo is of that ilk. I'm surprised he doesn't do more preaching at me.

My parents, also Wesleyan, thought of John Wesley, with all his talk of good works and hearts burning within, as almost another incarnation. Our little church down in Essex drove me crazy. Sister This. Brother That.

Oh wait, it was Wesleyan Holiness. Did that make a difference?

But where did all their Holy Roller ways leave Mom and Dad? Just as dead as anybody else. So much for all of that. I believe if God "calls home" those who loved Him so much, and right on a set of train tracks in Highlandtown for crying out loud, maybe God and love really aren't one and the same. And maybe He's not so creative as people say. I mean, please! Hit by a train? How could such devastation be mixed with such unoriginality?

I expected a bolt of lightning for that, or at least a shock when I plugged in my blow-dryer. It's not really that I'm mad at God. I just think maybe we've made Him a little too earthy, as if Someone capable of setting this world in motion is fretting over the fits and starts we call our days, arranging them like tiles on the celestial bathroom floor as if we honestly and truly believe our lives even register when dropped on the scales of infinity.

As far as I'm concerned, the deists had it right.

Hort would have strongly disagreed. As would Solo, I'm sure.

Georgia

Uncle Geoffrey calls at 7:00 a.m. as I stand before my window watching and listening to the day's prelude. And good night, my head hurts! I know better than to mix my alcohols, but Mr. Beam gave out before I did, and all that was left was some of that Wild Turkey, curse that gobbler.

Who knows where UG is? London? Bangladesh?

"Twenty-two years ago today, Georgie."

He never says hi first. No need with Uncle Geoffrey, truly the only steady man in my life now and maybe ever.

"Where are you?"

"My house."

So he's home in Lexington, Kentucky.

"Are you doing all right, hon?"

"Yeah. I have a hate-hate relationship with April 26."

"Me too." He takes a long drag on his cigarette. Uncle Geoffrey smokes like a barbecue grill and somehow manages to not smell like an ashtray. Don't know how he does it. And he's so granola otherwise. "So let's talk about her. I'll start."

Uncle Geoffrey tells me a new story every year.

"Good. I haven't made my coffee yet."

"If I was there I'd make it for you Moroccan style."

"And I'd drink it."

"Well, then go ahead and brew away while I tell you about the time Polly and I put on a concert in the neighborhood to make money to buy a guitar. Have I told you that one?"

"Nope."

UG played a beautiful guitar. Classical mostly, but he could jive when the desire struck. Mom always said I was like her baby brother in many ways, a hybrid able to straddle two worlds at once.

"Well. Mother decided she'd buy no more musical instruments for us. Polly went through clarinet, flute, and trombone before she finally settled on the piano—an instrument, I might add, we'd always had around the house. I tried out violin, trumpet, and oboe—oh yes, and the French horn. Wasn't bad on the horn, but somehow, inside me, I knew the guitar would usher me right to the Promised Land. So your mother, the consummate benevolent big sister, decided to take matters into her own hands."

Everybody loved Polly because Polly cheered everybody on, all the while dancing to her own tune.

I choose the strongest coffee in my cupboard. Knowing what the morning's bringing with it, is it any wonder I was mixing my alcohol last night? Twenty-two years later and the day she died still feels like stepping on a nail, only this year it's more rusty than last. I need to get a job, to think beyond this, to weave some sort of purpose from these strips of people who compose me. But old Gaylen left me enough cash to live this simple lifestyle just fine.

Fine, fine, fine.

I don't know whether to thank him or curse him. If I were hungry I'd find a job. If I had no bed, I'd be filling out applications. If I were naked… well, if I were naked, I guess I'd be beyond anything remotely constructive. Unless I were taking a shower, and I barely need to do that anymore with Sean still in Richmond. Sean, who hasn't knocked on my door for years now, not since Dad's funeral.

"We decided to go all out, utilize every instrument we had some measure of proficiency with. Polly invited the entire neighborhood as well as our school teachers, fellow students, and the parishioners at church. We even worked up Schubert's 'Ave Maria' for the occasion."

Another big drag. Another long exhale.

"Mother just shook her head and said, 'Do what you want, but don't expect any help from me.' We wanted to do it all on our own anyway.

"We charged a dollar a ticket, and as the day grew near, we realized our living room wouldn't hold all the people who said they'd attend. Polly made an appointment with the principal at a nearby church school and asked if we could use their hall and that we'd be willing to pay a fee if necessary."

Sounded like Mom, who never relented when something was important to her.

I press the button on the espresso machine, the grating sound of the grinding beans flinging away any remainders of sleep. I smell the essential, strong yet bright aroma, watch the stream of black liquid flow into my cup. Mom loved a good cup of coffee. And crisp bacon. I begin to root through the fridge. A stupid activity, as the frigid, fallow cube only advertises that yes, Georgia Bishop has nothing to live for.

Oh, sorry. A hard chunk of sharp cheddar hulks jacketless, shivering in the corner of the veggie drawer. I have no idea where it came from, but I'm sure I bought it with the best of intentions.

I slide some Chunky Monkey ice cream out of the freezer instead. My stomach lurches, but oh well. I'll dodge the chocolate slabs for now.

"We pulled it off. Well, Polly pulled it off. Even then her talent evidenced itself in a way mine never would.

"Afterward, she was hired by several people to play at their parties, and her weekends were full from that day forward. Sometimes I joined her, on the guitar, of course." A melancholy drag this time. "I miss her, Georgia Ella."

Georgia Ella Bishop.

See? Mom liked Ella too. She even accompanied the great lady once when Ella showed up at the Ten O'Clock Club unannounced on a humid night in June 1968. June sixth to be precise. Upon recalling that day, Mom would hug me tight and say, "Next to you, baby, that was the highlight of my life."

"I miss her too. I wonder what she would be like now?"

"Just the same. With some wrinkles."

"Sort of like you." My uncle and my mother looked like the perfect couple.

"Have you been playing your organ, Georgie?"

"Some." Lie.

"Piano?"

"Some." 'Nother lie.

"Did you take the job at that church on Charles Street I found out about?"

"No." I'm a liar, not an imbecile. At least not until two in the afternoon.

"Georgia…"

"It's gone, Uncle Geoffrey. The music's just gone."

"No doubt you feel that way. But I know better. It's on a little hiatus."

"And now the fingers aren't what they were."

"Oh please, Georgie. You could get that back easily enough."

He's right. "I don't know…"

"Well, anyway. I'm trying to convince Fairly to come visit me."

"As in Fairly Superficial?"

"Not nice, dear. Funny, but not nice. Have you heard from your cousin recently?"

"No. And that's just fine. I only call her if I need decorating advice."

He laughed. "Too true. I wish I could have convinced her to come down. Despite the perceived glamour of her life, I think she's as lonely as you get."

"I doubt she has one free night a week."

"Busy doesn't mean warmly loved and cared for."

"Good luck convincing her, nevertheless."

"Oh, I think I'll get her here eventually. I'll pull the Hort card. He really would have loved coming to Lexington. It's a nice little town, Georgie. You'd know that if you deigned to visit."

"And lose my stool at the Ten O'Clock Club?" I mean, without my showing up every afternoon, they'd lose half their profits.

"Well, who can compete with that?"

I add some sugar to the brew. "So tell me what you're working on these days."

"Mountain-top-removal mining awareness."

"What? What's that?"

"Precisely."

So here's my uncle in a nutshell: *Something's wrong. I'll fix it. I am the Atom Ant of societal ills.*

Fairly

When Krakatau, or Krakatoa as I always called it, erupted back in 1883, the fine ash and aerosol cultivated such vividly crimson sunsets, the afterglows were mistaken as fires. Fire engines rushed out, clanging their bells, spotted dogs barking, in New York City, Poughkeepsie, and New Haven.

Did they just keep driving toward the scarlet light? And was it like keeping pace with the sun as they sped along the highway? Oh yes, I suppose they would be driving horse-drawn fire engines. Hardly the same thing.

Over thirty-six thousand people died after Krakatoa blew, mostly from the resulting tidal waves, but impossibly beautiful sunsets delighted people for three years following. Hardly a fair setup.

Funny how life works like that. Funny and sad, and for some reason it angers me that beauty is almost always birthed from pain. Many's the day I wonder if God realizes just how silly that plan really is.

Oh no, not again! This note from Solo sat on the counter, and it was only three o'clock. How long he left before that was anyone's guess.

> Dear Fairly,
>
> Andrew is sick, and I must go pick him up at school and take him to the clinic. Tavern on the Green will seat you at 8:30 for that business dinner—I figured you forgot to make the reservation.

He was right about that.

The coffee company called and left a message. They cannot come to repair the machine until next Tuesday.

Just lovely. Another thing to do.

I need to work out or these abs will be flabs.

Why not simply order a new espresso machine directly from the supplier?

Great thought.

But first, I need to find out who murdered the director of the tea museum in my latest book. Too bad the Le Corbusier lounger I ordered for myself isn't being delivered until tomorrow! That would make for a comfy read.

Cost a pretty penny, yes. But I deserve it.

I dial my boyfriend, Braden. The fifth in the string of men since Hort died. They're always pretty. Always smart. Always talkative. Hopefully he'll agree to meet me for dinner, because I forgot to schedule that client. Good. Another night out of the apartment, and I found the cutest shoes to wear with the vintage cocktail dress I picked out this morning.

Clarissa
1994

The father leans down on his haunches and takes the little girl's arm, gently rubbing her hand.

"Clarissa? Will you be all right here on the sofa? I won't be out long."

He remembers the day he and his wife brought her home from the foster parents who cared for her before the adoption. He couldn't have imagined this scenario. But his wife changed one day. He honestly didn't mean to get so angry at Phyllis, and he hadn't touched her since. Why couldn't she forgive him?

The little girl looks at her father with her dark, colorless eyes, blinking her bangs out of the way.

She likes the TV, the little girl. The happy people who get mad or sad but always get happy again. The pretty clothes and the way the mothers and the fathers smile when their children enter the room.

The little girl watches them for hours and hours. Inside of her, when the nice TV father puts a sandwich in front of the son or the daughter, or when the nice TV mother sits on the edge of the son's or daughter's bed, the little girl makes a place for them to do that for her as well, and she sometimes believes that they do, that maybe someone nice just dropped her off here and left to go shop for brightly colored groceries in crisp brown sacks, and that maybe they'll wake her up in the middle of the night, gather her in their arms, and take her back where she belongs.

After the show she runs to the window, the big curved window in the kitchen. She can see the next-door neighbor's driveway from there. They're like the TV family, they are. And the next-door mom has just shut her own car door and is walking around the car to help the man sitting in the other seat.

The leg that settles on the pavement is encased in a heavy woolen sock, and the shoes are thick and hard, with rubber-tire bottoms and slick black laces. The old man stands to his feet and touches TV Mom's face.

He pulls out a cane and starts toward the kitchen door. TV Mom opens the hatchback and lifts out a suitcase—the old kind that looks like a box with a handle. So the nice old man is staying with them?

It's like a show. But real live. And it's fascinating to the little girl. She watches TV Mom unlock the door, let the old man in. Granddaddy, the little girl will call him. She watches until the side door is closed, then watches for several minutes more.

Perhaps they're having coffee now, warming their hands around the cups, and maybe they're talking about all the fun things they're going to do while Granddaddy visits.

Georgia

Bits of mirror and silver glitter all pressed into slick black laminate lines the Ten O'Clock Club. The original art deco bar reclines like a tired bon vivant across from the corner stage. I shrug out of my spring jacket, cover the black leather seat of the barstool, and rest my elbows on the padded perimeter.

And now I am a drunk. I'd flirted with the bottle since eighth grade, when Bobby Martin invited me over to play video games and we raided the liquor cabinet and how cliché, right? But it felt so good to feel happy like that. Free and able to laugh at anything.

Jesse pours me vodka, straight up with a twist, and slides it forward. "You're a little late today, Georgie." He rests his forearms on the bar in front of mine. "It's after four." Twice as much hair grows like rye grass out of his ruddy arms than grows out of mine.

Jesse used to spin me around on these stools, his booming laugh blending with my childish giggles. I don't recall a time when the meaty bartender didn't remember a birthday or bestow upon me some odd present for Christmas. One year, he bought me my own box of Halloween decorations.

It amazes me, now that I think about it, how many people tried to step in after Mom died. But how can a woman like Polly Bishop be replaced?

I can't see much change in him, considering he's worked here thirty years. Aunt Drea's loyalty assures almost no turnover at the Ten O'Clock Club. The barmaids are now barmatrons. And Aunt Drea smokes her little Tiparillos, all the while patting them on the rear and saying, "Good work, doll! This club wouldn't stay open without you."

Aunt Drea and Mom became friends in the fifth grade when Drea punched a girl in the face for making fun of Mom. No one can remember the reason.

Jesse taps the space between our arms. "What's up, hon?"

"Rough night."

He shakes his head, and I raise my hand. "I know, Jesse, I know. You can't imagine what my mother would say."

He points at me. "Here's the thing that gets me about you, Georgie. You're not bad looking, you've got talent oozing from your pores, your dad left you enough to live on—while maybe not extravagantly, definitely enough to get by in the everyday—and here you sit tying one on."

Jesse usually doesn't talk like this. Jesse usually minds his own business when it comes to things like sex, drinking, and any questionable behavior he's been guilty of a thousand times or more himself. Jesse usually isn't this annoying.

He turns around and pours himself a cup of black coffee. "Thing is, there are people who aren't born into any sort of opportunity the way you were, and they'd kill to have a skill, a little cash. I don't know what you're thinking."

I just shake my head. "Give me one more year of this."

"Two's not enough?"

"I don't know. There's something about the number three that seems just right."

He sips his coffee and rubs a hand over his slicked-back hair. "You weren't even close to your dad. And what's wrong with a job? All I know is, this isn't right."

I set down my drink. "Do you honestly think I believe it is?"

"Maybe not."

"Maybe nothing, Jesse. I live a stinking life. Nobody knows that better than me." I pick my drink back up, throw it against the wall of my throat, and grimace. "Keep 'em comin', as they say in the movies."

"Drea's coming in early today; you'd better get your drunk on quick."

Wow, that stung. I really do need another drink after that.

Drea circles her arms, and the billowing, swirling, yea, dizzying Indian fabric is enough to render me nauseated. "It's time for you to leave, Georgia. Get out of the club now."

She came in thirty minutes early, and how rude was that?

I try to pull my purse off the floor, but I slip and fall, hanging off the barstool beside me by my jaw. "I am an owner here."

Aunt Drea used to be my friend.

"Jesse, help her to the door. And I'm not seeing to your safe trip home today, Georgia. You're on your own."

Good night, Aunt Drea. "I'm fine."

"Baloney."

Baloney? Who says that anymore? I start to giggle. Baloney.

"I can't imagine what your mother—"

"Save it. Jesse already speeched your spoke."

Speeched your spoke. Her spoke. Oh, that's hilarious!

"This isn't funny, Georgia Ella."

Oh, but it is. I feel the laughter popping up like woodchucks from their holes. Ha. Ha. Ha, ha, ha.

Ella? What were they thinking, those two crazies who called themselves parents? Ella? Georgia and Ella go together as much as—

Cinder and Ella! Cinderella. Georgiaella. Cinderella. Georgiaella.

Jesse takes my arm. "Come on, hon. Let's just get to the door. It's a good first step."

I touch his face. "You know, you're still a beautiful man. A beautiful person. You're so nice to me, Jesse." His beauty makes me want to cry.

My eyes fill with tears.

I turn to Aunt Drea. "And what in the name of all that's decent did Ella Fitzgerald ever do for me? That's what I'd like to know!"

Jesse squeezes my arm. "Come on, baby doll. Just go down to the bench and get the bus." He reaches into his pocket. "Here's the fare. And please, go right home."

So I sit on the bench in the spring evening, brain twirling pleasantly, my fanny spreading out like warm batter on a wooden griddle, loose and flappy-like, and when the bus arrives, I stumble on, hoping I can fit the coins into that stupid little machine.

Fairly

My contact lens ripped! Right in half like a slightly-dried-out Jell-O saucer. And I'm out of replacements. So I rolled it around on my fingers, figuring I might as well have a little of that curious fun I used to have when I was child and the thermometer broke.

Lucky me, I may land myself in a cancer ward someday due to the effects of the mercury I allowed to skate and pill across my palm.

So there I sat at the Tavern with Braden, who said we needed to celebrate the finishing of his MBA. He's a Mr. Smarty Pants. Did I tell you Braden's only twenty-three? A whiz kid. My boy toy.

Man, he looked cute, that brown, curly JFK Jr. hair sweeping his brow.

"Those glasses are sexy, Fair. You know, there's something alluring about a smart woman."

I heaved a dramatic sigh. "Well, you'll just have to accept older and more worldly wise."

He raised his brows. "Wanna get out of here?"

"No." I batted his arm. "I'd rather eat. I'm easy, not cheap." I feel as if I'm watching a movie. This can't be me, for goodness' sake.

Our waiter, Jim, arrived. "Are you ready to order?"

I set down my menu. "I want two thick pork chops grilled for five minutes, then rubbed with pepper, garlic, and brown sugar and baked for ten. Then throw them back on the grill for another three."

Jim leaned forward, bald head catching the candlelight. Looked both ways. "Come on, Fairly. You know I'll catch it from the chef."

"I'll tip you forty percent."

He leaned back and nodded his head, the expression of disgust bobbing up and down. "Okay, okay. I swear. But only for old time's sake."

One time, during our senior year of high school, I kissed Jim behind the school gym. I had my cheerleading uniform on too. I'll bet he thought he'd died and gone to heaven. He went off to school in New York, just like I did.

A theater major.

And he didn't have a Hort to rescue him for a sweet little while.

"Caesar salad with something sweet in it like oranges or apples, and I'll take the grilled artichoke."

Braden ordered the filet mignon, a baked potato, and a green vegetable.

What's for dessert, my dear? Jell-O?

I should swear off these frivolous relationships. But wading around in "intimacy light" is a whole lot easier than diving into a committed relationship, and it's all I can handle. It's a good thing my parents are dead. I don't know if they could stand to see what I'm doing. But I am rather successful in my business, if not my ability to function emotionally.

No, I haven't been to a shrink about all this, but I am aware that I simply can't face the issues of life as they've come to me.

Diversion is good. Diversion is good.

I sipped my cocktail. "I heard a rumor that my friend Leo Jacobelli—remember him from that party I took you to last week?—he found a Laverne settee. Quite rare."

"Ah! So you're getting furniture from old TV shows now? Cool!"

What was I doing there with this guy?

"Not *Laverne and Shirley,* Braden."

Still, however unartistic, Braden was rather cute. I believe I said that already. I feel rather sorry for him, however. I don't believe I'm going to want to live this fast and loose for much longer. When I see Solo with his boys and think of his dead wife back in the Congo, I feel more than a little silly. I feel downright fetid and not a little sloppy, as if people like Solo are a wheel of Parmigiano-Reggiano and I am a can of squirt cheese. As my friend Jim used to say when Sally, the loosest girl in school, would walk by us in the cafeteria, "Don't touch that, you don't know where it's been."

I can't be that girl much longer.

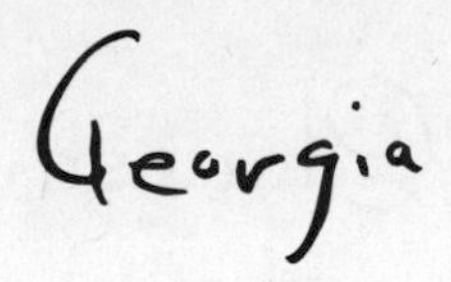

We married young, right out of high school where we'd met as freshmen. Sean sang, I played, and we loved each other. The most beautiful boy I'd ever seen, he grew up slim and lithe, golden and brown, smooth and calm. The lovemaking was great. The music was great. The food was great.

But four years into our marriage, he left to go to a monastery for a time because Sean could never be contained and he loved God in this very mysterious way, accepting of pain and the thorny existence all humanity must live, a feed-the-poor kind of way.

Like me. I'm so accepting of all that. I can handle the ways of the world so well. Or at least with such economy. I mean, why not the bottle? In the scheme of things it's cheaper than a big house, less time consuming than an ubercareer, and even more numbing than therapy.

He's still at the monastery, in fact. So I'm married, but I'm really not. Even at Grove Church, after a few years of asking when he'd be coming home, the people stopped wondering.

But what if I returned to work? Would that really be so bad? Jesse may be right, really. A lot of people would give almost everything they've got to be in my shoes.

Clarissa

The mother slams in through the door. No car in the driveway. No man at home apparently, the creep!

She tramps over to the sofa, pokes the girl on the shoulder. "Clarissa."

The colorless eyes move their gaze from the shoulder to the mother's face.

"How many shows have you watched since Daddy left?"

The girl thinks. *Saved by the Bell, Full House, Family Ties.* "Three and this." *Growing Pains.*

"Almost two hours, then." The mother's lips curl inside themselves, and she mutters, "Phyllis, Phyllis, Phyllis. Phyllis, what have you done?" She turns and steps toward the door.

"Where you going, Mommy?"

"Upstairs to lie down. I have a headache. Go outside and play. You watch too much TV, Clarissa."

The little girl presses the button on the remote and jumps down from the couch. Then she heads out the side door. Maybe that nice next-door mom and the old man will come out at the same time.

The little girl skips down the steps and into the backyard. Her father brought home a swing set a few days ago, and she's pretty good on the teeter-totter, even by herself. Her older brother, Reggie, who is really her cousin, is at school during the day. She's glad for that because Reggie can be mean sometimes. He calls her Ugly Girl a lot.

She climbs on the teetertotter and, testing her balance, whizzes back and forth across the beam, feeling the cold winter breeze nibble her nose and cheeks.

So why not try the swing? She's not sure she can do it on her own, but her mom has a headache.

The little girl jumps down from the teetertotter and slips her bottom up onto the swing. She grasps the chains and jerks her body, trying to get it moving forward.

Oh, this is frustrating!

A shadow falls across her lap. A shadow wearing a hat with a pompom on the top. "Can I give you a little help?" it says.

The little girl looks up. It's the old man. It's Granddaddy Man!

"Okay."

He pushes her gently. "Now tell me if I push you too hard."

Georgia

Uncle Geoffrey's ring, "A Whole New World," lights up my cell phone as I practically plaster my face against the bathroom mirror, trying to pop the menstrual zit I'm blessed with on the right side of my chin each month.

I press the button with the green phone on it and turn away from the blotchy sad sack in the mirror.

"Guess what, Georgie? There's an opening for an organist here in Lexington!"

"Uncle Geoffrey, come on."

This is a little freaky, like God's suddenly going to start caring or something.

"I'm serious. You've got to get out of that hole you're living in. You'll soon become one of those peculiar hermit women who wears long skirts and black hats with veils and buys everything in bulk over the phone."

"What do you mean 'one of those'? I've never seen anybody like that in my life!"

"It does sound a bit like Emily Dickinson with a phone line, doesn't it? I promised your mother I'd see to it that you lived your promised life. Enough is enough, oh niece of mine. If you don't come down, I will come up there and drag you out by your hair."

"I don't know if I'm ready for that yet, much less an organist position." Last night I was just muttering crazy things, things only a raving lunatic or a drunk would say. Who in her right mind thinks about getting a job?

"The interview and audition are next Wednesday. I already set it up."

What a meddler!

"Georgia, you can stay here. You can even move in here if you want. I'm always gone anyway. And I'm serious about the hair thing. You've got enough of it for me to grab a hefty handful, you know."

"I need to think about it."

"You've got five days to make up your mind. But I'm telling you, Georgia, two years is long enough for anybody to get their head together. You've made your last excuse."

"Am I becoming one of your projects, then?"

"Well, that's up to you. I'm not above making you one."

That sure is the truth. Still, I thought that was a pretty good line, and he worked his way around it beautifully. I'm definitely off my game.

"I'll think about it."

"That's all I ask. For now. You know, I was thinking about your being such a fine organist. I used to take a great deal of chest-puffing credit for all that, but now I wonder if jazz piano wasn't supposed to be your gig."

"Am I that pathetic?"

"You can answer that better than I can, Georgia."

"Why did you ever convince me to drop jazz, Uncle Geoffrey?"

Silence strains until, "It's something I've been asking myself a lot over the past couple of years. I probably should have kept my mouth closed on the matter."

So now, as I sit once again on my barstool, I have to wonder how I got here. Really. What was the one thing that ushered me to this place? What? Or who?

And why? That's something I don't think I can answer.

Do you know what it's like to watch your fingers dance on their own? Do you know what it's like to ride on a wave of sound, not seeing ahead but somehow knowing where you're going? Do you know what it's like to close your eyes in a cool, dark place, spinning on a discus of warmth that is notes and beat and the odd place to rest?

Fairly

East Lae`apuki continues its ocean entries, with lava pouring into the water in the August 27 collapse scar and near the tip of the lava delta."

I found that entry earlier in my little sketch journal. I frequent the Kilauea updates on the Internet. I used to think of volcanoes as either-or. Either they're dormant or they're exploding. Silence or kaboom! But now that I know a little better, I love the way lava can gently dump its heat into the ocean, mounds and mounds and mounds, creating footholds and crevices for future inhabitants of the island. I feel some similarities sometimes, as if the heat inside me is dumping out into something cooling and soothing, building toward something I cannot name or even imagine, creating a place to stand.

I can tell you what that something is not. Braden. That's for certain.

Every time he comes home with me and Solo sees him kiss me or take my hand or make a much-too-familiar joke, I feel such shame.

Maybe I should just ask Solo to marry me!

Oh, Hort would have loved the idea.

Solo would make me face things I'm not ready to face.

Perhaps he knows this, because he forces me to do nothing right now. His presence is a megaphone from which I shrink but cannot turn and walk away.

He's all of Hort I have left, you see. I've changed the apartment, launched my career, switched from flats to high heels. Solo remains the same, and he still laughs and laughs when we remember Hort together, and he still cries. Solo still cries.

The summer of my fifteenth year, Mom, Dad, and I stopped midtrip from Virginia Beach to Baltimore at a stuffy old inn on Route 3. By the time we were shown our seats in that old house built in the 1700s, we almost fell to our knees in thankfulness for the umpteen layers of paint that most likely kept it all from crashing down atop our heads.

We opened the menus, large cardboard covers with gold tassels, and Dad began to laugh. When my father laughed it seemed as if the entire room were dying to join in.

"Look at number twelve."

Smothered chicken.

We giggled.

And then our waitress arrived: stoic, crabby, German.

"Vud you like to order?"

Oh heavens. I could see it coming before Dad uttered one word.

Smothered chicken, a crabby German waitress, and my father. If a combination more destined for impish trouble exists, I've yet to find it.

Dad pointed to his menu. "Smothered chicken? Truly?"

The waitress, reminding me of a matron at an orphanage in a book by a Brontë, merely blinked.

"How awful for the poor bird." Dad set down his menu, leaned on his elbow, and twirled his hand in that artistic yet manly fashion. "I mean, I can see strangling it, chopping its head off, or even hitting it over the head with a shovel...but *smothering* it?"

He waited for a response.

Nothing. Dad kept eye contact.

"Really? Smothering it? That poor chicken never did a thing to hurt anyone, did it?"

Her expression more concrete than a lingering slab of the Berlin Wall, her lips barely moving, she said, "Are you ready to order?"

Mom covered her mouth with her hand, I jumped up and ran to the bathroom, and Dad ordered a club sandwich, taking great pains to assure himself that the turkey had been killed quickly and humanely.

I want to mean something to somebody again. I want private jokes that reach back into the fabric of life and pull a thread from near the beginning of the bolt. I want history and hilarity wrapped up into something plush that will warm my chilled torso, knowing that more is being woven. And more and more and always more.

Georgia

Planes frighten me these days.

So now here I sit at Union Station on the ancient wooden benches, the waxy marble floors and high ceilings amplifying the pounding of everybody's heels. I'm trying to read something that's good for me, a book Sean left behind years ago, but I glance up at the board every thirty seconds to see if my train has arrived.

I've read the same paragraph ten times now.

And what did this Thomas Aquinas know about imitating Christ anyway? He was a monk! They're not really tempted like the rest of us, are they? Walking around with heads bowed, hands folded in their sleeves, copying Scriptures, singing chants, leaving their wives behind in Baltimore while they cloister themselves from the world can't possibly allow much space for sins of the body.

And am I really headed to Lexington?

I sat on these benches years ago waiting for my grandmother to come home from a train trip out west to see my aunt Bette, Mom's youngest sibling, the mother of my cousin Fairly, before she had Fairly and moved back to Baltimore. She's dead now too. Almost everyone is dead now.

Mom and I arrived at the station early on a sunny summer day, most likely in August, and I climbed all around these high-gloss benches, sliding longways across the tops, slipping down the curved wooden arms to land on the floor. They were the closest things to church pews I ever knew at the time, and even now there's something sacred here in the idea of people traveling to places more important than where they find themselves.

I dig my fingernail into the varnish now as then.

We eventually explored the snack shop, where she bought me a small box of Nabisco chocolate chip cookies, the kind where the cookie on the box sported cat ears, face, and whiskers. Why do we remember these things? And how much would I pay for a box of them, eaten beside Mom, right now?

The slats on the board rotate, and I look up again. Yep, it's here. The train to DC, then on to Chicago; then I'll take a bus from Chicago to Louisville, then down to Lexington. Why I am doing this instead of flying for an hour is beyond me now. How silly can a woman be? So I drag my old suitcase across the floor, down the iron steps, and wait with strangers on the platform.

There's nothing like riding on a train. I'll admit they don't travel along the scenic areas of the cities through which they speed, but more's the charm. I wonder what it was like when hobos loitered near the tracks? when drunks lingered a few stops farther down the line, nothing to live for with the Depression and all? Something about the Depression has always intrigued me. These days, while we may not be deprived of material possessions with our nice cars and houses, we certainly are deprived in how we live among one another. We live in relational Hoovervilles, always waiting for the other person to do the reaching out.

I'm the perfect example.

But UG knows a little bit more about how to live than I do. Maybe I'll get better at it in Lexington.

Bus stations disappoint me every single time. Here you long for something out of a movie: people bustling about with a full basket of business, an atmosphere of time gone by, when folks dressed up to travel, stored their food in iceboxes, and swept their front stoops every Saturday morning. But that's the airports' job these days. I hate it. The big beasts burp you out to the curb all the more quickly, providing no incentive to dillydally in the past.

Lexington hides under a mantilla of fog, and cars roll past me on the street, their passage sounding like zippers—up, down, up, down. Soon I find myself in a cab driven by a woman with short, spiky blond hair, leather wristbands, and tattoos. Middle twenties, I guess.

Grrr!

"Where to?"

"540 East Fourth Street."

We're on our way, and thank God, she's not blasting her way along the streets as though someone bolted jet engines onto the car. I truly hate that. But then, this isn't New York or anything, is it?

"Cool place you're going to. You know the guy who lives there?" Her voice fills the space, deep and resonant, yet husky.

"My uncle lives there."

"No kidding."

"Yeah."

"Geoffrey Pfeiffer?"

"Yep."

"Small world."

"How do you know him?"

"Long story. Maybe for another day. Let's just say I probably wouldn't be driving this cab if not for him."

"He got you the job?"

She barks out a laugh. "No! He kept me alive."

Oh. We drive along, and I'm feeling more embarrassed than I probably should. "You lived here long?"

She nods. "All my life. Give or take a year here and there."

"Are there a lot of people in Lexington who look like you? No offense."

Her eyes crinkle in the rearview mirror. "What? The tough yet somewhat artistic type? None taken, by the way."

"Yeah." I laugh.

"There are some. Let's just say I've found it works for me."

"What do you do when you're not driving a cab?"

"I act some. But I do radio voice-over work mostly. Oh, and I was in this really weird play last year. They had us all wear bright white, slather white greasepaint on our faces and hands, and jump around on a glaring white set. Blue lips too."

"Sounds strange."

"You said it. Especially for Kentucky. There's a theater at the library that pretty much is anything goes. My favorite so far was Act Out's *Southern Baptists Sissies.*"

I look out the window. "How come you never tried to make it in a bigger town?"

"Who said I didn't?"

"Was it bad?"

"Let's just say I came home even less of a person than when I went. Seems to me that's just backward."

We're in what seems like downtown now, old houses queued along the streets. No row houses like those in Baltimore. Most of these have small yards and a tree or two.

I tap the window. "Look at those long skinny houses. I don't think I've ever seen anything like that."

"They're shotgun shacks."

"Huh?"

"They're called that because you can stand in the front room and shoot a shotgun clear through to the back. The rooms are lined up one behind the other."

"Ever been in one?"

"I live in one. There's a bunch around the corner from your uncle's house, on Ohio Street. They're all over."

"Cute little town."

"Oh, wait till you walk around. Our route isn't going through the nicer sections. There are some nice old sections. Maybe someday…"

Yeah, there's always a someday tucked inside everyone, isn't there? But maybe someday what? Tattoos and spiky blond hair won't land her in a house in the nicer section, will it?

But what if some rich entrepreneur came along and got to know—

"I'm Georgia, by the way."

"Alex."

—Alex for who she was inside, and said, "Don't care about the hair. Don't care about the tatts," and whisked her off to his place on—

"What are some of the nicer streets?"

"West Second. Broadway. Gratz Park."

—West Second, where her every need was met and she was loved just exactly for who she was? What if that happened?

Would she go?

I kind of think yes.

I've got to give my cousin Fairly credit for capturing a dream. She married an older guy, defying all conventions, because she really loved him. I haven't seen her since before Hort died. I'm not exactly in any position to offer comfort or guidance.

And if she knew the truth about my relationship with Sean, why he actually left me for good, she'd probably disown me.

I guess I wouldn't blame her.

Clarissa

The little girl pulls out a pad of paper and begins to color a picture. For Granddaddy Man. A few days ago, after he pushed her on the swing, he brought some hot chocolate outside in pretty blue-and-white mugs. He said, "Warm insides make cold outsides almost nice."

She agreed.

They sat and drank their hot drinks at the picnic table near his kitchen door, and when Clarissa's mom woke up and called to her, Granddaddy Man introduced himself and wow, was the mother different! "Of course Clarissa can come over and do crafts. She's so lonely—her father doesn't pay much attention to her, you know, and I'm working all the time, it seems."

Granddaddy Man actually lets Clarissa use a penlike iron to write her name in wood!

He had to go to the doctor today, so she's going to draw him a card while the mother screams at the father as he gets home.

"You can't leave a five-year-old home alone so you can go prowling around."

"I wasn't prowling around, Phyllis."

The little girl decides to get herself some milk before she starts the card.

"You must think I'm short a brick. I'm not an idiot."

"I won't leave her tomorrow. I just needed to get the oil changed. Leonard was probably home if she needed something." Oh, Leonard. Leonard the Granddaddy Man. But he was at the doctor's!

"And you couldn't possibly have taken her along. Let me see the receipt."

The father slams out of the house. The little girl sets her milk on the counter and tries to run up to her room, but the mother shoots out an arm, takes the little girl into her arms, and sits on the couch.

Reggie comes home from school. He's the son of Phyllis's brother Alan. Reggie is always telling Clarissa that he's been here four more years than she has.

"You know I love Clarissa more than I love you, Reggie. I always wanted a little girl. She's so pretty."

The little girl squirms to get down; the mother's arms constrict like a wire twist tie, tighter, tighter. She squirms more and feels the crack of the mother's hand against her baby thigh. So the little girl doesn't cry. The little girl stops moving.

She hears TV Mom's car in the driveway but doesn't dare to climb down. Leonard the Granddaddy Man will be glad to see her even if she doesn't come over until tomorrow.

Georgia

I'm feeling jingly inside at seeing my uncle. The music I'll hear, the restaurants we'll visit, the down comforter, a thousand books lining his walls. His coffee and homemade rolls. If I wrote a composition about my uncle, I would have to compose at least three movements to reflect his various tones.

A composition? Who am I trying to kid? Those days are about as gone as boy bands.

Alex the cabby pulls over for a funeral procession, and I try to snatch a good look at the mourners' faces as they pass us, but the sun glares off the windshields.

Funeral processions weigh more once you've buried someone you love.

I can hardly believe Gaylen Bishop grimly made his way off the planet almost two years ago. But I still turn on the news every once in a while and expect to see him, with Big Ben towering in the background.

"Big Ben's not so big, Georgie," he'd say when I was a child. I wish I'd had the guts to ask him to take me along.

Sometimes life throws something your way for which you had fully prepared. Or at least you think you did. But it's not the nice soft lob you expected. It's a fast pitch you can't even see, let alone get a nice piece of. And your reaction feels so completely different; you shake your head, try to gather your feet beneath you, and pray you don't drive into a tree some dark night when the temptation strikes.

What I suspected the night before I buried Dad came true; I never went back to the Grotto.

The thought of getting up in front of people, like my father did every day from various places around the globe, sped up my heart, weighed down my stomach, and clouded my vision until dread formed like dough inside of me, raised by my fears, punched down by the little hope remaining, and raised again by my fears.

How could I do that? Just get up and...play? Who really wants to listen to some half-baked church pianist-organist playing the same old things every year? And as much as I liked "Shout to the Lord" when I first heard it, who can wallow in that kind of predictability, world without end amen? Why isn't a jazz waltz tempo heartily embraced by the believing masses? It is without a doubt the most joyful tempo ever created.

Fairly

We couldn't afford extracurricular lessons, so in ninth grade I saved up baby-sitting money to enroll in a furniture-reupholstering class at the community college. I was hooked.

So, I admit it. The feel of the fabric, the curve of the wood, the smell of it all, well, call me a drip or what have you, but I kept saying to myself, "I love furniture. I love furniture!" And soon I was sketching my own designs, checking out scads of books from the library. Great, square, slick books on modern design ushered me through the gates of heaven, and I began sketching on everything I could, searching to recreate the peacefulness those pictures allowed my soul to find. Such simplicity, such cleanliness, such order.

Naturally, Dad pronounced it fabulous. "A designer in the family. Pretty soon you'll be designing for Knoll!"

And I understood what he meant! I felt so proud.

Mom sparkled, delighted.

So off I went to Parsons in fabulous New York City and learned everything my ultrahip professors threw my way, gathering it to me like ripe peaches. My taste became so discriminating, I realized the unremarkable qualities of my own creations, something I've found rather amusing since. I assembled roomfuls of others' brilliance, sometimes doing a little design dalliance of my own when something needed to be built on-site. And fresh out of school I went to work for a communications company, designing executive spaces and even apartments for employees coming in from around the globe. The job provided me with a budget far beyond anything I'd imagined.

It wasn't until after Hort died that I realized I was a good bloodhound, the fresh scent of a rare find easily reaching my nose. Being in on the kill at an auction house or (less frequently, but generating five times the buzz) walking by a thrift shop and seeing a Karuselli chair for forty dollars made every day feel like I'd been handed back a math test with "A+ 100%" scrawled across the top.

A better feeling than anything Braden's ever offered.

My life has seemed set for so long.

And I do like it that way, really. I subconsciously vowed to live the grand life when I sat down in my first Egg chair—tenth grade, Jocelyn's Finds: A Rare Furniture Place, Fells Point. I remember the cans and cans of corned-beef hash Dad fried up for supper, pretending it was ambrosia. I remember going to the Goodwill and praying I wasn't picking out something one of the upperclassmen's mothers had donated. I remember redoing them with different buttons or trim or tie-dye or reconstructing them altogether just to make sure no one recognized them for the castoffs they were.

Oh yes, Bette and Rodney were great parents, but a dollar only stretches so far, doesn't it? And they lived high on the hog of good deeds. I don't begrudge them all they stood for, and I'm not angry because of their sacrifices to make the world a little more just and a lot more beautiful. But I paid my price.

My recent trip to London was brilliant.

Maybe I've bolstered up enough fortitude to fly down to Kentucky. Won't Uncle G be surprised?

"Solo!" I called from my desk in my den. "Are you in need of a coffee break as much as I am?"

"Yes, I am!" he called back.

"I'll make us some!"

"Oh no, no, no. Let me!"

I can't make a good coffee to save my life.

He appeared five minutes later, two cappuccino cups in hand.

I pointed to the Eames leather couch. "Have a seat." And I sat on the other end.

He took a sip. "There's nothing like a coffee."

"I know. I had some good coffee in London. Of course."

"Of course. Did that Braden man meet you over there like he said he was going to do?"

I nodded. Even saying the word yes to soon-to-be Reverend Solo felt wrong to me.

"I don't like that man, Fairly."

"I know."

"He does not respect you. And so then you fail to respect yourself. Jesus, now He wants more for you than that."

I rolled my eyes.

"Don't you dismiss me like that. You know I speak the truth. Now, let us change the subject."

"Good. I think that's about all I can process on the matter."

He smiled. I love Solo's smile.

I reach forward to my drawing board and pull off a sheet of paper. Oh, I do adore the crisp feel of heavy paper. "Look. I'm designing a restaurant for a friend. I've never done that before."

"Ohhhh, Fairly Godfrey. Look at that!" He held the paper at arm's length, obviously in need of some half eyes. "You are a talented lady."

I return the paper to the board.

"Shame you wasting your time on that rapscallion," he said under his breath.

His worry anointed me.

Georgia

I plop back on UG's couch, coffee mug ready for lifting. UG makes great coffee. I spooned a heaping mound of Golden Syrup straight into my mouth, and he laughed.

Mornings with Uncle Geoffrey have always been quiet occasions. He broke the news of Fairly's impending visit. Just what I needed to think about with this interview-audition at All Souls Church ahead of me. If I need personal grounding, Fairly is the last person I should be around.

I really thought the death of Fairly's parents would change her for the better. She'd always been a bit flighty, going through that phase some girls do of wanting to be a model, then a fashion designer, and practically having an affair with her art teacher, cutting her hair short, growing it long.

We don't have a lot in common. Fairly loves European techno music.

Fairly makes her bed.

Fairly reads cozy mysteries.

Fairly wears Chanel perfume.

Fairly stops at one glass.

Fairly is twenty-eight, six years younger than I, bound to me only by common grandparents and Uncle Geoffrey.

And she's beautiful.

I've never begrudged her that, to be truthful. Some girls possess a beauty so natural, so honest and carefree, you can't even give them credit for it. While my brown hair falls straight to my shoulders, hers contains shoots of gold that swirl around in the loopy curls she was born with. She seems to take it in stride though. Accepts compliments easily and without false pride and gives them back lavishly. There's nothing less appealing than a beautiful woman who's stingy with her compliments.

Sipping the coffee, I decide I'll play at least one Mendelssohn. Too bad I can't play a little Peterson! But I doubt old Oscar would be welcomed in an Episcopal sanctuary on a Sunday morning. But then again…

One time, when Fairly was still in college, I was practicing at the Ten O'Clock on a Saturday morning, a rare solitary jazz session. She walked in unexpectedly and remained quietly in the back. I didn't realize she sat there until I finished.

I heard her sobbing as the last note faded off.

"What's the matter, Fairly?"

"You made me feel like I could kiss the moon, Georgia."

Something rubbed up against my heart at her words, like a love-starved kitty in need of a good scratch behind the ears.

It was the only moment like that we've ever had.

Maybe Fairly knows more than I give her credit for. Maybe I should listen to her words right now. Maybe I should want to usher people to the moon so they can give it a big, beautiful kiss.

Do I really want to be a church organist?

I set down my mug, walk over to the window.

It should be a no-brainer. I'm a good organist. Really good. But the thought of returning to that life… And shouldn't I quit drinking before I get another job? So then, playing in clubs would be a really bad idea, right?

I'm helping in my uncle's kitchen, one of those great old city kitchens with magnetic knife strips on the wall, a porcelain sink, pot racks, pegboards with utensils. All of these, fueled by a little elbow grease, promised more of UG's great meals.

While I slice potatoes to "thin perfection," as UG says, on a mandolin, he cubes lamb for a curry. Basmati rice will soak up his spicy gravy, the golden juice flowing in between the grains, the meat tender to the teeth, and we will eat to our hearts' satisfaction, and we'll talk about important happenings and people, and I'll remember that the world is a much bigger place. Bigger than a little condo in a high-rise building, bigger than a stool at the Ten O'Clock Club, bigger than a hangover.

It's my second night here in Lexington. Tonight a group of people are gathering to eat with us. Some crazy commune type of group who are all about Jesus, Jesus, Jesus. I really thought Jesus freaks were ancient history. Don't get me wrong. I love Jesus. Sean made sure of that before we married, and I've never regretted becoming a follower inasmuch as I really am one. I mean, when compared with the likes of Mother Teresa or someone, I'm just clinging to raw grace, you know? And verses like "make your calling and election sure" scare me silly. But I'm just not comfortable wearing Him on my sleeve, if you know what I mean. "Praise the Lord, Sister This and That" feels about as comforting as a bed full of sand.

Anticipating the gathering doesn't help my appetite any. Let's hope they've had baths recently and aren't trying to conserve water too drastically.

I'll bet they're just plain weird.

UG isn't totally weird, but he tends to attract utterly weird people.

Of course, he is unconventional—wears organic clothing and shoes that appear to be sewn by elves. He isn't a vegetarian, and he just can't quit the cigarette habit, which seems a little surprising given the stereotype of socially conscious people like him. He is down to half a pack these days, however.

And is he gorgeous. Though fifty-two, he still possesses this fleecy head of dark-blond hair that's never seen a blow-dryer and only occasionally a pair of scissors—kind of a Jesusy do. Always tan from being out in the sun of all seven continents, he screams Peace Corps. His eyes aren't really blue or green or gray. They're "light." Every time I think I've nailed the shade, he turns his head and I realize I was wrong.

With a lineup like that, I'm not sure why he's never married. He's never seriously dated anyone either. He says he's just playing the Saint Paul rag, but I wonder if he's really one of those people who just doesn't need sex. But whatever. It's his business.

A loud knock practically shakes the house down. UG hurries out of the kitchen saying, "And that'll be Old Al."

Old Al, always the first to arrive; Old Al, an electrician who used to be a drug addict; Old Al, who tells me all this right up front within thirty seconds of our introduction.

"Oh, then!" I smile with both my mouth and my nostrils.

Brian and Teresa are seminary graduates who work for almost nothing at the Catholic Action Center. He's a Charlestonian, and she's from Bar Harbor, and they're trying to get pregnant. It's anyone's guess what that baby will sound like!

Then I meet Gracen, Phil, Blaine, and Peg. All of them carry a bowl or a platter or a bottle to add to the meal, as well as a story they don't mind telling right up front either.

Gracen: searched for God all over the world, found Him in Jesus right here in his hometown of Lexington; homemade three-bean salad.

Phil: still searching but liking what he's seeing with this group, although he's still not sure about all that violence in the Old Testament, or Jerry Falwell either, for that matter; hummus, pita chips, and Chilean merlot.

Blaine: former alcoholic (Oh really? Hmm), businessman, originally from Cincinnati; potato salad from Kroger, a bag of nacho cheese Combos, a carton of Ale-8 ginger ale, and if that isn't the best soda I've put in my mouth, I don't know what is.

Peg: one-time teenage runaway and almost prostitute; baked macaroni and cheese, totally fattening, and cheese bread, and I totally love her!

I sidle up next to UG and his curry. "Well, they're not ones to keep secrets about themselves, are they?"

He bumps me sideways with affection. "Should they be? Haven't you had enough of that?"

"Oh, good night, yes."

"They already know about Sean, Georgie."

"What?!"

"So you don't have to pretend you're not one of the walking wounded like the rest of us."

"Why did you tell them?"

"So you don't have to pretend you're not one of the walking wounded like the rest of us."

"It's my story to tell though, isn't it?"

"Not just yours. Mine too. Get out some salad dressing, won't you?"

I open the fridge. "How do you figure?"

"If Sean had done right by you, I'd have a lot less worry in my life."

"Sorry I'm such trouble, Uncle Geoffrey."

He sets down his knife as I place the bottled dressing on the counter. Seeing a bottle of Kraft blue cheese comforts me. "Georgia, look at me. You're not a drain. I worry for you because I want you to be happy. This thing with Sean…"

"I know, I know."

"Do you ever hear from him?"

"He hasn't called since Dad's funeral."

"You've got to decide one way or the other here. Do you want to stay married and make this work, or do you want a divorce?"

"How can I choose something like that?"

"I can contact him for you if you'd like. It's time the man stepped up to the plate."

I take a deep breath, suddenly realizing that Sean's continued absence, when faced with a viable alternative, is actually an easy out. How could I tell him about Jim and Jack? How could I just…be? "I don't know if I'm ready for that yet."

He nods and continues cutting. "Okay. Let me know. But as your uncle, I'd just like to say this isn't good for you. That's all I'll say."

"Thanks."

"For speaking or stopping?"

"Stopping."

"Yeah, I figured." He chuckles, shakes his head, and looks very uncley.

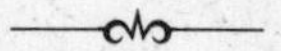

Okay. So. Weirdest thing ever. This group passes around a loaf of the cheese bread that Peg made, fills up a glass of the Chilean merlot, and feeds each other communion before beginning the meal! Crazy.

I don't know what's wrong with little cups and bread cubes, for heaven's sake.

But I watch as Peg tears off a piece of the bread that Gracen holds and dips it into the wineglass in his other hand, and a tear slips down her cheek as he says, "Peg, this is the body and blood of Christ, broken and shed for you so that your sins may be forgiven."

Before the elements can get to me, I excuse myself and head for the bathroom. But I make a detour into my bedroom first, unscrew the cap from a bottle of Stoli, and have my own sort of communion. A communion with myself, because with the way I'm headed, if I don't kick this soon, myself is all I'll ever have.

Come on, Jesus! I've been waiting for You to commune with me for years. I've set out my bread, just the way I like it, filled my cup with my favorite wine, and still You do not come. I pray for deliverance, and still You do not come.

I'm down at the Dame, listening to a regional band named the Crooked Sniders. The monthly calendar the club prints up makes me want to hoot.

If you like the Dave Matthews Band—you'll love Granite Encyclopedia.

If you like Limp Bizkit—you'll love Grounded Till Tuesday.

If you like Coldplay—come hear Giddy Gadfly and the Sainted Redundancy.

I'm sitting with Porky, Jones, Hildie, Amos, and Marty. We've been laughing like crazy and living it up. I haven't had this much fun in years. Communal drinking is so much better than perching on the lonely stool at the Ten O'Clock.

Jones brought me home. I know this only because Uncle Geoffrey told me.

Remember that feeling when you know you did something wrong and you know you got caught, but still you're hoping like crazy you won't get a talking to?

Yep. That would be about right.

And tomorrow's my audition.

I slink into the kitchen. A skin-topped cup of chai sits cold on the counter. UG left the CD player on loop.

Keith Green, oh my goodness, singing, "To Obey Is Better Than Sacrifice."

Man, is my head pounding.

Clarissa

The mother slams in through the door. No car in the driveway. The father is not at home apparently, the jerk!

She walks over to the sofa, pokes the girl on the shoulder.

"Clarissa."

The colorless eyes look up.

"How many shows have you watched since your father left?"

The girl thinks. *Saved by the Bell, Full House, Saved by the Bell, Full House.* "Four and this one." *Moonlighting.*

"Over two hours, then."

The mother's lips disappear.

"Turn off that TV."

Clarissa grabs the remote, praying the mother won't sit down and hug her. She runs outside into the summer sun, hoping to find Leonard the Granddaddy Man.

Last week, he took her to Six Flags for her birthday and let her ride on the carousel twenty times in a row. TV Mom came too. Leonard is TV Mom's father. She said that sometime Clarissa could come over and spend the night if her mother ever goes out of town.

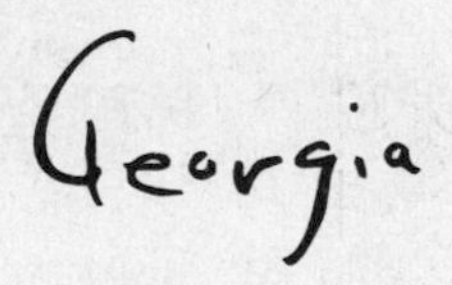

Georgia

This old church up on Sixth Street smells funny.

Today is my audition, so I figured I'd better get some practice time in beforehand, and the rector seemed agreeable when I called him to ask. He's from England.

"Absolutely fine. Come when you'd like. I'll be in the offices in the back. Just knock and someone will hear you and let you in."

An elderly woman with a thick Kentucky accent, mop in one hand, escorts me to the sanctuary, her other bony, dry hand resting between my shoulder blades, comforting and foreign and itchy all at once.

Entering a church sanctuary for the first time is like stepping into a blooming rose. My feet clop on the wooden floor; light flickers in warm dusty streams through the large, arched window over the balcony; and there she sits, a relic of the glory days this church must have once enjoyed.

Saliva pools in my throat and under my tongue, a thickened dread, and my pulse begins to slam in fear. How can I do this, really? After all this time? I am crazy, crazy, "Crazy as a loon. Sad as a gypsy serenading the moon."

Now or never, Georgie.

I hear the words in my mother's voice, and I find myself almost running down the aisle toward the back staircase, wondering who she is, this wooden, piped, genteel lady who lounges in humble submission, a work of art in her own right, yet bound to the whims of us humans. Poor grand thing.

Oh, Mom.

I believe it's an Austin, which means I can do pretty much whatever I want on her, which also means this church's past glory was indeed glorious! The walnut cabinetry, simple and refined, needs a good polishing, but I can return the dame to her place of honor. I'm glad she's in the balcony. It's about the music, not me. And I know this organ would say the same thing if she could speak in anything other than notes.

And I truly mean that! I'm an artist, not a performer. Imagine me, a Liberace? I have to giggle at the thought, and yet, had it really been about me, maybe that would have kept me on the piano bench. Life always cuts both ways.

"Now, sweetie, you just play to your heart's content. We'll all enjoy it from the back. The noggineers are meetin' today, so we sure will appreciate your music."

"The noggineers?"

"We knit booties and hats for the newborns at Saint Joseph's. The sweet little things."

I smile. What a nice thing to do.

And so I play the first song I learned, picked out really, at Mom's piano years ago: "Twinkle, Twinkle, Little Star." Or "A-B-C-D-E-F-G," if you prefer. And I begin layering in the harmony, the song content to stay within my right hand.

Oh, little star, perfect little star.

My left hand jumps up. How I wonder what you are.

And when my feet find their places upon the long, narrow pedals on the fourth time through, the church is filled with stars, bouncing off the floor, flinging themselves against the sturdy beams overhead, peering out the window and whizzing away again to circle the baptistery, the lectern, and the pulpit.

And I laugh! I laugh as they dance and spin in this forlorn little place, breathing life into the wood, the glass, the very air itself.

The rector runs in from the door through which I'd come, hands waving in the air, yelling, "You're hired! You're hired!"

I lift my fingers from the keys.

"No! Do not stop! Please, don't stop, Ms. Bishop. I'm a dry and very thirsty soul."

And I, of all people, understand. At least the thirsty part. The dry? Well, that is surely another matter.

He sits on the first pew, and I continue, playing with all I used to be, and I throw it all the old man's way, remembering the feeling of trying to fill the empty places in other people with my music. It has been so long since I wanted others to kiss the moon.

Sean would listen to me play for hours, and afterward he'd kiss my cheeks and fill his fingers with my hair and say, "You own me."

I stop, lifting my fingers off the keys I don't know how much later, after simply trailing through the book of hymns, playing my favorites, letting them bleed through my skin, letting the life of each song pump and slide like blood through arteries, letting stray chords and themes swim their way into my heart.

The rector opens his eyes. "Thank you."

"Thank you. I'm sorry I was a little rusty. It's been a while."

"Sh, now! You're very gifted. When can you start?"

I gather my music. Poor Bach. Never had a chance today. "I've got to close up my apartment in Baltimore. Find a place here, I suppose."

"We don't have much of an endowment, I'm afraid."

"We can talk about money later." For it's not about the money. How expensive can living in a city like Lexington be?

He pats the back of the pew. "Right. It's mid-June. How would the first Sunday in August work for you?"

"That would be fine, Reverend…"

"Smithers."

Smithers? I almost laugh. "Reverend Smithers."

He's a sort of sheepdog in a clerical collar. Older than he looks, I surmise when I see the brown spots on his hands. The hands tell no lies, my mother always said.

"Is there anything you'll need to have done to the organ before you come on?"

"No, not that I can see. I'll know better when I've played her more. The sweet girl." I pat the cabinet. "Organs have personalities, you know."

He stands. "Oh, I certainly do know. Every church I've been in seems to hold an organ that has its own ways and means despite the vestry!"

I'm going to like him.

"Your write-up for this position said organist. Do you have a music minister?"

"No. As I said, we're not that well endowed."

As you said. "How many members?"

"About a hundred and twenty."

I cross my arms.

He clears his throat. "Eighty are regulars."

"Older people?"

"Ah—yes. You could say such."

"Any interested in singing in a choir?"

He smiles, open mouthed. "Some. Mrs. Hanover possesses a beautiful soprano voice. And John Davies's bass booms like a tuba, really."

"Perhaps we could come up with a quartet or something. Would you mind if I did a little more than just play organ? I promise I won't charge you extra."

"I suppose. But don't tax yourself. If all you did was play like that every Sunday, it would be an improvement so vast there'd be no room on anybody's part for complaint."

Oh yes, church people do love to complain. I'd nearly forgotten.

"By the way, Reverend, do you like jazz?"

"Oh yes!"

Fairly

I married Hort in Hawaii near a lava channel flowing out of Kilauea. We had to rely on some mail-order clergyperson, but our hearts were sincere. Really they were.

So we took helicopter rides, trekked to waterfalls, tried to surf. Honestly, men in their late forties are hardly old geezers now, are they? And people were always telling Hort how young he looked for his age. He loved life to the full. Maybe people are allotted only so much life to live, so much filling to cram in between the slices of life and death, and once they do, poof, they're gone.

If that's the case, my cousin Georgia should be around for the next five hundred years. Uncle G called and reported on her visit. Getting drunk at a place called the Dame. She needs to find that Sean. She needs to tell him to come home and be who he promised to be. I'd give anything to have Hort back, and I'd like to think if he went off to find himself, I'd go along for the ride, eager to be the first person to see what he'd find. Why doesn't she just tramp on down to Richmond and demand his return?

The doorman came up with a box. I tipped him and opened it up.

Just as I lifted out a gorgeous new brassiere from a catalog company, Solo walked in. The man makes me feel a little cheap regarding my behavior with Braden, but he can't possibly understand how lonely I am. I never thought I'd be this kind of person when left to my own devices. A lot of people think they know who they are, but I believe we only learn the truth after the loving people who formed our boundaries are dead.

I am who I am, and honestly, it's not pretty anymore. Slick and shiny and striking perhaps, but not pretty.

Solo sighed a while later as we looked through upholstery swatch books and a page of African prints came up.

"You still miss her terribly, don't you, Solo?"

"Yes, Fairly, I do."

"I'm sorry."

"You miss your Hort, too."

"Yes."

"The young man who disrespects you will never take his place."

I try to smile. "Exactly, Solo."

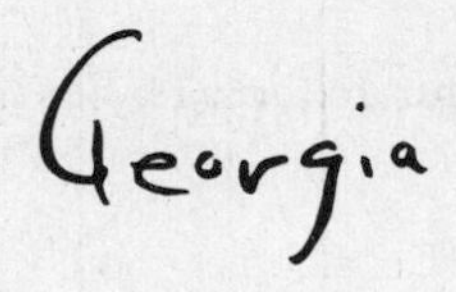

Today I'm frying up some garlic and onions we bought from the Blue Moon Farm's stand at the farmers' market Tuesday afternoon, and boy was that a hike! UG walks everywhere.

"Just doing my bit to conserve fossil fuels."

Uh, okay then.

First step Lexington, next step some pueblo somewhere.

But now, this aroma and the chili destined to result, assures me the trek was more than worth it.

Which reminds me of a piece of advice my mother gave me when I was ten. We lay on the couch, Dad creating his red sauce in the kitchen. The aroma of sautéing onions and garlic settled in with us as we read, she down at one end, I down at the other, our legs twined together on the middle cushion.

My father's sauce, scented with garlic, onions, sweet Italian sausage, peppers, and fresh herbs before fresh herbs were de rigueur, filled our hearts with love in one of the few ways he could express it.

He'd toss up a green salad with homemade blue-cheese dressing, set the table with candles, place the cutlery just so, slip on a little Billie Holiday, and we'd all feast on the pasta, the sauce, the candlelight, the music, and Gaylen Bishop. For Gaylen created sauce only when he was at his best.

I don't remember what I was reading that day, but Mom was reading *Atlas Shrugged.* She was always reading *Atlas Shrugged.*

"Georgia, a man's got to nourish you. Now, now, I know people say it's the woman's job, but I tell you, find a man who can cook. A man who cooks understands something essential about living."

Gaylen making red sauce. I haven't thought about that in years. And I really do need to read his cards and letters. But they're back in Baltimore, so there's no help for it now.

UG peers over my shoulder. "Looks good. Go ahead and add the cider."

Sean made an Irish stew that drove us between the sheets every time. Why didn't I think about that stew before now? Or the sauce?

"UG, let's make a red sauce soon."

"You got it, dear. I'll bring home the ingredients tomorrow."

"And maybe an Irish stew sometime."

"Why not?"

So we're sitting on the front porch, chili in stomach. Peg and Blaine, who stopped by with some more of that yummy Ale-8 to share, headed out to take in some artsy film at the Kentucky Theater a while ago, and I'm thinking there may be a budding romance in the works.

"What time does your bus leave in the morning, Georgie?"

"Ten twenty."

I'm heading back to Baltimore tomorrow to close up the condo and collect my cat from Aunt Drea. At least Miles is already a city cat. At least I'm already a city girl. Maybe that was part of my problem at the Grotto. Stuck out in the middle of the country, it never felt like home. Maybe All Souls will be a healthier alliance. Maybe I won't feel the need to compensate with Jack and Jim. Or Ben and Jerry, for that matter.

"So what's up with Peg and Blaine, Uncle Geoffrey? Something going on there?"

"Seems so."

"They seem like the two most normal people in the group."

"I know. Peg with her butter and meat, Blaine with his business."

"He should be at some big church out on Tates Creek Road." I'd already heard about Battleship Boulevard, as the group called Tates Creek Road, where some of the area's biggest churches lined up like boats at the dock of the road front.

He shrugs. "Some people just need a little more in-your-face community."

"I'll bet she likes Point of Grace."

UG laughs. "She does, Georgie, she most certainly does."

"Good for her."

"That's what I say. Even a countercultural mold is just that, a mold. This little fellowship isn't about anyone having to shed their skin to pull on another one."

But I don't know. I'd like to shed the skin I've got if I could trade it for a skin that didn't like to drink so much.

Clarissa

The little girl loves her crayons. Once Reggie broke them all in half. She cried, but then she didn't mind because she figured she has twice as many now.

The things she likes to draw the best:

unicorns

Pegasus

butterflies

birds

Sometimes she wishes she were a unicorn—just a whisper of tail and horn. Or Pegasus. Because then she'd have wings.

Pretty wings. Strong wings.

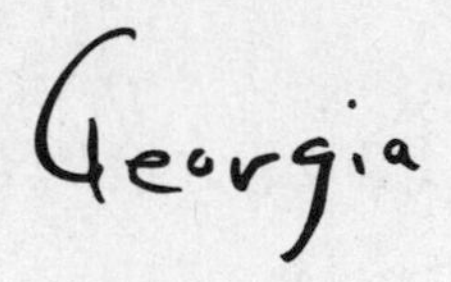

I walk along Charles Street, somewhat glad to be home. Sean and I lived here, right above Mick O'Shea's Irish Pub.

We squirreled ourselves away in an apartment the size of a linen closet and just as dusty. We scrubbed and wiped the wooden floors, laughing and throwing sponges at each other. And often, when Sean lost himself in the circles of foam and fingers, he'd sing, and I'd lose myself in him.

Sean had always been a mystical sort of guy, retreating for hours with a prayer book, hiking through the woods with nothing but a song in his head, coming home hours late always saying he'd lost track of time. How I let something I once valued so deeply, this soulishness, this connected heart, become a matter of contention isn't a mystery.

Sean didn't know about my drinking.

It really was a bit easier to do without him around.

I stare up at the window that once held a bouquet of flowers or a sleeping Miles the cat but now glows with the pallid light of an office. I grieve the people we once were.

Because the truth of the matter is, he didn't leave me.

I left him.

Fairly

I've decided to wow the people of Lexington with my fashion sense and good taste. So I've packed my vintage items; I'm much more into vintage these days, and my olive green cocktail dress is going to be stunning when I take Uncle G out to dinner.

Uncle G says his home is a hundred and thirty years old and sits on East Fourth Street. But since I have no knowledge of Lexington, or anyplace else in Kentucky for that matter, I don't know if it is a posh area or not. Still, those old houses are dreams to redo, and it does have central air conditioning. I made sure to ask.

He could gut the entire place and remodel in modern. Would I love to get my hands on a project like that!

Today I'm flying out of Kennedy. If the morning is a harbinger of the trip in general, I'm doomed. Braden stopped by on his way to work and said he wanted to come along.

"Braden, dear, what delights could Kentucky possibly hold for you?" I made him an espresso.

"Why, you, of course."

"And that's all. Can you imagine how backwoods this city must be?"

"What exactly is it they do in Kentucky?"

"Horses, I believe."

"The thought of you on a horse makes me want to laugh out loud. Remember what you said when I asked you to go fly-fishing with me?"

I nodded. "Who'd want to fish for flies?"

He laughed, reached over, and rubbed my arm. "You're priceless."

"How romantic."

Truth is, Braden comparing me to money is like Georgia O'Keeffe comparing me to a flower.

Braden went for more toast as Solo came into the kitchen for a coffee refill. I have to admit, well, my boyfriend embarrassed me. Frivolous. Smarmy. Smart but not wise.

Solo finished helping me tote my suitcases down to the front entrance, and I invited him to stay at the apartment with his children while I'm gone. But he declined.

He entered the kitchen as I drank my final cup of good coffee, because does Lexington even know what coffee is? "The desk called up. The taxi is waiting."

"Oh, Solo. I don't know why I'm doing this."

"Kentucky will be good for you. Get you away from that rapscallion."

"You really think he's that bad?"

Solo winked. "I see much, Fairly Godfrey."

"I don't doubt that for a minute. All right then. I'm off. Feel free to make yourself at home."

"Thank you. And when you get home, I'll have a nice pot of Moambé stew on the stove."

A few hours later I settled into my seat on the plane. A gorgeous young businessman type sat next to me and asked me to close the window blind if I wouldn't mind.

Mind? For a winning fellow like him?

He made a call on his cell phone before the flight attendants told us to turn them off. I couldn't help but listen in.

"I'm sorry, Mrs. Gregorio. I just can't be home by four."

...

"I know you need to get to the doctor appointment."

...

"Here, let me give you my sister's number. You might be able to drop them off there."

He said good-bye and smiled, a little embarrassed. "Sorry. Most people hate to hear worried fathers making childcare arrangements."

"Is your wife out of town?"

"No. She's in the hospital."

"Will she be all right?"

"I doubt if she'll be home again this time. Cancer."

"Oh. My aunt died of cancer."

He shook his head, then leaned it back against the headrest and closed his eyes.

I couldn't tell him about my parents or Hort. I knew he thought me flighty and didn't understand when I mentioned my aunt. At least he didn't know I was only five when she passed away.

The grace and generosity of my parents bolsters me even now. And if I could do justice to their character and their capacity to love, perhaps I'd be a writer and not a design maven. Suffice it to say, I've never felt love like that from anybody else. Who can love like a parent? And who can love like a truly selfless parent? And who can *not* truly give her heart away once such love has squeezed her shoulders with such abandoned affection? It's easy to see how I could love Hort the way I did.

I didn't deserve to lose my parents so young. What child does? And the thought that I was blessed to have such parents at all, even for so short a time, only goes so far when I'm listening to insipid mealtime gossip from the glitter people. So opposite of Hort.

And Hort. How could I have told the man on the plane that I sat in his place once? Well, sort of. I don't have children to grieve over, but I sat by the sickbed, then the deathbed, heard the big clock ticking and ticking. But children can be a blessing as well as a curse at such times. How much different would I be if I had a little Hort Jr. running around?

The thought made me smile.

A little Braden perhaps?

The smile jumped away.

Perhaps Solo was right.

The plane landed, and I gathered my effects.

I laid my hand on the lawyer's forearm. "I'm sorry I sounded so callous about your wife. I lost both my parents eight years ago in an accident. It may not be the same kind of loss, but I understand grief. I'm so sorry."

He shook his head. "Thank you." And he cleared his throat and blinked his eyes.

I still couldn't tell him about Hort. Some things will always remain too precious. But I felt sorry for his children. So sorry.

People see me as a birdbath.

I am a well.

Georgia

Sean played percussion and sang smooth as a ribbon of saltwater taffy. Add my piano and our friend Rick's bass, and the resulting equation formed a sound unlike anything I'd ever heard before. I've never experienced a groove like that again, in love or in music.

Especially love.

I've never wanted any other man.

When I first met Sean in ninth grade, at my school of the arts no less, he glistened like copper, thick dreadlocks stuffed with cinnamon and walnut. The product of two musicians of the classical bent, both parents given to reading obscure literature and essays written by people I still haven't heard of, both inclined to Eastern thought and foods, Sean oozed a certain aloof mystery. But he also possessed a faith his parents never could understand, something buried deep within him at birth, ready to germinate with the first nourishing ray of light. Faith in everything and this thirst for something bigger and grander, able to flower inside a happy, curious childhood that took him all over the world and inside the homes of intelligent, talented, and spirited individuals who saw children as the last vestige of purity and, therefore, to be learned from and appreciated.

As Sean always joked, "That's because most of them didn't have any kids!"

His parents reminded me of Fairly's parents, only my aunt and uncle followed Jesus. Sean's folks didn't understand their son, but they recognized that faith was his pathway to follow and believed discouraging it would be like breaking the fingers of a child who loved to draw.

I met Sean in the lunchroom at school. He sat by himself, eating an apple and looking out the window. He didn't seem to mind the solitude. I've never liked it, though it defines my life. I couldn't bear to see him sitting there all alone, so I approached his table and set down my tray. "Hi."

He turned and looked at me, saying nothing. When I was about to pick up my tray in embarrassment, he smiled.

I'd like to say we were bound together by pain, that he rescued me from bullies who'd been bothering me for years, that he filled the empty space my mother left behind and my father seemed to be unaware of; I'd like to say we felt some amazing electrical charge; I'd like to even say I felt the touch of God when I sat down, some sort of destiny awaiting.

But no. I simply sat down, and he smiled more broadly.

When he started reading the Christian mystics, people like Saint John of the Cross, Madame Guyon, Saint Teresa of Avila, and Saint Francis of Assisi, he went somewhere else—first in his mind, then with his heart, and finally with his body, retreating to the monastery in Richmond and leaving me, a twenty-four-year-old organist, heartbroken.

Not at first. Somehow I understood back then his need to follow his heart, to find some sort of fountain that would satisfy him like the woman at the well was satisfied. It was only for six months, he said, begging me to come too.

Sean should never have married. Period.

When he came back, I crossed my arms at the doorway and told him to leave. But he brought his bags inside and unpacked his clothing. The scene didn't go at all as I'd rehearsed during that half year as my resentment built up. Go off to some inner-city commune and leave me here? What? I'm not good enough? The music's not enough, and how long will it be before nothing's good enough? Oh yeah, I saw it all in that time.

I walked out of the room fifteen minutes later, telling him, "If you think you can walk in here, unpack your bags, and start up our marriage again like nothing's happened, you're delusional."

So he packed up his things again, stood at the doorway, and begged me to let him in.

I said—and I shudder to this day to think I actually uttered something so old hat—but I said, "Don't call me, I'll call you."

I was a little drunk. Big surprise.

He gave me the address of the monastery and told me he would wait. And despite the fact that over seven years passed without word one from me, he resurfaced during the time surrounding my father's death, looking much more settled but even less sure. He met me at the Ten O'Clock Club around midnight the day I buried Dad. My refusal to answer the door obviously hadn't deterred him. He waited and followed me into the bar. "This is silly, Georgia. Please, let's make this work."

"It's been too long, Sean."

"I've been waiting for you to change your mind. I don't want to give up, Georgie, but I don't want to force you to love me either, or to live out a commitment you don't feel or want."

"Oh, how very monastery that sounds. Very wise. Very grasshopper."

He was beautiful. Older looking by that time. The bright blue eyes sitting more loosely them in the burnished skin. He filled out too, solid, like a real man.

I told him, "I want a divorce."

"I meant what I said all those years ago."

"It's too weird now."

"No divorce, Georgia."

So we chitchatted, both of us raised to be polite, and I found out he'd never strayed to another female, that he still wanted to try. Please.

"My father just died, Sean. I can't think about this yet."

He said he'd come back later, and he kissed me. So sweet, his lips the same, yet somehow more than they were before. The next day he helped me box up my father's things at the condo.

"What are you thinking, Georgia?" He handed me some ties for the Salvation Army. "Are you ready to make a new life?"

"I don't think so."

He squatted in front of my father's bar and opened the cabinet. And it became clear to me why I didn't want him to return, this holy man who fed the poor and turned to Jesus while his wife worshiped at the altar of Bacchus.

He grabbed several bottles by their necks and turned to face me. I handed him an empty box.

"Georgia, I'm sorry I didn't try harder."

I stared at the bottles. "They're Dad's."

"I should have—"

"The damage was done."

"I won't divorce you."

"Yeah, so you said. Maybe you'd better go home to Richmond."

Ten minutes later he stood at the door. "I'll be waiting for your call. Man, Georgie, someday call me. Or write me back. Or something."

And he told me he loved me. And I believed him, but I realized he didn't know even one half of who I'd become.

But it's time to drive this car one direction or the other. Uncle Geoffrey's right. And maybe I could make a right turn into Alcoholics Anonymous or something while I'm at it.

Yeah, like that'll ever happen.

It's funny. After that high from playing at All Souls, I actually thought it would be enough to get me to stop drinking. I remember at church hearing stories about big, big prayers, mothers praying God would do "whatever it takes" to bring their children back to Him. I used to think, Dear God, I hope nobody's praying me into a cancer ward or a wheelchair.

Today, I might feel a little differently.

I am torn.

I don't want to play the organ in a church. I loved playing in that church the other day. To be engulfed in the sound. But today, I only want to run.

I want to play jazz again, like I did when I was in high school. I want to slip on Polly's shoes, the only shoes that ever really seemed to fit me all the time, match any outfit, go with all my pocketbooks.

But can I do this? Can I walk down to that rector and tell him I quit before I even started? And honestly, if I did, would the jazz shoes fit anymore?

Who am I? Where am I? Why don't I know what to do with myself? How do I stop what I'm doing to become who I am?

God, God, God! Step in. A little help. Not my will but Thine, all right?!

So I sling my purse over my shoulder and walk down to the Ten O'Clock.

Jesse raises an eyebrow as I walk straight past him and sit down at the piano.

Twinkle twinkle little star.

How I wonder what you are.

Only this time those stars whiz like lightning bolts and fireworks all wrapped up in a gauzy sensuality that makes you want to sway and love and kiss.

Up above the world so high.

You diamonds in the sky are beautiful here now. Come and play with me. Come and play.

I look up.

Aunt Drea and Jesse stand with their mouths open. I stand up, walk out, and go home.

Jazz is a slang term for copulation. *Boogie-woogie* for secondary syphilis. *Gig* refers to the female sexual organs. And *swing*? Well, the term *swingers* didn't come from nowhere.

I play my piano all night. I improvise. I pull long-forgotten melodies from somewhere deep in my brain, and I feel as if God, despite the names for what I am doing, sits on the edge of His throne and sways. Maybe a little?

Please?

Sinful music, Georgia, coming from a sin nature. And if not sinful, well, surely not the best option. You were living the best option before this, don't you remember? And you could not be satisfied. It's not the music, it's not the expression, it's you. If you couldn't be happy playing in church, you couldn't be happy anywhere.

YOU ARE THE PROBLEM!

Remember, girl…only one life.

Only what's done for Christ.

And Jesus is in church. Not on any of those records, not in those clubs, not, obviously, in those jazzy fingers of yours.

You're getting on my nerves. You're a loser who's been sulking for years. You're pathetic, and I don't like you one bit.

Pull yourself up by your bootstraps, girl! This act is boring me now. Get moving. Moving, moving, moving!

Oh, God! Who is this voice in my head? Is it light or dark? Tell me, please! I can no longer tell on my own.

Clarissa

The father helps the children into the backseat of his car and tells them they're going to spend the night at his sister's house, with Aunt Wanda and Uncle Buck. Phyllis needs some time away from the kids. Too much pressure on her these days.

Remember Jimmy and Scott and Sue? Your cousins?

The boy says he's old enough to stay home.

"No, Reggie, you're not. Not overnight."

"Aunt Phyllis says she hates you. And I do too."

The father recedes into the bags under his own eyes.

The little girl remembers the last time they went to Aunt Wanda's, how Jimmy and Sue held Reggie down while Scott peed on him. Even on his face.

"You're adopted, you don't belong," they always sang, dancing around and wiggling their behinds at Reggie. But the girl was too little to really do anything. She tried once and received a blow to the head for her heroics, Reggie telling her not to embarrass him like that. He could take care of himself.

She's not going to go to sleep, she decides, because she never wants to get peed on and not know it.

She told the father that TV Mom offered to let her come and stay next door, but he said family is family.

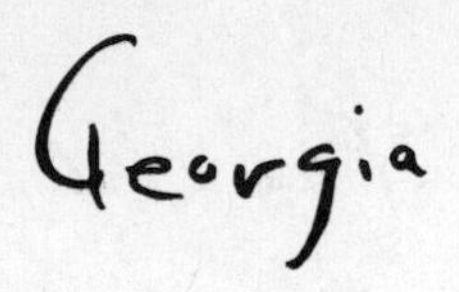

And then there's John Coltrane. I look up at the ceiling in my bedroom as I lay naked on the bed. My AC is on the blink.

If I could design the ultimate jam session, Coltrane would naturally be in the mix. You see, there's a part of me that loves these musicians for their music...but a truer part of me loves them for their struggles.

Coltrane was an addict. When he emerged from the prison of his substance abuse, he wrote *A Love Supreme,* my mother's favorite jazz album. He wrote it for God, he said, which to me means he wrote it for all of us.

What is it about some of us, the old runners of our art so pitted and worn, we jostle and bump and sometimes grind to a halt, needing the wax of booze or sex or drugs to lubricate our very existences and send our creative urges whizzing down the mountain of truth?

Fairly

I met a darling girl on the way to Uncle Geoffrey's house. This cabby named Melissa even looked like a Melissa because the true Melissa requirements are sparkling dark-blue eyes, white teeth, shiny brown hair, and laughter. She laughed for three-quarters of the ride, and I thought, "I need a friend like that, goodness knows." I mean, people like Melissa are easy to be with, and while she's not unfashionable or anything, she doesn't seem so affected and blasé like the majority of my tribe in the city.

She knows Uncle G. Everybody knows him, she said. Frequently she drives him to the airport, and he's sure cute for an old guy. That tickled me.

Uncle G purchased a fan for the guest room, so I will be able to sleep. It hummed as I read myself tired with another cozy mystery, this about a headhunter in Maryland who has the most adorable house, and don't people's lives in books hold such appeal?

Oh, and Uncle G's little house is just darling! Despite his normal Big Lots–Sal's Boutique fare, he has managed to intersperse his collection of items from his travels the world over. Very eclectic. The guest bedroom needs a nice coat of paint and new draperies. So I figure I'll make myself useful and help out a little during my stay. I'm thinking caramel with honey and butter overtones.

Thank goodness the mattress is new.

It feels more settled than any place he ever lived before, which makes me wonder if something new is around the corner. I have a theory, really, about how our dwellings affect our lives and decisions. But I'm no sociologist. Rather, it's more of an observation that people tend to stay in places they love, especially if they've done the work on them themselves.

Mary-Margaret

With fine-boned hands, sweet yet strong, Mary-Margaret unfolds the square of wrapping paper, pushing aside the cellophane wrapper. Cute, wispy fairies float like wishing weeds beneath the glossy surface.

Six years old she'd be.

Sliding the gaping scissors along the paper with a tidy zip, she sighs, then casts away the excess and sets the present, a jewelry box, in the center. She opens the lid and listens to the song, "Music Box Dancer," as the tiny ballerina twirls on her peg just like the dancer in the jewelry box she'd had when she was growing up. It took her forever to find one like this, old-fashioned and displaying the tenderness she feels in her own heart.

She prays one day Miranda will find her. And when she does, the ballerina will be waiting to dance to such a pretty song.

She loves this child just as she loves the children God let her keep. Just as much. She's been waiting for her heart to harden, to find a place in it where there is no room for Miranda, a separate place, but it just won't happen. And so she bleeds.

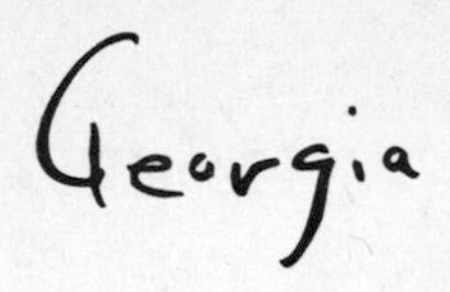

Sean asked me to marry him when we were eighteen, a week after graduation. We sat in the back of Sacred Heart Church in Highlandtown, holding hands and listening to the organist practice for the upcoming weekend's Masses.

"This brings me such a sense of peace, Georgia."

I laid my head on his shoulder.

He pulled me close. "And you bring me such a sense of peace too. I know it sounds sentimental."

I felt the same way about him.

When the final note echoed around the sanctuary and the organist lowered the cover, Sean slipped the ring on my finger as he said, "In the sight of God and the Blessed Sacrament, will you marry me?"

And I accepted, though I wasn't quite sure what the Blessed Sacrament had to do with it. But that's Sean for you.

We walked down to Fells Point, his arm around my shoulders, and I felt young and old at the same time. Very ready to commit my life to him. My entire life. But still happy about the tassel hanging from my rearview mirror.

We married at the end of July.

Each day, before he returned home from his job at the bike shop and left for night class, I'd look at the clock and get the same wonderful feeling I used to get when my mother and I walked hand in hand across the parking lot of Kings Dominion, jingly excitement speeding up my heart as I thought about the roller coasters, the shows, the dolphins, holding my mother's hand as we ran from ride to ride.

I should get back together with him. He's asked my forgiveness many times. He grows more beautiful each year. And I haven't had a drink in two days.

Maybe if we start out slowly, maybe if we go back to the cafeteria or Sacred Heart Church. Maybe. Maybe. Maybe.

"Okay. Sit down and let me tell you a story, Georgie."

UG. On the phone. "You need to hear about Ella Fitzgerald."

"Please, Uncle Geoffrey! I know Ella like the back of my hand."

"Even better. Listen up." He inhales from the cigarette I cannot see but know is there, snuggled between the lower portions of the first two fingers on his right hand.

He tells me about Ella's childhood, how she lost her mother at fourteen and her father six months later. How she started doing poorly at school, skipping classes; how she got in trouble with the police; how she landed in reformatory school, where she was regularly beaten.

"She managed to escape that school, right in the middle of the Depression."

I knew that.

"She was quite a lady, Georgie. She didn't give up."

"So what does this have to do with me?"

"I contacted Sean. He's coming to Lexington the day after you arrive."

Okay, so two days without a drink was a good start. Maybe next time I can make it three. But who knows when that will be?

Fairly

I love these people! Uncle G didn't tell me he was part of an adorable little cult! Ex–drug addicts, businessmen, an almost-prostitute, and a cab driver–actress with tattoos and spiky blond hair! Theological students and a cashier from the Save-a-Lot round out the group and make them even more delightful.

And a beautiful man named Gracen. Love him!

They meet in the park on Sundays and seem to eat dinner together all the time, if what they tell me is true. I have no reason to believe it isn't.

Their idea of church sure beats sitting in a stuffy old sanctuary, sitting, standing, sitting, standing. And even though it's so Jesusy, I don't mind. Hort loved the liturgy and the quiet worship at the early service at his church, but I convinced him I wasn't Episcopalian and had no intention of doing anything on Sunday mornings other than coffee and lounging with the *Times.*

Uncle G tells me Georgia's moving down soon. He actually asked me if I'd go around with a real estate agent to "separate the wheat from the chaff" for her. Nice little Bibley reference. My parents would have loved it.

To be honest, I kind of miss Solo. People who revere God in quiet ways fill me somehow.

I'm all about houses and style, so tomorrow I'm heading out with an agent named Howard Huckleberry. Dreadful or adorable, I can't say. He's got some cute houses to show me as well as a few apartments for rent. Georgia would have a conniption if she knew I was doing this, but as I said to Uncle G, "Mum's the word!"

The city celebrated World Refugee Day today, and so I trudged over to the park with Uncle G. Why must he walk simply everywhere? Fossil fuels, my foot. How much gas would it take to drive from East Third down to Main and Broadway? And my feet will end up looking like some shoeless pioneer woman's feet. Most of the people in the cult wear walking sandals, and I have to admit they *are* cute in their own hand-milled-flour way, but a woman has to uphold her standards. And Lexington, judging by the looks of the pedestrians, could use a little more panache. In the meantime, I thought I'd just stretch out on the park lawn and take off my YSLs. I do love the old designers.

A man as dark as graphite stepped up to the podium and began to speak of his experiences in Africa. He lost his wife and daughter and now lives in Kentucky, making a brand-new life for himself and the child who survived, another little girl. He held her high above his head, and we all cheered as they smiled.

My goodness. How could anyone smile after seeing his wife raped and hacked to death with a machete?

And then he told us he was a Methodist minister, that the key to life is forgiveness, that Jesus is the way to learn to forgive. I would say that was easy for him to say.

But clearly it wasn't.

He seemed to just be warming up when a few of the more blue-state people became a little uncomfortable at his Baptist-style preaching. I couldn't say I adored it either, but in my book, this man should be allowed to say whatever he wanted after what he'd been through.

Uncle G has mostly blue-state views but behaves with red-state friendliness. I, myself, am yellow. This minister named Jonah seemed yellow too. For some people, I've always thought, political views are too much of a luxury, what with trying to survive for the day and all.

On the way home from the rally I called Solo.

"What are you doing?" I asked.

"Researching Incan religious rites."

Oh.

"How was your wife killed, Solo?"

"She died of a terrible sickness. The diarrhea, I believe you would call it. I tried to get her to the hospital in the city, but by the time we got there, she was too far gone. We had only the most simple of supplies in our village. I did all I could for her, but…a man can only do so much."

"I heard a man speak today whose wife died at the edge of a soldier's machete."

"Ah yes. Much quicker way to go. She was lucky."

His mind-set astounded me.

"Solo, will you finish work or take a post somewhere when you get your degree?"

"That's up to God."

"Well, I just wanted to talk."

"I can do that too. Always here for you, my friend."

Talk about getting something you don't deserve. I wish Solo traveled with me everywhere.

Clarissa

The little girl cries out and clings to Reggie while the aunt, hair teased out like that Cruella De Vil lady on *101 Dalmations*, leaps around, flashlight under her chin, yelling, "I am the devil! I am a demon! I am the devil!"

The aunt whirls out of the room, and the little girl lets go of the boy's arm as he turns his back and cries. She knows he's crying only because his shoulders shake a very little bit.

"You know your real mother and father didn't want you, Clarissa," Reggie says, sniffing and wiping his nose with the back of his hand. "They had other children they loved more. Six before you. They didn't want you at all."

Clarissa doesn't believe him. She knows the lady who had her loves her. The lady who had her misses her.

Besides, as soon as she gets home, she's going next door to Granddaddy Man. He's already promised to watch *Annie* with her. The little girl knows he'll make popcorn too.

Fairly

Uncle G toasts sesame seeds in the kitchen. A gorgeous aroma. When will air-freshening products become available in scents like this? Or baking bread? Or Sunday pot roast?

I don't know who is coming for dinner tonight, but I have to admit, I actually enjoy sitting around the table with Uncle G's friends. You never know who will join us for the meal, but Uncle G is a warm host, and smiles in various shapes and sizes accompany the food and the conversation. People seem to smile more in these parts in general, I've noticed.

I noticed something else when walking around with the real estate agent this afternoon: fewer angry drivers. Drivers respect pedestrians and always allow them to cross the street before making a turn. I never before realized how aggravating the lack of such politeness is, but now that I've experienced the opposite, I fear I'm ruined for life in a major city.

We're heading back tomorrow to a one-bedroom apartment I found above a bistro so Uncle G can give his seal of approval. It's the most charming little place. Loads of appeal, new appliances, and vast windows. Two flights of steps put a bit of a damper on the arrangement, but if Georgia's in the same condition as the last time I saw her, she could use the exercise.

Howard Huckleberry, surprisingly subdued and cosmopolitan in dress (and yes, I admit I expected loud plaid pants), showed me a small, older house for sale on Jefferson Street. Not the best neighborhood, and surely a fixer-upper, but the woodwork, leaded windows, and stained glass screamed, "Buy me! I've got potential!" I doubt if Georgia's interested in a fixer-upper, and while her father left her with an income substantial enough for one person, I doubt she'll be able to afford the price as well as the cost of improvements.

I could do wonders with a place like that.

Braden just called me on my cell phone. My ex–Pilates instructor, Camille "Shoes du Jour" (I've never seen her in the same pair of trainers twice), is throwing a cocktail party tonight to raise money for her daughter's cheerleading team. She became a suburbanite three years ago when her daughter started school. Now, I realize I'm not the most charitable person in the world, but a cheerleading team? I'll throw some bills into the bucket at the red light for the man from the soup kitchen, but I draw the line at funding the neuroses of parents of overcommitted children.

If Camille cut back on prepared food from gourmet markets, she could finance the entire team herself.

"Are you going, Braden?"

"Of course not. Can you imagine, really?"

No. Even Braden has more sense than that.

Maybe it's not so bad being here in Lexington.

Jonah, the refugee minister from the rally at the park, came to dinner tonight with his little girl. I can't remember her name as it's something very foreign and not easy to recall, let alone spell.

I mean, we hear about people living through horror all the time, but when you meet them face to face, it's another matter entirely. What do I do with this information?

People like my parents, like Uncle Geoffrey, rely on their faith to guide them. And surely there are many others who don't but still seem to find it in their hearts to make sacrifices for the common good.

But don't I do enough already?

All right, Hort. I can see you shaking your head.

The minister shook my hand. "You have beautiful eyes, my dear. So brown and large."

Did they remind him of his wife's? I didn't want to ask. I didn't want to know. I didn't want to think about what this man had survived. I didn't want to think about what he'd seen and how he still found it in him to tell me my eyes were beautiful.

But I reached out and touched his arm. And it was warm and full of life and living and pain and even death. "I'm sorry she died," I said.

"Death is death, Fairly. How it happens doesn't make it any less final. Geoffrey tells me you lost your husband."

"You have beautiful eyes too, Jonah."

My brown eyes met his.

"What does Jonah do here in Lexington? Does he have a church here?" I dunked several bags of tea into a pot.

Uncle G pulled down a loaf of bread from atop the refrigerator. "Not yet. He owns a restaurant. Della-Faye's, it's called. Soul food. Home cooking."

"Really?"

"Yes. Bought it from the original Della-Faye. She still cooks there most days. Little place on Sixth. You should try it sometime."

"Oh dear. Me at a soul food restaurant? I'm just trying to locate some decent sushi."

Georgia

I didn't realize until I got older that he did it to give Mom a break. But before my dad began traveling the world, he would take me to Mass every Saturday night. We'd sit in the beauty of the sanctuary, sing more loudly than most people, and say the creed with conviction.

Afterward, we'd drive to McDonald's for a hot apple pie or french fries, blowing on the deep-fried food and placing it in our mouths before we should have. We loved crispy food back in those days.

Sometimes we'd drive to the Little Professor Book Center, its sign sporting a small owl with round glasses and a mortarboard hat. He'd head off to the magazines, to the politics or history section; I'd sit cross-legged on the floor of children's literature. And he'd buy me Laura Ingalls Wilder, the Bobbsey Twins, or John Bellairs.

All the next week, I'd hold my new book in my hand, rub my fingertips across the glossy cover, and breathe in my father.

Okay, so while sorting through the condo I found the cards and letters and opened one up, and honest to goodness, I don't know how I missed the fact, all those years ago, that he was trying.

> Dear Georgie,
>
> I'm in Paris, France, right now. I went to Mass this evening and found a McDonald's afterward and had fries for old time's sake.
>
> Any news yet from Sean?
>
> Love, Dad

Maybe not opening the letters had something to do with it. Good grief. Notes from the dead. It's way too late to do anything about it. I didn't even know he'd returned to his faith.

Some people don't open bills. They feel that rush of dread drive down into their stomachs, knowing money they don't have in their accounts is due.

When love comes due and you have neither the strength nor the reserves, isn't it just easier to leave it in its envelope? Besides, he'd leave me for weeks at a time. What's a little slip of paper compared to years of that?

My little cat jumps up on my lap, and his green eyes shine. I love him. It's so easy to pet Miles, and kiss him atop his streamlined, feline head. Why can't it be this easy with humans?

Fairly

Sean McCafferty showed up this morning, a few days early according to Uncle G. They found him a room at a boarding house farther down the street, and it's quite possibly the creepiest place I've ever seen. Sister Pearl's Boarding House and Rest Home appears to have at one time been a small elementary school, a motel, or an asylum for the criminally insane. The brick seems destined to crumble if you so much as cough.

Heavens, but you couldn't have paid me to step into the place.

I was eighteen when Sean went off to the monastery. My parents encouraged him to go; he was talking inner-city ministry and a commitment to simplicity. They never saw their way back through the guilt when he didn't return.

So here it is: Georgia was once a delightful person! She even played rock'n'roll when the mood struck. She pierced something new and let others grow over all the time. Colored her hair pink or orange, sometimes both.

She threw herself into her music, and then into Sean, with this intense verve because I think she realized, with her mom dead and her dad gone all the time, it was up to her to make life interesting.

One day I snuck into the club and heard her play when she didn't realize I was there. The music took me to a place I'd never been. Gifts like that don't come along every day. And as good a designer as I am, my skills can't compare to the likes of Georgia's. That'd be like comparing a Ryland home to Fallingwater.

When Sean left, she lost her inner fire, changed her hair back to its natural brown, and only worked at the church, never making it down to the Ten O'Clock.

Then her father died, and she lost her music altogether. My theory is that she started losing it years before, when Uncle G convinced her to go classical. Why she listened to him, I'll never know.

Honestly, she plays sacred music with such depth and beauty. But when she used to play her jazz, well, I've already waxed on about its effect.

I shook Sean's hand, remarked how good he still looked, and he said he was delighted to see me again after all these years.

"Yes. It has been a long time." And I shook my head and walked back to my bedroom. Georgia and I may not be close, but I'm not going to let that guy think he can just walk right in and all's well with me! Georgia had no mother and an absent father and was a young woman, and Sean *still* chose to go.

Uncle G and Sean went for a very long walk. I don't know what my uncle said to him, but Georgia's coming back tomorrow, and I have no idea what she'll do!

I made us both a cup of tea. Just Uncle G and me. Sean went back to Sister Pearl and the old folks.

"So what really is going on, Uncle Geoffrey?"

"Something that should have happened a long time ago."

"Do you think Georgia can forgive him?"

He raised his eyebrows and picked up a spoon. He stirred his tea and licked the spoon. "Funny thing, Fair. All these years I had the story wrong."

I scraped out a chair and sat down.

He sat opposite me. Outside I heard some kids yelling as they kicked a soccer ball up Ohio Street.

"She kicked him out when he came back the first time."

"He should never have left to begin with. 'A man shall cleave unto his wife,' my grandmother always said."

"But punishing him for almost a decade? That's a bit heavy-handed by anyone's standards, don't you think?"

"It's not like he was hanging around her door all that time." He smiled. "Looks like that's about to change."

Clarissa

The mother slams in through the door. No car in the driveway. No man at home! Again!

She marches over to the sofa, pokes the girl on the shoulder.

"Clarissa."

The colorless eyes flicker up.

"How many shows have you watched since Daddy left?"

The girl thinks. *Saved by the Bell, Full House, Saved by the Bell, Full House.* "Four short ones and this long one." *Law & Order.*

"Almost three hours, then."

There's a last time for everything.

Georgia

Jazz drives me crazy. Crazy like New Orleans on a day so hot the heat rises into your nostrils and steams your brain like a peach dumpling. You feel the humid heat waves as they spill onto the pavement from the lips of a saxophonist who loves his horn more than any woman he's ever met because the horn never disappoints him. He may disappoint himself, his woman, his mother, and the holy church, but the horn stays true and pure and loving, shining into his heart with a brassy passion, licking his soul tenderly, lapping up his affection like crème de la crème.

And then he shares it with the world. Somehow, though his heart is sore—his mother left him when he was ten, his girlfriend cheated on him with the no-account drummer—he shares the love.

And the pain.

He shares the confusion, too, because sometimes pain and love hold each other's hand, then sway like cats on a fencepost.

So when people say, "Jazz just sounds like a bunch of noise to me!" I want to show them a picture of my mother or the man on the street corner with nothing but a horn and his love.

Unfortunately, only the occasional city sends out radio broadcasts on the way down to Lexington, and then I hear mostly gospel music or hellfire preaching or the local Swap Shop show. John at 555-1111 is selling a table saw and a brand-new pair of sheep shears, oh, and a used shed if you'll haul.

I stop for gas, choking on the prices, when an older van, bright yellow with wooden panels, pulls up.

The door slides open with a slam, and two older kids jump out, a boy in his late teens, judging by the growth of stubble and a certain ease that tells me the black cloud of school has cleared out of his sky. The girl is perhaps fourteen, her breasts still not full underneath, her face still rounded. A woman steps out. Her ponytail, probably once high on her crown, now rests by the nape of her neck, tendrils waving about in the breeze around her weary face. Dark circles hide the color of her eyes and any beauty she must have once possessed.

"Clarissa! Go get us a couple of Cokes. Reggie, don't forget to make a pit stop."

Reggie pushes his sister forward.

"Hey!" she cries. "Stop that."

She's tall and thin and gorgeous, dark haired, dark eyed. He's athletic and blond, a good five years older than she is.

"Stupid."

"Whatever." She hurries into the store.

The woman looks at me and shakes her head. "We've been on the road for a couple of days now. I think everybody's nerves are stretched to the breaking point."

"I know how that can be."

"You got kids too?"

"No. Just bad nerves." I slide the nozzle back into its slot at the pump.

She twists open the van's gas cap. "Where you headed?"

"Lexington."

"Me too. We're moving there."

"I'm moving there myself."

"Well, maybe we'll see you around." She turns her back on me.

And that is that.

I guess luck will have to be on our side.

Fairly

Here's a list of pets I've owned: Scooby-Doo was a rat terrier; Bare, Naked, and Jaybird were three ferrets; Licorice was a black guinea pig; Liz and Richard were lovebirds; Nat, King, and Cole were gerbils; Goodness and Gracious were two black cats.

Only twenty years old when my parents died and Hort and I started seeing each other, I hid my relationship with him from the world and the school. We'd meet up in obscure places: fifty-year-old coffee shops, unsung Chinese restaurants, airport bars, New Jersey.

We dated for over a year and married after graduation when I was twenty-two. And when he died, I'm not sure what happened to me. It's not that I'm not loved. Uncle Geoffrey adores me.

So, okay, in the realm of love in your life, one uncle seems a bit spare, doesn't it?

Maybe I should take a lesson from Georgia. It would sure save me a lot of money to become a hermit instead of buying furniture and shoes! But in the long run I couldn't afford the isolation. People, no matter how vapid, keep me going somehow. Hopefully I'll soon be trading up for more-genuine models. Sort of like finding the real thing when all you've been sitting on is a reproduction.

Uncle G's friends are the genuine articles, I'm finding. And it's not as if they're all rosy, either. Yesterday, Alex got angry at Blaine because he said something, well, a bit backward. He called some woman a "broad" in the story he was telling.

Well, it tickled me to no end, but Alex gave this speech, the rest of us sitting around, wide-eyed. Then she left.

I turned to Uncle Geoffrey. "Well, that's that, I suppose."

"Oh no. They do this sort of thing all the time. Somehow they manage to work it all out. They have to, really. We all do."

And then he went on and on about Christian love and how we don't have an option to not be in fellowship with a brother and sister in Christ, that we must be vulnerable, loving, and yak, yak, yakety-yak.

My crowd in the city may not be deep, hence vulnerability isn't something we even consider. It's all safer than it appears.

I flew in and out to an auction in Grand Rapids, Michigan. Some hermity woman collected Joe Colombo's weird home units, those crazy living pods that enabled a family of twenty-five to live in something like ten square feet. Never mind most of them were just plain ugly, and some looked like a miniset from the campy old sci-fi movie *Logan's Run.*

Joe designed some decent chairs, though, which I bid on and won. And I bought lamps. I have a soft spot for the Coupé wall lamp. In yellow, particularly.

He died young.

Georgia

As I draw nearer to Lexington, I think about the lady at the gas station and her children.

"You got kids?" she had asked.

"No."

Sean always talked about having kids. Kids, kids, and more kids. He said all the corny things about the girls looking like me and the boys looking like him, but with mixing our races, I doubt any would have looked like me. And that was fine. Sean did the compromising on looks in our match, anyway. Man, could he turn heads.

When my mother died, I sat in my room after the paramedics had taken her away, and wished I had never been born. And I told myself I'd never do that to a child. Have them, nurture and love them until they thought they really must have hung the moon, then up and leave for good like that. That's a lousy thing to do to a kid. I know she didn't do it on purpose, but I was left in the same position notwithstanding.

I always pretended with Sean. Oh yeah, pant pant pant, kids are for me! Wonderful things, aren't they? Don't you just love them? I even came to think little dresses and sailor suits were the cutest things imaginable.

Now I'm getting a little too old to think about having kids. And that's just fine with me. Sean, if he wants me that badly, will have to lay some of those dreams aside. Whether or not he is willing remains to be seen.

Hello, Sean! Good to see you after all these years. Wanna get back together? Sure? Here I am, an unmaternal drunk. Let's renew our vows right away, but first, a vasectomy, please, and a promise never to mention kids again.

You should have divorced me, Sean. If you had a brain in your head, you would have seen we were destined never to make it work. I honestly don't know why you were even attracted to me in the first place. Talent can only take a relationship so far. If anywhere.

Here are the lyrics to the first song I ever wrote:

When you hear the crackling of the fireplace
You will know that Christmas is near
When you see the gifts beneath the Christmas tree
You will know that Christmas is here

I wrote that the last Christmas Mom was alive, and she loved it so much she made a little jazz recording of it and slid it in my stocking. The following Christmas, Dad and I found ourselves at the Ten O'Clock Club with a group of musicians gathered around the long table, actually about five tables strung together, straight down the middle of the club. There's something rather tired and frayed about a nightclub during the day, the house lights up, the dark romanticism exposed to the naked eye in all its shabby exhaustion: the sticky floors, the dusty corners, the peeling paint.

I sat and cried the entire time, and Dad said nothing, only ate with his head bowed, lifting the fork and setting it down in a perfect one-two rhythm. There was something so pitiful in his posture that I clipped off a little corner of my heart and gave it to him that day because, you see, he just couldn't muster up the brave face he'd been using since the April day she died. He still smiled for the camera and acted so big and booming, barreling through life just like he did before her passing. But that day, the strength was gone.

Christmas is the hardest day to pretend.

Yes, I've got issues. No, I didn't really know him. But I loved him anyway, like a girl loves a movie star even though he does stupid things like fawn all over a younger woman, or leave a perfectly good wife behind for some hypersexy costar.

I think I've progressed beyond "the crackling of the fireplace." But how do I know? And it doesn't matter anyway.

Mom loved to hear me tap out tunes. She'd sit and listen with her eyes closed, hands folded across her lap. Then again, Mom used any excuse she could get to "rest her eyes."

I never asked my dad how long my mother was actually sick. For all I know, she was battling the disease for years and only shared the pain when it became too great to hide. They did things like that back then.

Fairly

I rang Solo today and got an earful.

Why I'm prolonging my stay in Lexington baffles me somewhat. Uncle G seems a bit sad these days. I'm thinking all his activism has sucked the life right out of him. He needs to take a break for heaven's sake. But saying so would be like telling someone on a ventilator he needs to breathe on his own for a while.

"So is everything okay then, Solo?"

"Well, Fairly, that Braden fellow is up to some terrible tricks, and I do not mind telling you."

"Yes?"

"I think he was over here last night."

Oh dear. "Why?"

"I found a used…what do you call them…on the floor by the sofa…oh, very embarrassing."

"Never mind. I understand."

"He is a very bad young man. Very bad. You can do better than this scoundrel."

"You said it."

"You gonna break up with him, then?"

Oh, Solo, you are my good friend.

"You think I should?"

"Who wouldn't? I mean, really, Fairly, the man disrespects you most terribly. And you, a widow. It's shocking."

"You're right, Solo, as usual."

"Yes. Solo knows these things."

So I called down to the security desk and confirmed that, yes, Braden had ventured upstairs with a woman he said was my sister. I read the riot act and found myself in a stew, and not one of Uncle G's lovely lamb curries either.

It's not as if I was completely attached to Braden. It's not as if I was even somewhat attached to Braden. But cheating on me in my own apartment? What did I ever do to him to deserve that sort of spite?

Or maybe he's simply the mealy-mouthed little gold digger I've been suspecting him to be.

I dialed his number.

"Baby doll!"

"Get everything out of my apartment by the time Solo leaves this afternoon."

And I pressed the button.

There. Done.

How very, very nice.

Yes, actually. Hoo! Relief.

I called Solo back. "Braden will be over sometime this afternoon to get his things."

"I'll put them together myself. I'll take them down to the front desk so he does not darken this door again."

I called Braden back and told him not to darken my door again. His belongings would be at the desk.

I slipped on my shoes and took a walk toward the university, and kept walking, milling among the UK summer-session students, some of them earnest and glad to be at university, backpacks hanging like Santa's pack off of their burdened shoulders, others there only because college is expected and they look trendy and cute. I sat on benches too, here and there, enjoying the sun on my single-woman face, Braden being gone.

Perhaps I need to go back to school.

Maybe I should learn about volcanoes. I do love volcanoes.

Georgia

Fairly and I sit with UG at his old Formica kitchen table. Tomorrow I move into my new apartment. I love it. New appliances and white paint, old yet decidedly not creepy. The back wall, almost entirely windowed, looks out over the rooftops of Lexington. I felt like singing "Chim chiminey, chim chiminey" as I gazed upon a wide-open world.

Maybe I just needed a fresh start.

We've been waxing sentimental as family members who haven't seen one another in eons do. UG is talking about his sisters. My mom, being the old-est, gets first description.

He looks into his cup of tea, then points at me. "Polly Bishop was the kind of woman who turned heads wherever she went. She always wore dresses and high heels and had a sparkle in her brown eyes that said, 'I'm ready for anything you can dish out.' "

"That sounds like Mom."

"How did she and Uncle Gaylen meet?" Fairly.

"The practice studios at the University of Maryland. Gaylen walked by and heard her playing. He loved music back then. He played piano too. When he was younger."

Fairly lifts up her coffee cup. "No wonder you're as talented as you are, Georgie. Sad, though, because never once in all the times he visited me while I was at design school did we ever go hear music."

"Visited you?" Me.

"Oh yeah. He used to visit all the time when I was in college. After Mom and Dad were killed. I mean, he moved to New York and all, right?"

He visited *Fairly*?

UG. "Polly played the piano like a man, although you know I'm not sexist. But she had strong fingers and purposeful meanderings over the keyboard. Oh, but when she skittered across the keys so light, she worked magic. Whereas Georgia doesn't realize the scope of her talent, Fairly, Polly knew exactly how good she was. She played all over the East Coast before Georgia was born and even recorded several albums."

UG takes a sip. He's smoking like a country ham house too.

He points at me again. "Georgia has always lived in her mother's shadow. A benign shadow, surely. Polly made it no secret that she'd cut off her fingers for either Georgia or Gaylen. That much passion is a tough act to follow."

"Wow." Fairly pours herself another cup of coffee. "We have some sort of family, don't we?"

UG raises his mug in a toast. "You're not kidding."

Let's see. A jazz pianist and a reporter. A social worker and an artist. And a free-thinking, liberal, free-wheeling, social-justice-seeking lawyer.

A ditz and a drunk.

Oh great.

I raise my cup as well. "You poor, poor man."

Fairly snorts her coffee, coughing, sputtering as the liquid sprays us all.

Count Basie's mother helped to oversee his musical progress. His dad did grounds work and maintenance for several families; his mom took in laundry. He left his home in New Jersey for Harlem in the 1920s. And he became a great man. I'm not sure when his mother died, but I'll bet he was older than twelve.

Fairly

Georgie excused herself around midnight, went into the bathroom, and started throwing up.

I didn't realize she'd been slipping a little Irish or something into her coffee. Come to think of it, she seemed to be excusing herself a little too often.

Uncle G helped her to her feet in the bathroom, and she pushed him off with a scathing "Do-gooder" scraping from between her lips, and the sneer uglied her up two hundred percent.

He must be used to that sort of thing, because he acted like he didn't even hear it, and believe me, she kept going with it. Whispering soothing words I couldn't hear, he simply put his arm around her back and walked her to her bedroom.

I followed them in, and there it was, right on her nightstand, a bottle of vodka. Cheap vodka to boot. And the signs are adding up now.

I had no idea she drank like this. But couple tonight with the night some stranger brought her home practically passed out from the Dame, I'm beginning to wonder about her. The signs sure are there. No job. No friends. No purpose. And it's not like this runs in our family. You can say what you want about Uncle Gaylen, but he always kept a clear head. Tonic and lime, his drink.

What is her problem? Yes, her parents are dead. So are mine. Her husband is gone. So is mine.

I mean, we both loathe the cards dealt to us, but you don't find me passed out, do you? She has entered the realm of beyond excuse.

Uncle G returned to the living room with a cardboard box in his hands. He set it on the coffee table—one of those high-gloss, tree-stump-looking affairs. "Here. I saved these."

I flipped up the flap. "My goodness! I thought they'd gotten thrown out with Mom and Dad's other stuff."

"*Nyet.* I managed to salvage a few things you missed." He raised his brows. "You did miss these, right?"

I held up my hand. "Gospel truth. I certainly did."

"Because I wouldn't put it past you, my dear, to throw these away simply because they fail to fit your image."

I feel the heat rise to my face.

Uncle G gets down on his haunches in front of me. He takes my hand. "At least have the decency not to pretend with me, Fairly. I don't buy this artsy persona you've crafted over the years. I know you."

"And you love me anyway?"

He squeezes my hand, leans forward, and kisses me on the cheek. "Next to your parents and the nurses, I was the first person to hold you after you were born. Even then, it was obvious you had something unique within you."

All the pictures are nestled inside. All the memories my parents and I made. Mom was a shutterbug, one of those delightful people who posed everyone at the smallest provocation. First time eating steamed crabs? Let me grab the camera. Getting together for a special lunch at Haussner's? She rifles through her purse, and oh, I put that thing in here somewhere. A visit from long-lost friends? Let's line you all up there on the sofa.

But I look up at the gibbous moon now, the house silent and filled with that hulking wonder other people's things possess in the dark, and I hold a picture of a young couple in my hand. And in the woman's arms a baby rests. And the woman sits on a threadbare couch, and the man sits on the arm of the couch beside her. And my heavens, the way they look at the little baby, you'd think she was destined to save the world.

The baby is warm and safe and has no idea the sacrifice they made just to bring her into their family.

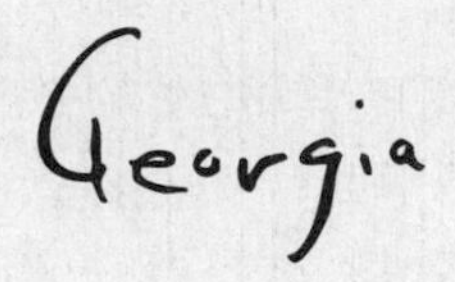

Georgia

We sit on the front porch in the pink of morning. Fairly still sleeps, and UG and I rock in the early coolness.

"Feels good out here," I say.

"Yes. Your head hurt? You were really in a bad state last night."

"Yeah. I did manage to get up around four and take some aspirin. Had some crazy dreams about human flowers."

I can hear his thoughts, but I close my ears. Na na na na na.

"When are you leaving for your trip, UG?"

"Day after tomorrow. To eastern Kentucky. Want to come?"

"Sure. Why not?"

He sits up straight. "Really? We'll be gone for three days."

"Why not? Anyone else going?"

"Maybe Fairly."

I snort. "Yeah, right. Eastern Kentucky is hardly a fabulous hot spot."

He sits back, smiles. "There's a lot more to Fairly than you think, Georgie. But then again, that might just be a loving uncle speaking. You two have never been close."

We rock some more in our chairs, the traffic thickening with each quarter hour that passes.

"So is Sean still in Lexington?" There, I asked. And it didn't take two hits of vodka to do it.

"He wants to see you."

"I can't yet. It's too sudden, you know?"

"Sure. But you can't put it off forever."

"How about after the trip?"

"Okay. I'll call him and let him know."

The world heats up a few more degrees, lights up even as Uncle Geoffrey does the same. I know I've been around bars way too often, but even so, cigarette smoke and a hangover are about as compatible as consommé and a double-chocolate, peanut butter milk shake.

"What's he going to do in the meantime?"

"I think he'll probably look for a job."

"Really?"

"Sounds like he's pretty serious about reconciling with you."

Good night. Just when I thought I was going to finally get my life back together, paint in some shadows and highlights, somebody comes along and replaces it with another picture altogether.

Who am I kidding? I knew this day had to come sooner or later. I stand to my feet and stretch. "Well, I'd better get a move on. Big day."

"Excited about your new place?"

I kiss him atop the head. "Nope."

"Didn't think so."

Clarissa

After the little girl jumps off the bus from first grade, she stops by the crab apple tree. The father's clothes litter the front lawn. There's the red plaid shirt. The workpants. The Fruit of the Looms, and she wishes the fruit guys on the TV ads were real, especially right then, for maybe they'd make her laugh even as the mother screams a string of words the little girl cannot understand.

She especially likes the purple grape guy.

More briefs, undershirts, and creamy sport shirts flutter like doves down onto the overgrown lawn.

Pretty doves.

Pretty father. He was so nice. When he was home, anyway.

She stands, the patterns of fabric swirling like a kaleidoscope.

Paisleys, plaids, polka dots. Pajamas—soft pajamas.

The mother grabs her by the arm.

"Oh!"

"We're going away for a few days. I have your clothes."

The cousin follows behind, tears striping his cheeks.

"I hate you, Clarissa. It's all your fault. We were happy before you came."

The little girl turns to the mother. "Can I just go stay next-door? Please?"

The mother sighs. "Oh, all right. Run on over and see if it's okay."

Fairly

If I ever have children, the names I'd pick are these: for a girl, Marcella or Georgia; for a boy, Inigo or Winston.

The strange thing is, I'd pretty much written off the idea of children. I'd love to get married again. Someday, maybe.

Can you imagine the children Braden might have envisioned? Children with names like Spencer or Harper who we'd give over to a nanny so we could pursue our individual desires because fulfilled parents are better parents. Happy parents have happy children! And we'd run them in our shining black foreign imports to five different extracurricular activities each week including some language lessons in Japanese or Russian so that we could feel so good about ourselves because they make us proud.

Jonah, the refugee minister and restaurant owner, dropped by for a cup of coffee this morning and told me the special at his restaurant this afternoon. Ribs. Mmm, mmm.

So here's a new theory: perhaps children don't need to be experts at anything other than how to be kids. Wouldn't that be a lovely thing?

Jonah agreed with me. And I called Solo, and he did too.

These men are brilliant.

Clarissa

The little girl steps on the thermometer by mistake. She picks it up off the kitchen floor, and the silver spills onto the palm of her hand.

Pretty shiny balls. Skipping and moving. Swallowing each other up. Scattering.

Pretty shiny balls.

She runs next door and raps on the screen door. "Hello? Hello?"

TV Mom answers. "Hi, Clarissa. Come on in. We're just about to leave."

"Where you going?"

"Just to church. Wanna come?"

"But isn't church on Sunday?"

"Yes. We're just going to help plant flowers. Mums for the fall."

"Okay."

The little girl stands there.

"Should you go ask your mom?"

"She's not home."

TV Mom turns her head and looks at Leonard the Granddaddy Man. "See, Dad?"

He stands up. "All right then. Let me find my garden gloves."

"How about a sandwich before we go?" TV Mom asks.

"Okay. I really like peanut butter and marshmallow cream."

"Me too. My son, he's all grown now, used to call them buzzies."

The little girl laughs. "I'll have a buzzie."

Georgia

My real estate agent in Baltimore suggested I leave my condo furnished so it would be easier to sell. Stupid me, however, didn't think about the furniture I'd need here in Lexington.

I'm leaving all that up to Fairly. She said she'd pick out some furniture befitting the place. She said the cool white paint and the clean architectural lines with that wall of windows, buzzy, buzz-buzz-buzz, buzz. Great. Thanks. I could care less about what it looks like as long as I can lay my head down and sleep it off.

I hate it when I think thoughts like that. I didn't used to be this way. The old part of me is actually grateful to her.

UG is having a big dinner with his Jesus freaks before he leaves for his trip, as if this is the last meal anybody will eat until he gets back, as if he really is responsible for ending hunger in Lexington.

Sean wanted to help me unpack, UG said.

I just gaped at him. "Yeah, right. I don't think so."

So a couple of the Jesus freaks are helping me haul the boxes from my car. The bistro on the first floor is cooking something right now… I don't know what, but I'm suspecting bacon and onions and garlic are in there somewhere. A little too early for that kind of smell. Too glorious for the likes of someone like me.

Gracen, the African American man and maker of three-bean salad, smiles as he passes me at the threshold, stereo in his hands. "Mind if I get some water?"

"Let me find you a glass."

I run up the two flights of steps and locate the small box of kitchen supplies. Knowing I'm not going to entertain UG-style, I packed only the necessities. I fill a glass from the tap. "Sorry, it isn't really cold."

"But it is really wet. Just what I need."

I've never seen someone so thankful for a glass of water. Peg, the maker of mac'n'cheese, enters the kitchen, wiping her forehead with her forearm. Her auburn hair is pulled up on top of her head in a chaotic ponytail. She has cellulite hanging down from her upper arms and doesn't seem to care.

"Water, Peg?"

"Absolutely."

"Thanks, you guys, for helping me."

Gracen drains his glass. "Why wouldn't we?

I shrug. "Because you don't know me?"

"You're Geoffrey's niece, aren't you?" Peg asks.

"Yeah."

"You needed help, right?"

"Yeah. But I'm more comfortable doing things by myself, I guess."

Peg sits down on the floor and leans her back against the cabinet. "Me too. Then I ended up on the streets where there were a whole lot of people ready to help, if you know what I mean."

Gracen says, "Did you believe in God then, Peg?"

"Oh sure. Alex is the former atheist, not me."

"Oh yeah. That's right."

"I just didn't believe in church. Still don't, if you want to know the truth. I'm a work in progress."

"I heard that. I just kind of lost myself—long story. Geoffrey brought me around, though. The man practices what he preaches."

"He picked me up when I was down, that's for sure."

Uncle Geoffrey? I mean, sure he's a nice guy, but…

Gracen rubs his calf. "And then we picked up some others as motley as we were, and voilà! Church!"

Peg nods. "Pretty much the history of us."

Gracen heads toward the door. "One more box and we're done."

I like these people and all, but they sure are weird. Too closely knit. Makes me feel a little creepy-crawly.

"So, tell me about Blaine, Peg. You two a number?"

She smiles and nods.

Love, Jesus-freak style.

And you know, there's something nice about that.

Fairly

So after lunch, organic BLTs, Uncle G pulled out his guitar, Georgia plucked on some Celtic harp only some musicologist would know the origin of, and I blew away on a flute that Uncle G borrowed from a friend of his. I haven't played the flute in years.

And we played old songs like "American Pie," "Proud Mary," and "Yesterday." And only "Yesterday" sounded like much of anything. Really, "Proud Mary" on guitar, harp, and flute?

Gruesome.

We laughed ourselves blue.

Clarissa

The little girl cried when she realized her father would never come back. The mother grabs her arm.

"You should be thankful I didn't kill him the way my mother tried to kill my father. Now we have to stick together because he left. If I see you crying again, I'll spank you."

The mother looks at her watch.

"I've got to go to work. I'll be home at six. I want you to make us some sandwiches for dinner. They'd better be ready by the time I get home."

The little girl looks into the refrigerator. No lunchmeat.

Tuna?

She cannot find a can opener. The cousin is staying after school for sports. She cannot find a can opener!

Her stomach feels sick, and she wonders if she can scrape together some change to buy a can opener at the convenience store.

The little girl rummages through the couch cushions, in all the pockets of the coats in the closets. She doesn't know if she has enough, but she pulls on her winter coat and heads out the door.

Can opener. Can opener.

Wait. Oh wait.

She switches directions and knocks on Granddaddy Man's kitchen door.

Of course he has a can opener. Of course.

Georgia

On my thirteenth birthday we walked out of church, and Dad said, "This is it. I can't pretend anymore."

He'd had it with God and the church. "There aren't any answers there. My questions have no answers. If you want to go on your own, Georgie, fine."

So I'd set out on Sunday mornings. Sometimes I walked to the Baptist church because I liked the rousing music. Sometimes I walked to the Catholic church because I liked the reverence. Sometimes I walked to the park, lay on my back, and looked up at the clouds, and I'd think about how Jesus came as a little baby, just like I did. And I'd allow myself the luxury of hanging out with Him in my mind.

Dad: Jesus is here, Georgia!

Me (in the basement): Send Him down!

Jesus (clopping down the steps): Hey, Georgie, what's up?

Me: Watching TV. Come on down.

Jesus: Cool.

And He sits on the other end of the couch, and I get Him a Coke and me a Sprite, and we eat popcorn until it's time for Him to go home and get His homework done, and maybe we could switch lab partners and be together? Of course everybody wants to be lab partners with Jesus; He's that good at science.

Sometimes I'd fall asleep and dream about God. Startling dreams. Vivid in all the senses. Senses mixed. I could taste red and see sweet and salty. I could hear velvet.

And I'd go home and play the piano, trying to feel what I remembered. Trying to play what I felt.

I wanted to be Oscar Peterson when I grew up. One thing I had in common with Peterson was that I, too, had a teacher who told me I had a special gift to give the world. "The Gravy Waltz" makes me want to stand up, take the world by the hand, and run it around the block while I yell, "This is my best friend, everybody!" And then me and the world, we'd sit on lawn chairs in my backyard, sip lemonade, and talk about the best day we ever had.

One day the dreams stopped, like all dreams seem to do. I couldn't say when that happened.

Fairly

For some reason, I've never been afraid while walking around the rougher parts of town. I may not have taken away much from my religious upbringing, but the sense that God watches me and guards my footsteps has never left. I'm not proud, thinking I deserve this type of care due to my own merit; for despite my glossy veneer, I know what a frivolous life I really lead. At least I've been more aware of it lately. But I had parents who prayed like zealots concerning every little thing, any time of day. It annoyed me growing up, embarrassed me when friends visited even though some of them connected with their religiosity. So when I say I feel safe no matter where I find myself, it's because of Bette and Rodney Godfrey, not me. And I am confident that even now they're still making sure I'm okay.

I suppose that's what bothers me about life and death. I'm very sure there's a heaven when it comes to my parents. But when I think about my own life, I can't begin to come to grips with heaven's existence. First off, it must be very ornate. At least I picture it like the sets on TBN. Second, how creative is one allowed to be? Really? I mean, we're talking God all over the place. A tough act to follow, surely.

Thoughts like these ushered me down the street earlier this afternoon after I ordered some furniture for Georgia's new place. The Internet's a wonderful thing! Georgia moved her belongings over to the new apartment with the help of Peg and Gracen, and Uncle G had a meeting with the city council after we played music on the porch. I must say, he cut a dashing figure in his suit and tie. I hope someday he finds a woman to settle in with via a blazing, exuberant romance, of course. Squandering all that gorgeousness doesn't sit well with my modernist sensibilities against waste.

I headed down Upper toward the northern end of the city, and, as usual with cities, the scenery flattened out like a gauzy train trailing from Lexington's three skyscrapers.

Three skyscrapers.

How sweet.

I passed shotgun shacks left and right. Some huddled in sparse disrepair; others lined up in decorated shabbiness—rusted wind chimes and faded lawn chairs, plastic daisies in truck tires, forlorn little birdhouses. And a few shone with fresh paint, flowers, and breezy curtains at the windows.

Of course, folks measured me with suspicion, but who could blame people for that? A Caucasian woman in vintage garb and an "it" bag doesn't really belong on Upper between Fifth and Sixth Street.

But I waved or nodded or said hello, feeling a bit like Reese Witherspoon, that combo of blond and bloom, and I received a couple of smiles in return. Mostly from men. All in all, however, I felt like "a total poseur," as Braden's ten-year-old niece used to say. Now she was a cutie. Too bad her uncle wasn't more like her.

I turned down Sixth feeling a tad hungry for some lunch and doubting there'd be a place to get some decent food in these parts. Heavens, was I mistaken!

A little place called Della-Faye's VIP Restaurant sat just behind the veined sidewalk. Jonah's place! A shoe box of a business holding, at first glance, about as much promise as a two-dollar umbrella. But, I thought, why not investigate anyway? Jonah could probably use the business. The handwritten menu in the window advertised home-cooked food: roast beef, meatloaf, homemade fried chicken, mac'n'cheese, pigs' feet and cabbage, cheeseburgers, green beans, beets, limas, collards, apple cobbler, and chocolate pie.

And today's special—ribs!

I pushed open the door, the bottom of it sticking on the weatherstripping.

The place smelled like a home where a grandma with five children underfoot cooks three hot meals a day for the farm workers, the postman with worn shoes, and the minister, who happens to drop by most days at lunchtime. And she does all this with a smile on her face and a song on her lips.

The song would be something like "Blue Moon" or "Ain't We Got Fun." Or if she was religious, maybe "When the Roll Is Called up Yonder." My father loved that one.

A Formica counter, white with gold flecks, I'm guessing circa 1960, and eight chrome-rimmed stools of the same ilk, lined the right side of the cramped establishment. To the other side sat one table with a view of a small television perched atop the drink cooler. A middle-aged black man wearing a trucker cap nodded as I passed. I set my purse on my lap and swung into place.

Woo, hot in here! No AC apparently. I guess I'll be taking this old dress to the dry cleaner, praying all the while they don't ruin it.

Oh my, fried chicken, fried chicken. The black words scrawled on the whiteboard pulsated like a beating heart, and my nose searched the air for that singular aroma.

So, New York isn't exactly the mecca of fried chicken. We act like we have it all there, but we don't have a plethora of fried chicken. Something I've not shared with many people is that fried chicken, in my opinion, eclipses every other known food. Of all people, I realize that isn't glamorous, but my mouth knows the truth. That first bite is as good as a blanket out of the dryer after sledding or a gulp of cold Coke after a day of yard work.

Now, there's an art to consuming fried chicken. The first bite must include the moist, steaming meat as well as the crispy, savory skin. You feel your teeth break through the crust, sink into the flesh, and as the steam hits your nose with the aroma, the morsel explodes into your mouth, setting your taste buds on high.

Next, you strip the skin off and set it aside. You eat the meat, picking up the piece of chicken if it's a drumstick or wing, using your fork to peel it off if it's a breast or thigh.

Once every bit of meat is off the bone, you leave a tiny bite in your mouth, then pick up the crispy skin and pop it in your mouth, and that, my friend, is the most perfection a mouthful of food can ever hope to achieve.

Someday, I may write a guide to the best fried-chicken places in America. Imagine, eating my way around the country.

So I hoped Della-Faye or Jonah did a decent fried chicken. I thought I saw a leg or two peeping out from beneath a sheet of foil in the warmer.

"What can I get you?"

And Della-Faye appeared behind her voice, an angel of nourishment, the saint of fried chicken, covered in sweat. At least I guessed that was who it was. She'd pulled back her thick curls into a little bun on the crown of her head. Her white T-shirt, covered by an apron, contrasted with her red-brown skin, and the slant of her eyes and cheekbones boasted of some Cherokee somewhere up the line.

"How do folks like your fried chicken?"

"Been makin' it since I was eight years old. I done perfected that chicken years ago!"

"I'll take that."

"Breast and wing? Or thigh and drumstick?"

"Oh, thigh and drumstick."

"You get two sides with that."

"Green beans and mashed potatoes."

She picked up a paper plate and began setting up my meal. "Gravy on the potatoes?" she hollered from the giant stove in an alcove at the back of the room.

"Yes ma'am!"

I am such a chameleon.

"Corn bread?"

"Yes, please!"

And I sat and ate while men, the slick sweat of their working day thick upon their faces, filed through, ordering cheeseburgers and ribs to go. Mostly black men, a few Hispanic men. No whites, no women. I seemed to be breaking some unspoken rules, but Della didn't appear to mind because she asked if I'd be settling in for some dessert.

So I took my time. I savored each bite of that chicken and the honest-to-goodness real gravy on real mashed potatoes in which lumps of starchy potato soaked up butter and milk. I drank a chilled Pepsi from the cooler near the register, and I wondered what in heaven's name I had been doing in a Manhattan apartment, worrying about Le Corbusier loungers, dinners at Tavern on the Green, and underwear for Braden.

Solo was right. What a scoundrel. And a rapscallion to boot!

I miss Solo.

Well, okay. The lounger's okay to enjoy. Good design is important no matter where you find yourself.

But, for heaven's sake, I'm a woman who loves fried chicken! In that little house on Jefferson Street that Howard Huckleberry showed me last week, I bet I could perfect my own fried chicken.

I pictured myself in that place in a pair of comfy jeans and a T-shirt. Two bedrooms, a kitchen at the back looking over a tiny yard that screamed garden potential. Brick pathways to be laid and lots of hostas and coneflowers to be planted. A Japanese-style trellis bursting with morning glories. A fountain. What glorious possibilities.

Della-Faye set down the cobbler. "Here you go."

"Thank you. Is Jonah around?"

"Not right now. He went to shop for tomorrow's produce. I'm off, so he'll be doing the cooking."

"How long have you been here at this place?"

"Last week I celebrated my tenth anniversary!"

By the way, Della-Faye has no teeth. None that I could see anyway.

"This is the most amazing meal I've ever eaten."

"I was the oldest of ten chil'ren, so I been cookin' almost ever since I can remember."

"You grew up here in Lexington?"

"Oh no. Out in Nicholasville. My mother done passed, but my grandmother still lives out there. Ninety-five and still sharp as a tack. Now that's my son right there." She pointed to the man in the trucker cap. He nodded. "He done got the sugar, so I can't feed him like I used to. Got to be careful now." She leans forward and whispers, "It makes him sad."

I replied in kind. "With cobbler like this out of reach? I don't blame him."

I stuck my plastic spoon in the dessert and popped it into my mouth, and yes, I guess I can believe in heaven.

Twenty minutes later, after lingering over every little bite, completely cleansing my palate between each spoonful, I paid my bill. Della-Faye told me to come back, and I assured her I would, oh yes, and no doubt about that.

On the sidewalk I ran into Jonah, two bags of groceries in his arms. He smiled with a broad grin. "I plan on making an African dish tomorrow. Groundnut stew. Peanuts, if you prefer."

I stood on tiptoe and peered into the bag. "Ooooh, chicken!"

"And okra, onion, garlic, tomato."

"Bell pepper. I love bell pepper. Are those bay leaves?"

I wanted to touch the soft black skin of his sad face that smiles.

"Oh yes. And peanut butter, too."

I crossed my arms. "And what time will you be open?"

"Noon. Eleven thirty for you."

"All my favorite things in one pot. Who would have thought?"

"And where did you come up with this love of good food?"

I hold my hand up to my chest. "It's been in here ever since I can remember. And my father liked to cook."

"You bring your father tomorrow?"

"I can't. He passed away several years ago."

"Your mother?"

"Gone too."

"Well then, you come and eat my food and be blessed. I do cook with love." He held up one finger. "Very first ingredient."

Georgia

For some reason the sight of my cousin on her cell phone to some rich client—the way she pushed back her sunglasses atop her head, the way her feet looked so pretty in those shoes—sent me over the edge.

"You're wearing your mother's clothes, aren't you, Fairly?"

I don't know why I just let it fly out of my mouth like that when the realization struck. Fairly flinched. And I kept going. "You go on and on about vintage, but I recognize that dress. Aunt Bette wore it at my mother's funeral."

I pointed at it like it held leprosy within its weave, and Fairly blanched to a shade so white, so eerie, I shivered.

Then she ran out of the room, half the person she had been.

I honestly hated myself in that moment. I saw what I had become, my own rude pettiness a spotlight on the true state of my pathetic existence. Scum.

Ten minutes later she returned with a man.

The little brat. I didn't know she had that much fight in her, and if I wasn't so frustrated, I would have admired her pluck. But there he stood on the porch, a mere screen door separating us.

He gently pushed in the handle, and yes, I could have run, but my feet were smarter than their owner. He dipped his head into the room first, the dreadlocks now gone, the curly hair cut close to his scalp. But the eyes shone just the same. Blue like a summer sky above towering pine trees.

"Georgia?"

I couldn't speak. And no words came to mind. These people all knew what a washout I was. Fairly standing there with her hands on her hips, Uncle Geoffrey looking up from his documents at the dining room table, tortoiseshell reading glasses low on the bridge of his nose. And Sean. Sean knew the truth.

"Hi, Sean."

He walked over, and he wanted to hug me, even reached out his hands, but settled for a small rub on my upper arm. "Thanks for agreeing to see me."

I daggered Fairly with my eyes. She shrugged like a little girl trying to make up, apologetic smile pinching her mouth, eyebrows raised.

Aged afternoon sunlight spilled across the floor and traveled up to pool on the couch. I fell into it. What? What? Speak? Cry? Run? What?

"Nice shoes, Sean."

"They're practical."

"You look good."

He blushed, burning the caramel of his skin. He inhaled in soft, windy eighth notes. He seemed in a perpetual flinched state, hands crammed in his pockets, head pushed down between his shoulders.

And I saw it. I saw what I had done.

I took something so beautiful and treated it like a rarely used item in the back of the kitchen drawer. Like a rolling pin. A nutmeg grater. An extension cord or a pastry brush. Stay in the drawer until I take you out. Come back when I say so and not before. Only this wasn't some object, this was a man with a beautiful heart and an extraordinary gift—a one-in-a-million man—a rare pearl. I always said, in my darkest moments, "But I'm only hurting myself." And there he sat, the undeserving victim of Georgia Ella Bishop's choices.

He sat down beside me. But I got up and walked back to my room and put Messrs. Reliable in the bottom drawer of the nightstand.

What's my problem? I mean, take Billie Holiday for example. She scrubbed floors and ran errands for a house of ill repute. Her mother was thirteen years old when Billie was born. Billie basically grew up alone. She sang with the likes of Count Basie, Artie Shaw, and Benny Goodman. And then spent almost all of 1947 in jail due to her heroin addiction.

Well, at least I'm not a drug addict.

And at least Billie, though arrested on her deathbed for heroin possession, somehow found it in her to make music despite her problems. Tomorrow then, right? My new bed arrives tomorrow, and it's my last night here at UG's.

One more night. One more time to lose myself. Tomorrow I'll make a fresh start, okay, Ms. Holiday, Ms. Fitzgerald?

And yes, Mom, I know. How many times have I said that before?

But Sean is here, and this time he's not going away.

I unscrew the cap.

Hello, old friend.

Once more for old time's sake, and then tomorrow I must bid you adieu.

Miles mills around my legs, the poor thing ramming his head into my shins over and over, more forceful than ever before. He will not let me pick him up.

Fairly

Georgia failed to show for dinner, and the cult people have come and gone. But Sean's still here, and, well, Sean's the type of guy you can be yourself around no matter how ticked off at him you are, so when I told Uncle G what I did, how I got Georgie back by bringing Sean around, I wasn't afraid that Sean would ream me out.

In fact, Sean falls into the category of persons who quietly accept the events of life and see them as growth opportunities. Pretty sickening if you ask me. To be so mature and perfect. Still, folks like that come in handy when you, oh, say, use them to get back at somebody. He realized soon enough I had surprised Georgia with his presence, but he chose to remain mute.

We ate takeout tonight. Uncle G's current mountain-top-removal mining crusade has eclipsed his culinary pursuits. "Eastern Kentucky is one of the poorest regions in the U.S., Fairly," he answered when I asked why he cared so much. "If I don't try to do something about it, who will? It's not like these people have a voice on their own."

Of course, he brought in Thai food because who in the name of heaven orders pizza anymore?

"The coal companies are practically raping the region."

Or a pedestrian cheeseburger sub with lettuce, tomato, mayo, and grilled onions? And I'll take some onion rings with that.

"I'm just so tired." He stretches. "And I need to make some calls."

But I ate the Pad-Thai anyway, enjoying the peanutty taste with the green onions, egg, shrimp, and sprouts. The Thai really know how to do noodles, don't they?

What's happening to me? Tavern on the Green to Sonny's Thai Carry-Out Buffet in half a month.

I took a plate in to Georgia, but she rolled over on the bed to face the wall. "Get thee behind me, Satan," she said.

Dead mother's clothes, my foot!

Fine. That's just great, Georgia.

I knew one thing: after we finished, I'd walk my dead mother's clothes right down to Della-Faye's for some more of that addicting cobbler, and maybe Jonah would be there, for the simple fact that he survives, that he chooses to keep going, brings me peace.

When I went into the kitchen to announce my VIP intentions, I found Sean and Uncle G in an earnest discussion that my presence proceeded to stifle.

I crossed my arms in front of my chest.

Uncle Geoffrey set down his cup of tea, eyes skewering me. "Why in the world would you do such a thing, Fairly?"

"I'm tired of behaving myself."

Sean smiled.

"And I'm not going on the trip tomorrow."

"I figured as much from the get-go. Georgia said she'd go." Uncle G's face reddened. Interesting to actually see the man angry.

"I don't have any clothing now anyway."

Sean looked up over his teacup. "It's *all* your mother's?"

"Well, not my underwear!" Thank heavens. And even if that were true, I'd hardly admit it. "Or my shoes, either, Sean!"

He looked back down at his tea, and, of course, I felt just horrible.

"I'm going out."

They let me go, because men are usually like that, I've found. They don't have to work everything out right then and there. They realize tomorrow will come and tomorrow might just hold the key to making some sense of today.

Hah! Don't I wish!

I guess you could also call that a healthy case of denial.

But I simply refused to walk my high-heeled shoes down to the VIP. Not this time. So I pecked my way through the stuff on Georgia's floor, digging up her Wellington boots and a pair of socks.

Gorgeous with vintage tulle, not that she noticed. She was still facing that wall.

This time, I hardly cared at all what people thought of my ridiculous outfit as I walked down to Sixth Street. I looked silly, I knew it, so let's just not pretend, all right? I don't even remember making eye contact; all I wanted was that cobbler.

Della-Faye clicked off the light over the stove as I entered.

"You back again?"

"I had to get out of the house."

"I heard that. I'm about to go home. You mind taking your food carry out?"

"I'll take it over to the park. Lots of cobbler."

She turned her back and grabbed a foam container. "Then you'll be wantin' a fork."

I parked my mother's dress and my behind on the red vinyl of the stool. "Della-Faye, do you like what you do?"

She turned back around, the cobbler scooped out and glistening in its sugary syrup. "Now why do you ask?"

"I don't know you, but you seem peaceful."

She laughed. "Peace is an earned thing. You might just be too young to have done earned your peace."

"I've buried two parents and a spouse."

She raised her brows and set down the food. "How old are you?"

"Twenty-eight."

"Sweet Jesus." She turned back around, walked to the refrigerator in the back, and pulled out a chicken drumstick. "Lord, have mercy." After placing it on a plate she handed it to me. "Ain't nothing more soothing than a piece of cold chicken."

I bit into the cool goodness and had to agree.

She laid her redwood arms on the counter. "Now, I've got—hold up, there—what's your name?"

"Fairly Godfrey."

"Fairly, huh? Like that. Your mama and daddy good people, then?"

"I thought so."

"Mmm. So now this is what I got to say. It bein' Wednesday and all, I'm going to prayer meeting. As I see it, you look in need of some prayin'. Either you can witness it, or go to that park and eat your cobbler. It's all the same to the Lord and me."

"Will you be singing any songs?"

Her eyebrows shot up.

"Okay, why not? Do I have time to take a few bites of the cobbler?" It isn't hard to guess, it had taken me no time to eat that drumstick.

"Suit yourself. I'll make sure everything's turned off, and we'll get on out of here."

So I ate Della-Faye's cobbler. As many bites as I could shovel into my mouth while she closed up shop. The juices from the peaches dribbled down my chin and onto my mother's dress.

Clarissa

The mother swings her forearm, now covered with eczema, across the counter, sending the plates and cups flying onto the floor. The little girl watches them, her brain speeding up, the items slowing down, and they tumble like clowns, sad bright clowns, over and over, crashing onto the floor, spinning, exploding into colorful confetti shards.

The mother screams.

"If you can't wash the dishes, you can sweep them up instead! And if they're all gone, it'll be up to you to figure out how we'll eat our food."

The little girl holds a dirty dishtowel up to her mouth, flinching. The mother grabs her arm.

"Do you hear me, Clarissa?"

She nods.

She reels, pushed away.

"Now what's for supper?"

"Sandwiches?"

"What? I didn't hear you!"

"Sandwiches, Mommy. And some soup?"

"Where is it, then?"

"You're early. I haven't—"

And the mother turns her back on the little girl.

"Wake me up when it's on the table. I had a rough day at work."

"Yes ma'am."

She goes about her work, trying to whistle something, anything, but she can only think of the theme song to that movie about the doctor with the funny name that her mother watches over and over again on the VCR.

Somewhere my love, there will be songs to sing. Yes, that's it. That's the very song.

Fairly

Right then, I hoped that reincarnation truly explained life after death and that I would come back in my next life as a black woman. I'd wear my hair in long skinny braids I could tie into a knot at the crown of my head, and I'd dye the ends that sparked out of the plaited crown bright blond or black cherry. I'd swathe myself in African-print odds and ends and stain my lips maroon on some days and purple on others. I'd love my derrière.

And I'd pray to God with all the fullness of an angel choir spinning on the rings of Saturn, the giddy light of a newborn sun spilling on my face. I'd lay my hands on the back of a poor sinner like me, rock in the Holy Spirit, and shout, "Hallelujah!"

Mmm, hmm!

Thank You, Jesus.

And then I'd invite myself downstairs for a cup of strong coffee and a bowl of banana pudding. And I bet I wouldn't realize how important I was in the maneuverings of that mystifying deity who lurks around corners and surprises at whims.

I wouldn't realize it at all.

But maybe one of those sinners I touched would come back the next day, sit on a stool in my restaurant, and cry like she hadn't in years.

Then again, she might not. But who's to say what tomorrow will bring?

I pushed my forefinger into her blubbery side. Man, Georgie's gained a lot of weight this past year. She was out. I turned to Sean. "You know about her drinking, right?"

"What?"

Oh man.

He squats to see her face better. Sean's thighs are like tight hams. Why Georgia doesn't want to just jump the man, I don't know. "How long has she been doing this?"

"Years is my guess. She doesn't work. She doesn't have any friends. You do the math."

"Dear Lord." He ran his long, burnished finger down her deadened cheek. So loving. So in love with this woman lying on her side in a puddle of spittle.

How nice to be so adored.

"Since I left?"

"Talk to Uncle Geoffrey about it. He probably knows more than I do." I pulled the covers up to her chin and adjusted the blinds, cutting off the streetlight falling across her face.

So Sean sat down at the table with Uncle G, and, eavesdropping, I heard the history afresh, all at one time, like I never heard it before. Georgia finding the liquor cabinet the day after her mom's funeral, going into rehab at fourteen. The entire gory story of a motherless teen who was forgotten by her father and who spent too much time at a place called the Ten O'Clock Club.

Sometimes I don't think Georgia herself remembers the time for what it was. I honestly think she's somehow placed the blame on Sean for all of her problems. Or her dad. And I guess it's her mom's fault too, so that makes it God's, right? Or is it her dad's for not making up for his wife's absence, and if so… Oh heavens! The blame game is exhausting!

"How did I miss this?"

Sean's voice attests to his abilities as a vocalist. The promise of a song whispers out with his words. I've always had to bend forward to hear what Sean says. But I'm always glad when I do.

Uncle Geoffrey lights up a smoke.

"She was just good at hiding it, I guess. None of us knew. And she really didn't slide back in a major way until after you left. And then when Gaylen died, she spun out of control."

"I don't know what I was thinking going off like that. Georgia always seemed like the type who could take care of herself."

I settled my bottom on the floor of the hallway. Most people feel guilty about eavesdropping. I somewhat enjoy it. Hurts the tailbone a bit, but it's a small price to pay.

"She's never been, Sean. She got good at the act. Had to, with the way Gaylen was gone all the time. She had nobody to really connect to, other than me. And what good could I really do her?"

"She's always loved you, man."

"I know. But being shoved around between me and her grandmother and a host of babysitters, there wasn't a prayer she'd turn out capable of a decent relationship without some major compensation. I probably should have warned you."

"No, man. Love isn't like that. It doesn't keep a list of the things done wrong."

Well, Sean did plenty wrong, for sure. I only hope Georgia can be as magnanimous.

Sean. "You think I can talk her back to me?"

"I'd like to think so. The fact that she hasn't dated a soul since you left is cause for some encouragement. Or maybe not."

Someone drummed his fingertips on the table, and then a chair scraped back from the table. "Guess I'll go clean her up then."

"Thanks." Uncle Geoffrey gathered together some papers.

Well, I hopped to my feet, pins and needles poking my soles as I flew down the corridor and into my bedroom!

A few minutes later I heard Sean singing as though to an infant. What a complete waste. But I lay down on the floor by the crack beneath my door, raised my knees, and folded my hands across my stomach. And I heard music more beautiful in its simple sweetness than anything I'd ever heard as he sang in a melancholy minor key, "Would you like to swing on a star? Carry moonbeams home in a jar?..."

Clarissa

The little girl loves to color. With her tongue tucked into the corner of her mouth, she traces pictures of the pretty women in magazines onto onionskin paper, colors them in with colored pencil, and then outlines their curves of flesh and fabric with a felt-tip pen.

When the mother comes home from work, the little girl hides them. The mother will think she has too little to do. So she schedules her summer afternoons like this: wake up, find a lady in a magazine, sweep the kitchen and take something out of the freezer, trace and color, vacuum one bedroom, outline, vacuum another bedroom, watch a rerun of *Bewitched* on TBS, vacuum final bedroom, find a lady, scrub the bathtub.

And so she lives her small life on the corner in the house with green siding. The neighbors can't get over how helpful she is. She always smiles and waves when she's sweeping the porch.

What a wonderful child.

One day Leonard the Granddaddy Man knocks on the front door. "Clarissa?" he hollers.

She opens up. "Hi."

"Me an' Dianne are going for a drive in the country. Maybe get some ice cream. Wanna come?"

"I can't. Mom'll be home soon, and I haven't made dinner yet."

"You're cooking dinner? At your age?"

"Yes sir."

"Well now, I..." He looks at his daughter's house. "Well now."

Fairly

How do I even make sense of today?

Of course, *I* had to be the one to find her. I'd just wrapped the old white bathrobe with red poppies around me all set for a nice morning cup of Uncle G's Assam tea with honey, and I noticed her feet poking out from behind her bedroom door, which was halfway open. Why in the world would Georgia be lying on the floor?

Precisely. Of course, we all know why.

Somehow, she'd managed to awaken from stupor number one and do it all over again in the middle of the night. And why do I expect her to be rational?

Passed out, she was breathing so irregularly I'm certain I waited ten seconds in between each breath, not daring to breathe myself. And let me tell you, ten seconds becomes excruciating while waiting for someone to breathe. Made me lightheaded.

That woman!

Several empty bottles lay like struck bowling pins on the carpet.

I guess I am a little angry right now. What a horrid day. And it isn't so much that I feel put out, it's that Georgia has everything life has to offer right at her fingertips and she refuses to reach out and grab it. It's difficult to feel sympathy for somebody who has a gorgeous husband she rebuffs on a regular basis, more talent than the rest of us put together, and honestly, great hair and boobs. When I think of women like Edith Head or Madeleine Albright, my cousin infuriates me.

The room stank, vomit spewed like cooked oatmeal on carpet, walls, and bed linens, and she'd opened a window sometime during her binge, the summer heat overtaking the air conditioning.

How did I not hear her during the middle of the night? The desk chair lay on its side and a coat rack too.

Still, I knelt down, trying to avoid the throw-up, but it was simply everywhere. For someone who skipped dinner…

Oh, her hair was a clotted, sticky, matted mess, and I had to push it away from her face with my fingers, shoving down a wave of nausea—like we needed more regurgitation in the room. I've washed my hands at least five times today, and, like garlic or fish, the smell won't go away completely. Her skin felt so cold.

"Uncle Geoffrey! Quick!"

He came running in. "What's wrong?"

"Look."

"Dear God." Uncle G knelt right down in the puke. "Oh, Georgie." He turned to me. "Did you just find her?"

"Just a second ago."

He pinched her cheeks, called her name. "Call 911."

Just then a seizure overtook her, and I ran down the hallway to the kitchen, knocking my shin on the coffee table and my hip into the counter, and, boy, do I have quite the display of purple shiners there this evening.

Uncle G remained calm. He had turned her on her side by the time I came back into the room, still attached to the phone line. Her body convulsed in a slow, purposeful rhythm, as if her brain had told her, "Enough is enough! I'm gone," and left her body alone to do its own, jerky thing. All I could do was recite an old rhyme in my head in time with the jerking of her body. One, two, buckle my shoe. Horrifying, I know.

I wanted to fly away to the spot where Georgia's mind probably rested right then, lucky her, and didn't it figure? She's off to oblivion with the rest of us here running like lemmings about to go straight off the cliff.

"Why did you turn her? Aren't you supposed to keep people as they are?"

"I don't want her to swallow her tongue, Fair."

Three, four, shut the door.

I sat at the edge of the bed and gripped my knees. "This is scary. Will she be all right?"

He shook his head. "I don't know. She's probably got alcohol poisoning."

I believed him. He's seen enough stuff like this to know.

"See if you can find any more empties."

Five, six, pick up sticks.

I knelt down and flipped up the bedspread. I mean, that's where I'd hide them. "Good heavens."

"How many?"

"At least ten. But I'm sure they're not all from last night."

He sighed. "So we just can't tell, then."

The convulsions slowed down, then ceased.

We stared at each other.

Seven, eight, lay them straight.

"I'm scared, Uncle Geoffrey."

"Me too."

We watched for the rise of her chest, hoping for a breath. It didn't come. The next one didn't either.

"Georgia!" Uncle Geoffrey yelled out, leaning closer to her ear.

Nine, ten, do it again.

"Georgia Ella Bishop!"

His hand gently traced her face.

I grabbed her wrist, laid the tips of my fingers against the vein. "I don't feel anything."

Uncle G laid his head against her chest, felt the portion of her neck covering the carotid artery. "I think her heart stopped beating. Do you know CPR?"

I nodded. "You pump, I'll breathe."

I tipped her head back, cradling the back of her neck in my hand. So cold she felt, so dry. I checked for blockage, then laid my mouth on hers. I didn't taste the vomit then, and now, that thought astounds me. I only heard my pulse like a war drum in my head; I only felt my own breath burning in my lungs; I only saw pale, dead skin covering Georgia's face.

By the time the paramedics arrived she still wasn't breathing. They removed paddles from a carrying case, turned on the machine, and laid the paddles on her chest. Clear! Pressed the buttons, and her chest jumped a mile, and her heart began to beat again. They started an IV, strapped her to the stretcher as fast as they could, spouting their jargon, and Uncle Geoffrey ran behind them.

He pointed to the hook by the door as he followed the gurney. "There are the keys. Meet me at Saint Joe's emergency room. I'm going in the ambulance."

"I'll get her purse. Hopefully she has insurance."

And guess what she didn't have?

I got lost several times, went the wrong direction down a one-way street, ran a red light and almost hit a Budweiser truck, but finally managed to locate Saint Joseph's, a bloodless complex every bit as depressing as every other hospital at which I've kept a vigil. First for Mom as she struggled to stay among us after the accident. Dad was killed on impact. Then, of course, Hort. A much longer vigil, and so much more sad to watch him waste away like that before he finally refused treatment. Why God decided to let death have its fun for a while on my husband, I've yet to figure out. Not at all decent of Him, I'd say.

Can't we all have heart attacks, massive strokes, or car accidents where we don't know what hit us? Is that too much to ask?

I filled out as much of the paperwork as I could and tried to be as good a liaison as possible, and good heavens, this is the most pathetic little family imaginable. Me, Georgie, and Uncle G. Pathetic. We are all Georgia has.

And if that isn't about the most depressing thought I've ever had, I don't know what is.

About an hour after I'd arrived, Uncle G slipped out to where I sat in the waiting room flipping through a sun-bleached copy of *Redbook.* He looked as if two decades had come and gone since he hurried out of the house to the ambulance.

"She's okay, right?"

"Not really."

"What's wrong?"

"Georgia's in a coma."

Lovely, cousin. A coma. What a positively Shakespearean diagnosis. Tragic. Flawless. Not enough blood, though, do you imagine?

"Fairly?"

Horrible reaction, yes.

"Fairly?"

What were you thinking? How? How? How?

"Fairly!"

I shook my head, felt a bit of hysteria inside, prayed it wouldn't take the form of hyena-like laughter, tears being much more appropriate.

"You need to go home and get cleaned up, Fair. And bring me some clean pants, would you mind?"

I looked down. Dried vomit circled the knees of my pajama pants.

So that was my day.

I'm lying here on my bed. The house smells clean. That cab-driver-actress-voice-over-talent lady with the spiky blond hair named Alex came over and cleaned up the puke.

A casserole sits in the freezer. Not from Peg, obviously, because it's got barley and tofu and spinach in it. Ghastly. But…it really is the thought that counts at times like this, right?

Jonah brought over a container of groundnut stew, obviously made with love because it was one of the most delectable dishes I'd ever eaten, and I gobbled down at least half of it while watching *Wheel of Fortune,* and before I go to bed, I'll probably heat up yet more. Tomorrow morning, prior to the hospital run, I'm going over to Della-Faye's for some sausage gravy and homemade biscuits.

I've never been a stress eater before—but what is there right now?

And now we've got to worry about Miles the cat. He's under the bed, I think.

Oh no! Nobody called Sean.

Part III

Pink

Georgia

It's pink in here—a pale blush of a pink that fades into a fuzzy blue around the edges. I can remember lying on the floor of the bedroom around 3:00 a.m. and feeling the room spin.

I hate the spins.

I don't know how much I drank. I'd been so optimistic, and then the fear struck: Sean and me for the rest of my life, rehab again, accountability to a real live face. The next thing I knew, Fairly was cussing up a storm over my body. My goodness, talk about a potty mouth. And she always sounds so "cosmopolitan, dahling," but whoa, when life gets tough, apparently so does my cousin's vernacular! I could only hear her, and even then I knew my regular ears weren't picking up the profanity, but some other sort of consciousness was listening in. I had no idea she resented me so much, and I can't figure out why. Thank goodness she didn't kick my body like some burlap bag of grain. I really thought that was next on the agenda.

I entered some sort of pink zone once my body started jerking and popping. I like it better here in this cotton-candy world. It's actually quite nice, very watery too, as if I'm floating on something I cannot see. I feel as though I'm looking through binoculars, looking at the pink haze, which reminds me of the angel hair our next-door neighbor used to swirl around the lights on her Christmas tree. But that was before Mom died and we moved to the condo, closer to the Ten O'Clock.

Uncle G is talking to the doctors right now, and they're telling him it doesn't look good, that they'll have to do an MRI to see what's happening in my brain. There may be severe damage because I wasn't breathing for so long. Severe brain damage?

Does that mean I get to stay here in the pink?

I couldn't be more miserable than I was before, right? It's very sweet here. And very real. I didn't know comas were like this. Are they all? If not, they should be. I'll have to mention that to God. Maybe He actually listens to people in this state.

Footsteps retreat. And a hand grasps mine. UG is still with me, I guess. "Georgia? Can you hear me?"

I can.

"Oh, girl. Can you squeeze my hand?"

But my hand is a million miles away. His touch, normally so mortal and real, feels spidery and light.

A million miles away is a very long distance. Perhaps it's another dimension entirely.

Fairly

Solo picked up the phone on the first ring.

"Hello?"

"Solo, it's Fairly."

"Hello, Fairly Godfrey. You sound very upset."

Solo knew me that well. Something sweet flowed into my heart. I told him everything, and he offered no advice...for there was none to give. But he gave me plenty of "oh my's" and "poor lady's" to soothe me.

I just needed to hear my friend's voice. That was all.

And then—the Sean call.

Now or never, as people say.

I rubbed my hand over the tweed cover of Uncle G's address book. No PDA for this man, no sir. And sure enough, Mr. Organization himself had already recorded Sean's Sister Pearl number.

Why me? Couldn't I simply tuck myself in between the sheets, sip a cup of tea, and read a book, then get extremely sleepy so that the book kept slipping backward and I kept going to the same paragraph over and over? And *then,* I wanted to close my book, click off the light, roll into my pillow, and close my eyes until tomorrow morning.

Instead, I sat down on the brown couch, pushed aside obscure magazines on the coffee stump like the *Christian Century* and *Sojourners*—where is a copy of *House Beautiful* when you need one?—and set my heels on the shiny surface.

I gave myself two minutes to breathe in and out like I was about to do aerobics or something. Okay, so then I called. I bore the news. And when silence stretched on the line, I said, "Did you hear me, Sean?"

And I only heard one sob and a gulped "Thanks for calling."

When I finally went to bed, Uncle G had yet to return. I pictured him, slump-shouldered in the aqua blue vinyl hospital-room lounge chair, wondering how he got to be the one in charge of Georgia. No trip to the coal mines for him, I guess.

Georgia

Grandmom?

A dark, familiar shape forms in the pink, focuses more sharply as it ad vances forward. Yes, it is.

Grandmom, is that really you?

Hello, there! How are you feeling?

I can't feel a thing, Grandmom.

Good. It's nice in here, isn't it?

Where am I?

I have no idea. My place was green. I love green, though.

I didn't realize pink was my favorite color until I landed here. I like your dress.

Thanks. It was your father's favorite when he was growing up.

Will he be coming?

She shrugs. *I don't know. I'm surprised I'm here.*

She sits down on one of her old kitchen chairs, chrome and turquoise blue vinyl. *I came to tell you a story.*

I loved Grandmom's stories. *Which one? The one about the three kittens and the witch?* I'm sitting in a chair now too. This place gets niftier by the second and—did I really just use the word *nifty*?

Oh no, dear, you haven't heard this one yet. By the way, I think you're wanted outside. Do you hear what I hear? Somebody's crying. I don't quite recognize the voice. Sounds familiar. Listen closely. Tears like that ought not to be taken for granted.

So I concentrate.

"Oh, Georgia. Oh, Georgia."

Sean.

"I'm so sorry, baby. What did you do?"

I'd like to ask the same thing before we get started on the story. Grandmom.

I honestly didn't plan on drinking that much, Grandmom. I just kept going and going with it. Normally I'm more in control, but I saw Sean for the first time in years. That's who's out there crying, by the way. I really thought it would be my last hurrah with the bottle.

I see. That was a stupid thing to do, Georgie.

I know.

You've been doing a lot of stupid things for a long time, though, haven't you?

Yes. I've tried—

No, you haven't. Not really. Don't lie in here, Georgia. You can lie outside, but you can't get away with it here.

Oh.

Grandmom settles back in her chair. A footstool appears, the one she used to have in her living room. *I'll tell you what trying is. Trying is walking ten miles a day for water and a cup of grain to feed your children. Trying is going down on hands and knees and scrubbing the dirty floors of a hospital to make ends meet. Trying is setting aside the bottle even though it's difficult. Subjecting yourself to a goofy AA meeting if that's what it takes. My grandfather was an alcoholic, Georgie, did you know that?*

No.

One day, he walked away from it. She held up her hand, one I remembered well from childhood. *Now I'm not saying it's that easy for everybody, but it's amazing how powerful the mind can be.*

Grandmom, am I going to make it out of here alive?

Chuckles sound extra warm in here. *How should I know?*

Sean sobs and sobs.

Can we wait until he leaves for you to begin the story?

Of course, take all the time you need.

Sean feels very different from inside here. Transparent, in a way. Feelings transport themselves over to me as if the words that explain them are plastered across his forehead. Sadness, of course, because Sean always took in the woes of the world, stamped them on his heart, and tried to cast them back out. But they would never leave.

Grief.

Oh, wow. Grief. Sean knows, doesn't he? Sean knows that I'm never going to come out of this thing. Of course, he could be wrong. Sean thought I would go back with him, and he was mistaken then, so why should this be any different, right? But this grief feels so full, bloated like a corpse. I don't know how he can deal with emotions like this. Has it always been this way for him? I'm glad I can't see him.

Grandmom, you still there?

Yes.

There she is, floating in that chair. She sighs. *I always loved this kitchen set.*

Me too. I have a question to ask you before we start the story. Is it true, what you said all those years ago, that only Catholics go to heaven?

No.

But there are Catholics there, aren't there? Because this girl at school, she was a Baptist, she said that Catholics are idolaters and that idolaters don't go to heaven.

She was wrong too. You wouldn't believe how wrong most of us were about most things.

I kinda figured.

I truly feel sorry for those of you left on earth.

Do we ever get it right?

Some do more than others, but that's all I can say.

Oh, come on, Grandmom, I'm not going back there, am I? Can't you give me a little clue?

No. You're not dead yet. Besides, wouldn't you rather find out from Jesus?

I guess so. So am I going to die?

We all do.

This is obviously going nowhere.

Can I tell my story now, Georgia?

I guess so. I have a feeling I'm not going anywhere.

Grandmom's chair transforms into her old lounger, the rocking wing-backed kind she placed in her living room near the fireplace I never once saw lit. The rip on the side of the seat cushion is gone, though.

I didn't think about Grandmom Bishop enough outside here. Honestly, when Dad went on extended trips and she came to stay, she was much more quiet. She read her *Monthly Missalette,* cooked German food, packed lunches, helped me with homework, and didn't say half of what she's saying here. I never climbed up on her lap or listened to her sing a song.

But she had this way of touching my head, that comfortable, warm yet light stroke, which told me she was glad I had been born. And she raked from her imagination glorious bedtime stories that harvested tears, laughter, and sometimes cold fright.

That's who she is right now here in the pink zone. The lively, storytelling Grandmom: passionate and funny and bursting with humanity.

Yes, that was the real me. A lot of people hide behind stories. So are you ready to listen or are you still going to ruminate about who I was all those years ago? And I'm sorry I wasn't more outwardly affectionate. Old ways, you know.

You mean I can't even think in here without you knowing?

No. Isn't that wonderful? You can be completely who you are. You have to be. I wish I'd have understood that on earth. I hid myself from God all the time. Or thought I did.

I think I know what you mean.

Oh, you do.

That's right. Honesty first and foremost here in coma land.

Fairly

Della-Faye set down the breakfast plate, the country gravy liberally covering the biscuits with its peppery smoothness, the sausage links glistening on a separate plate. The coffee was strong, the sunlight gentle. And she hummed in the quiet. No television this morning.

Fine by me, truly. I don't believe I could have handled any extra stimulation.

I shoveled in that meal like I was about to leave the country and subsist on nothing but grubs for a year. And then, my coffee refilled, a radio whispering some gospel music, Jonah walked in and said some prayers, and I really didn't mind, much to my amazement.

And, oh my. What a good night of sleep does for a girl's compassion! As I sat sipping under the awning of unspoken prayer, I wondered if my cousin ever really had a chance. At twelve years old she lost the one person who loved her like a child should be loved. Uncle Gaylen traveled all over the place, and Georgia was shifted from Aunt Drea to Uncle G to her grandmother on her Dad's side, even to my mom and dad occasionally.

For four years this went on until, at sixteen, she told her father she'd rather just stay at the condo alone.

I wonder if she sent Sean away because she just didn't know how to be with someone consistently? Did she tire of his presence, no matter the benevolence it contained? Was it simply too much foreign stimulation? Even velvet rubs the skin raw after too many passes, doesn't it?

I wish I could crawl into her head and try to figure her out. Then again, I don't. She's in a coma, and we'll have more news later today.

Della-Faye said she'd put Georgia on the prayer chain at her church.

"You comin' to church on Sunday? 'Cause if you is, I'll save you a seat."

"Why not?"

She shook her head. "Child, your enthusiasm is shakin' down this building."

I just smiled and squinted. "I'll bet you're wishing I'd never walked into this place, aren't you?"

She leaned her forearms on her counter. "Now that's a funny question. There are some folks as come in here that I think should take themselves elsewhere, but you? Nope. You got problems. And I've got food. And a couple of good ears. I'd say you can come in anytime."

I don't know why, but that made me want to cry. Most people I know like being around me because they think I have no problems. I'm rich. I can do whatever I want with my life. I'm free, free, free! What's not to like about all that?

But Della-Faye somehow sees me as I am. Maybe because I walked in here as nothing else. Or maybe her fried chicken stripped me of my pretense.

Della-Faye knows.

I guess some women are just like that.

Della-Faye's scrumptious breakfast tucked inside, I hurried over to Georgia's apartment for the ten o'clock furniture delivery, which I inexplicably thought to delay yesterday while awaiting news of Georgia's condition. What does that say about me, that I'd remember furniture and forget Sean? Then it was on to the hospital where Uncle G, bless him, kept up the vigil.

Clarissa

The young girl listens as her mother talks on the phone with Uncle Alan, Reggie's real dad.

"I don't care if Dad's dead. I hope he's in hell, if you want to know the truth, Alan."

The young girl is glad Leonard showed her how to draw tulips. It's fun making the zigzags and inserting the little triangles in between. Red is the best.

"Too bad Mom didn't kill him when she tried."

Then yellow. Yellow's next.

"She can't hear. She's in the other room. But I'll tell you this, that man deserved to die alone, not that you let him."

. . .

"Do you think he loved you because you were there for him? No way, Alan. He went to his grave despising us all. The same cruel monster he always was."

The medium green is the best color for the stems and leaves, not the dark green. That's too much like pine trees.

"No. Demons like him don't change."

Roses? How did Leonard draw roses?

"Oh, come on. There's no excuse. You'll find he didn't have a dime once the lawyers sort everything out. And you're welcome to it. I want nothing from him."

Roses, roses, roses.

"He broke my arm, Alan."

Pink roses, red roses, yellow roses.

"He was lucky I didn't kill him myself."

Pretty roses.

"Well, more power to you. Now I've got to go."

The young girl flinches at the slamming of the phone.

Soft, smooth roses. So happy in the round sunshine that smiles down from the upper corner of the page.

"Clarissa!"

She climbs to her feet, the bedroom rug abrading her knees.

"Coming, Mommy!"

The mother pats the couch, holds her, squeezes her so tightly she can't breathe. She gasps for air.

"Okay then, little brat!"

The mother pushes her away.

"Why in the world would I expect *you* to understand? You've had everything. *Everything!* And you don't appreciate it for a minute."

The young girl runs to the kitchen, opens the refrigerator door, crossing her fingers and hoping the Jell-O salad will be ready in time for supper.

Georgia

Grandmom settles down into the chair, comfy. She still carries that extra twenty pounds as she always did. Unless. Unless that's the way we're supposed to look and, once again, we've bungled things down here. That wouldn't surprise me at all.

You're right. That skinny stuff? Nope. Eve has a nice little tummy and a real caboose. I think my generation was a little closer to a proper body image than yours, Georgia.

You don't have to convince me. I thought the dancers in White Christmas *were the cat's pajamas.*

So here's the story. Once upon a time—

I love it when they start like that.

There was a baby literally born in the dirt.

You?

Yes. Stop interrupting. Her mother was the daughter of a poor chicken farmer on the Eastern Shore. Poor, poor. So poor she went to school in bare feet.

Nobody gave her shoes?

Nobody.

Why not?

Mostly because they didn't have shoes to give, Georgia. One pair of shoes a year was all most people could afford. This was the Depression, don't forget.

Why am I sitting on a kitchen chair and Grandmom gets a nice rocker?

Suit yourself, Georgia. Leather or velour?

Velour, please.

So this is much better. And it's sky blue. Goes nicely with the pink.

Anyway, the problem was the chicken-farmer's daughter wasn't married. And she was slightly retarded.

Oh my goodness.

I know. And the chicken farmer had no time to raise a little girl. The mother obviously couldn't. And for several years a woman from town came in, but she wasn't very nice.

So what happened to the little girl?

Her grandfather put her in an orphanage. Just left her there with a little note pinned to her blouse. I was only six.

Who was my great-grandfather, then? Your dad, I mean.

Some sword swallower in a traveling circus.

What?!

Don't be so surprised, Georgia. You got the performance streak from somewhere.

Uh, my mother, perhaps?

My father too.

Anyway, I used to be quite miffed at my father.

What does that have to do with me, Grandmom?

That, Miss Smarty Pants, is for you to just figure out on your own.

She gets up from her chair. *Gotta fly.*

But she doesn't fly really, she just walks and walks and walks deeper into the pink.

You know, this place reminds me of the land of the witches and warlocks in the old TV show *Bewitched.*

That visit? Just plain weird, really.

Maybe somebody will come see me soon. Right now I'm being wheeled down the hallway, and the tech is laughing about his little son who's learning to talk. Calls him Bad instead of Dad.

I'd smile if I my face would let me.

Fairly

I used to think the theme from *Mission: Impossible* sounded so cute ringing out from my bitty cell phone. I mean really, finding a bona fide Gio Ponti Tavolo Rotondo table for less than ten thousand dollars completely warranted such a theme, and when I did, my client kissed both cheeks and pronounced me a miracle worker. But Georgia's condition causes the melody to hit a little too close to home. I swore as soon as I took the call from Uncle G that I'd switch it. I forgot. Which had an unfortunate consequence.

Earlier today after breakfast I dropped Uncle G off at the hospital and ran over to Target before the furniture delivery men were due to arrive. And oh my! The variety of adorable clothing floored me! Now my friends back home might laugh, but I must admit, I went a little loco. Faux-Bohemian peasant tank tops and skirts. Strappy little sandal flats. V-neck Ts and Capri pants. Slip-on Keds. It's adorable! And very Kentucky. I think they may have cornered something down here in regard to comfort. You know, those old clothes of mine can be as scratchy as an Easter dress from Great-aunt Hester.

I'm wondering if I should burn my mother's clothing or not. Now that I'm outed for my necro-couture, it feels creepier than Tony Randall, God rest his soul, fathering a child in his seventies. That really was a fabulous apartment he and Jack Klugman shared in *The Odd Couple,* though.

The furniture deliverymen arrived an hour late, so I thought I'd put some of Georgia's kitchen supplies away. Cute dishes. Cute teacups. All daisy patterned, and that surprised me a bit. She never seemed like the sweet-little-anything type. And how I never really saw her dishes considering I'm her only cousin gives me cause for shame. She's older, to be sure, but stunted and less experienced. If I had been more responsible, more sure of myself, and more comfortable with the fact that I care more about life than the Le Corbusier loungers it has to offer, maybe she wouldn't be in a coma.

A coma!

Heavens, who ends up in comas? I mean, it's something you hear or read about, but in your own family? And there's only three of us, and none in the immediate-family range. What are the chances?

Anyway, after unpacking the glassware, I opened up this mammoth Rubbermaid tub in that ghastly Williamsburg blue shade. Took some real strength to pry the infernal thing open, but I prevailed, and my biceps are better for it, quite frankly.

Quite frankly, I'm in danger of turning into pudding if I don't resume my gym time soon.

Inside the tub, hundreds and hundreds of letters lay like oversized confetti. I didn't read them, I promise, although I was dying to, but I thought I'd at least see who they all were from, and then the organization bug bit me, so I started arranging them by sender into piles. I figure if Georgia's in the hospital long enough, I'll get letterboxes and arrange them all by date as well.

So here's the final tally: fifteen hundred letters from Sean and three hundred letters from her father. Is that not incredible?

And guess what? All but one remained unopened. I don't understand. I simply, positively do not understand. If Hort had sent me something, I'd tear it open with my eyelashes if that's all I had to use.

So I waited for the deliverymen, and I felt relieved at the furniture choices. Modern design truly transcends any space, but well, there's always a first for everything. The place is already painted stark white, so the clean lines of the furniture render it peaceful enough. I had to go with reproductions, but the Mies van der Rohe chairs are perfect for reading with one's feet up on the coffee table, a Le Corbusier reproduction. Some handwoven throws warm things up so she'll be comfy enough during the cold weather, sitting there, drinking. Drinking. Drinking.

Oh, and the area rug! The one nonmodern item, my signature really, antique and art nouveau. This one sports a muted gold background and is simply the perfect accompaniment with the graceful, trumpetlike flowers that vine their way around the border. As a treat I ordered a baby grand piano. I can't think of a gift Georgia needs more. Call me silly, I don't care. I should have reached out well before this.

Beyond that, I took phone calls and managed to locate a gorgeous Noguchi Cyclone Table, 1955, for a woman in England who heard about me through the friend of a friend. Marvelous. Well, you can't go wrong with Knoll. I've said that for years.

So much for the businessy part of my day. While I was finishing up at the apartment, I called Sean and invited him to meet me at Duncan Park for lunch. Jonah packed us up some carry-out chicken, green beans, macaroni and cheese, stewed tomatoes, and apple cobbler. Della-Faye threw in some of her fried corn bread.

I sat at one of the picnic tables and waited for him. The basketball goals are dying for a coat of paint. He shuffled toward me, hand shoved in his pocket, and he looked so sad, kissed by the biggest, gloomiest rain cloud over the honey tree. I have no idea who said "No man is an island," but my goodness, he was right. Sean couldn't even make it as a peninsula!

He appreciated the food, no surprise. Sean would be thankful for white bread with American cheese.

"Why did you keep on writing to her?" I asked.

He looked up, caught. "How could I not? She's my wife."

"She said you didn't come back for three years. Three years is a long time. And by then, she said it was too late."

"I came back after the six months like I promised."

"Really?"

"I know Georgie tells it differently. It's a great wonder to me that you and your uncle will talk to me at all considering what you've been led to believe."

"Then why do you want to reconcile?"

He set down his fork and shoved his plate to the side. He really is the most beautiful man I've ever seen. The way he carefully folded his napkin and arranged the plastic cutlery atop the plate, his hands moving gently yet with such purpose, fascinated me. I stared, and I remembered how nice he was when he and Georgia first started dating and she'd baby-sit me. Sometimes he'd come over and push me on the swings as long as I wanted. He'd also color with me. He would outline the section he wanted to color with the crayon and then color it in with a lighter touch.

I just dug into the paper as hard as I could. Blues are bluer that way, greens more green. And reds. Well, who wants a red that isn't a bloody, glorious mess?

Sean thought about my question, and I marveled even more that someone with so much to offer would waste time on a case like Georgia.

"I love her, Fairly. I always have. I'm not the type of person who can just turn it off because it isn't returned."

"But she loves you, doesn't she? She seemed so wounded at your desertion."

He shrugged. " 'Seemed' being the key word there."

"She broke your heart, didn't she?"

He shrugged again and nodded. "Yes. She did."

"She sure had us fooled. I wonder what her problem really is?"

"It's theological."

I laughed and laughed. "You have spent way too much time in that monastery place, Sean."

"Maybe."

"Do you think she's mad at God or something? Do *you* represent God to her?"

"Now that I can't say. I sure hope not. Is she mad? I used to think so, but I think it actually goes deeper. I think she views Him as some capricious being who singled her out to suffer. And when you get that myopic, not only do you hurt yourself, but you fail to even recognize that others might actually be suffering too. She's holding a grudge against Him. Nursing it like a sick infant. Because if she forgives God for all that's happened to her, she'll have to do something about it. Like start living again."

"It's easier to drink."

"And to forget. This coma is probably the best thing that's ever happened to her if you could ask her. It's like being passed out drunk without the moral stigma."

Okay, that was harsh. But who am I to judge?

So if God's so perfect and all, is it okay to hold a grudge against Him? Do we sometimes need to forgive *God*? Is that okay?

I'm looking for the lightning bolt even thinking this as I now lie in my bed and listen to the sounds of a city falling asleep. It's late. So I think my cell-phone story will have to wait until tomorrow.

Sweet sleep. Sweet dreams.

Georgia

I don't know. Doctors can be wrong, right? Can an MRI machine have a bad day? I'm perfectly rational here in the pink. How can they say there's all this brain damage when I can think more clearly than ever before?

No visit yet from Grandmom, and I have some questions.

Sean came again, with Fairly. UG's been here all day. He shuffles papers and makes quick calls on his cell phone. I didn't realize how involved he is in other people's lives. How can he be around so much heartache and still have hope? I thought his involvement was all big stuff, fights against corporations, "the man," and the whole hippie, social-justice bit. But he advocates for individuals and families too.

I don't know where all that energy comes from. Maybe the lamb stew. Or the cigarettes, and no wonder he smokes. He deals with so much. He should be the alcoholic, not me.

So the doctor walks in. Stan Louis. He sounds dark-haired with dark eyes. Don't ask me why. And he tells them about the brain damage. Apparently, I'm what people used to call a vegetable, which always brought to mind this picture of an oversized piece of broccoli or a giant carrot in a hospital bed.

Sean starts tearing up, I think, because Fairly seems to be trying her best to comfort him and he's sniffling like a kid who's eating soup. "Doctors can be wrong, Sean. Maybe the machine wasn't working like it should." And she just about has him convinced, me too actually, when her phone rings about as loudly as a 5:00 a.m. alarm clock that was set at 2:00 a.m.

It plays the theme to *Mission: Impossible,* and Sean starts weeping again, this time like a mother by the grave of her only son.

Fairly didn't know what to do so she took the call. From that vacuous boyfriend of hers. Brendon or Brady or something. Thank goodness she took it out to the hallway, her final words in my hearing: "…putting things away for Georgia."

Poor Sean.

Oh, good night. I hope Fairly doesn't find the letters!

I've got to wake up. I've got to wake up. I've got to wake up!

Come on. Come on!!!

Nothing. Nothing but pink.

Pink, pink, pink, pink, pink.

Mary-Margaret

She already had enough children to know what eight-year-olds do. Her girls always loved dress-ups. Good thing she saved all those prom dresses and bridesmaid dresses. Would Miranda love dress-ups?

In the middle of the night she tiptoes down to the toy room and gathers the old gowns onto her lap. The lime-green chiffon was her favorite. Then the yellow taffeta with the silk daisies. Yikes, but the attendants' headpieces in that wedding reminded her of old-lady hats—hers went in the trash the night after the reception! She smiles, remembering her own horrid taste at twenty-one and the teal dresses she chose with the huge bustle-bows on the back, a single peach rose, silk at that, held in her friends' grasps. Mary-Margaret's parents didn't have much money, either.

Sometimes she dreams of what it would have been like if she had taken a shine to Grant Maugham, the rich boy in the sixth grade who made no bones about his affection for her. Sometimes she wonders what he's doing now. But not for long. Her husband loves her. Of that she's positive, and there aren't many things she's positive about anymore. Why throw the one sure thing away?

Her feet go numb as she sits on them, but she doesn't mind too much. Numb is good at a time like this. She pictures her little girl running around somewhere in some other woman's dress-ups. And she hopes she's happy.

Dear God, please let her be happy.

She figured she'd know something, feel a strange plucking on her heart if something was wrong, or a lovely warmth if all was well. But she never feels anything like that. She just wonders and can picture only a shadowy shape penciling math facts at school, or watching cartoons on Saturday morning, the sugary cereal she spoons from a bowl in her lap disappearing into nothing.

She opens the lid of the storage box and folds the dresses, laying them atop one another just so.

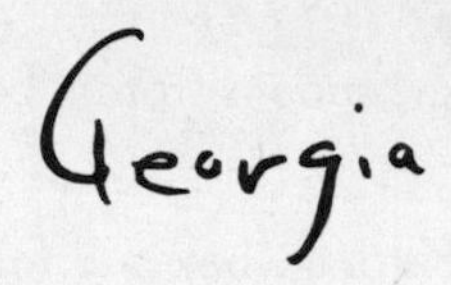

I wish I could see my day nurse. I think this is my second full day in the hospital, which means it's been three days since I went into this coma.

It's nice in here, though.

And Fairly did find the letters.

It's really nice in here. Nicer than anywhere I've ever been.

Sean deserves better than me. Perhaps that's why I fooled everybody, even myself.

Outside of me, Uncle Geoffrey talks with the nurse. Apparently only the machines are keeping me alive at this point, which is just totally weirding me out in here. I feel a little lonely, so I like it when she walks in and talks to UG. Her voice, soft and sweet, somehow changes his voice into something unsure and a little wavy when they converse. I may not be able to see things, but I feel things more fully. He's interested.

I'll bet she's beautiful.

"So will you be here tomorrow, Mr. Pfeiffer?"

"Yes. I can't leave her. I've cancelled my trips indefinitely."

Wow.

"You two are close then?"

He pauses. "Well, as close as we can be. Georgia has intimacy issues."

What?!

"Her mother died when she was young. I don't think she's ever trusted anything again. Except the bottle, you see."

"Unfortunately, the bottle always delivers," she says.

Oh, good night!

And she is so right.

Hello, Georgia, sweetheart!

Grandmom? You're back?

Of course. You don't think I'd leave you alone in here forever, do you?

That's what I don't get. Why do I have to be subject to time here? Surely this place is beyond time.

You're still alive, sweetie-pie.

Oh, so I'm sweetie-pie now.

She laughs. *I know. I wasn't good at affectionate ways back then. I figured I'd give it a try now.*

Works for me.

So, Georgia, are you figuring out some things, then?

Maybe.

I thought that last conversation Geoffrey had with Robin was rather enlightening.

Is that the nurse's name? Robin?

Yes. They're right, you know. About your addiction. The bottle is something you can count on.

Well, yeah. Like you can count on taxes in April, or a tetanus shot when you step on a rusty nail. I'd hardly say it was something that was a lovely experience. It's hellish, if you want to know the truth.

Oh, I believe you! No need to go there! She suppresses a chuckle. *Pun intended.*

Oh goodness. Otherworld humor apparently can be as corny in here as it is out there. Then again, Grandmom always did like those crazy old comedians like Henny Youngman and Groucho Marx.

We all hide behind something, Grandmom. I may hide behind the bottle, but you hid behind your pride.

What's that supposed to mean?

Maybe if you had been comfortable with who you were, retarded mother and all (and by the way, the word retarded *is a no-no these days), maybe I'd have been comfortable with who I was. I was made to play jazz, wasn't I? I'm sure you must realize that I was made to do that.*

The blue kitchen chair appears. *Well, yes, I do.*

Didn't you realize then?

She sits. *I suspected it. But I was never one to interfere.*

Seems to me people could have done a whole lot more interfering after my mother died. I never felt like drinking when I was playing jazz.

Then why didn't you do it more?

I thought playing sacred music would be more healing.

It's only healing to those it's supposed to heal. It reminds me of the story in the book of Acts, when the sheet with unclean animals comes down and the Lord says, "Rise, Peter; kill, and eat." Of course, they're unclean, not what was viewed as acceptable in the religious community.

Yeah, got it, Grandmom. Should've heard that sooner, don't you think?

Grandmom sighs. *If it makes you feel any better, I got it wrong too.*

How so?

I was supposed to be a scientist.

What? That's odd.

Why? I was always doing experiments as a kid. You should have seen the refrigerator at the orphanage.

Why didn't you then, Grandmom?

No money to go to school. I met your grandfather. It was the way things were back then. So many people miss their callings. You shouldn't feel too bad about it.

Yeah, right. *But I only had one life.*

Who doesn't, Georgia? Somehow though, God takes that all into account. He really is very merciful.

But I had a job to do and I failed.

Other people will pick up the slack. He's very resourceful. He'll use somebody more obedient to paint the larger picture if we don't do it. God wants us to live fulfilled and joyful. He knows how difficult the human existence can be. But our joy depends on doing what it is He's made us to do. It's never just joy for joy's sake. Always keep in mind the bigger picture.

That's nice to know. Now. Why couldn't anybody have told me that back outside?

Grandmom shrugs again. *The only thing I can tell you is that God gave you plenty of clues.*

Really?

Are you really that thick? A jazz pianist mother? The ability to play yourself? Being surrounded by musicians? Playing since you were three? Your obsession with that club?

I was drawn to that place for the booze.

Really? You can get booze anywhere, Georgia.

Oh, wow. *He could have been more obvious about it, Grandmom, that's all.*

What more could He have done?

Why don't you just take your comfy little chair and let me think on that one, Grandmom?

Don't be angry with me, Georgia. I didn't do anything! Well, other than not say anything but—anyway, one thing I've learned is that the clues begin in childhood.

I feel miffed. *This is just great, Grandmom. What good does it do me now?*

I have no idea.

I'm not going back, am I?

I don't know the answer to that question either. She stands. *Well, I'm off.*

Will I see you again?

Who knows?

I'm getting a little sick of pink.

Fairly

Sean and I visited Georgia earlier this evening. I picked him up at Sister Pearl's Rest Home. Make that Sister Pearl's Rust Home. Thank goodness he met me outside that ghastly, giant roach of a place. Take those corroded awnings down for heaven's sake, dear Pearl.

We walked into the hospital room and gave Uncle G leave to go get some supper. Peg the almost prostitute sat there too.

"Hey, Fairly! This is so awful, isn't it? I'm sorry for your whole family."

"Well, you're looking at all of us right here."

She laid a hand on Uncle G's shoulder. "Is that right?"

He zipped up his backpack. "I'm afraid so."

"Well, no wonder you like having us all around."

I said, "That sure is the truth."

I don't know why he feels the need to stay by Georgia's side all day. It's not like she realizes he's there or anything. Her brain has turned to mush by all medical standards, which means her fingers are useless. I realize her choices brought her to this place, but the thought that music will never come from her again makes me want to weep.

Sean squeezed Uncle G's shoulder. "Why don't you go on home, man? You look terrible."

And he was right. Dark, jumbo-marker rings outlined my uncle's eyes. And I think he forgot to shower because his hair shone a bit too much in that anemic fluorescent lighting.

"I am tired." He stood to his feet, bent over, and tightened the straps on his walking sandals. "Did you drive, Peg?"

"Yeah. I didn't think you'd be up to the long walk home."

"Thanks."

And when they walked out of the room, she led him through the door, placing her hand on his arm.

Sean set the little bouquet of flowers he bought in the gift shop on Georgia's tray table. Then he sat down on the opposite side of the bed from me and held her hand.

"She feels so dry, doesn't she?"

I reached for my purse. "Here. Why don't you rub in a little hand cream?" I tossed him a tube of cucumber-scented lotion.

He rubbed it into her hands so lovingly, and I sat and wondered how it is we humans can be so wasteful of our lives. We have so much time, don't we? Minutes full of seconds, hours full of minutes, days full of hours. And the years, oh, all the years.

I've lived twenty-eight of those years. And while I've been trying to forget the fact that I'm young and untried, I really, for the first time ever, do believe I'm graciously conscious of the fact that I have my whole life in front of me.

"Sean? How did you know you were supposed to be a singer?"

"Because I can sing. I always could."

"Did you sing much at the monastery?"

"All the time. Music was my chief responsibility."

"And now that you're out? What now?"

He set down Georgia's left hand, reached across the bed for her right, and began massaging in the moisturizer. The smell reminded me of summer days when I'd run in from playing out in the neighborhood and Mom would be setting out dinner. She always cut up a cucumber in the summer.

"I wouldn't mind being a music teacher somewhere. But I don't know. I guess I'll start applying around to schools. In the meantime, I've got to find something to support myself."

"Hey, listen. Why don't you move into Georgia's place? The rent's paid through the end of next month, and it'll buy you some extra time."

"I don't know, Fair—"

"Oh, come now. She's not getting out of here anytime soon. Why should it sit there empty? And Sister Pearl's should be in a Stephen King novel. Be practical, Sean."

He cocked his head. Then he laughed. "Remember who it is you're talking to. I've never won any awards for practicality."

I reached over and grabbed his hand. "I'm glad you're back. We need you to round out this family. I'm sorry she kept you from us for so long."

He squeezed my hand, smiled, then continued ministering to Georgia. "Don't be so hard on her, Fairly. I made my mistakes too. I'm not guilt-free. I didn't realize that your cousin lives in a world of pain. I was too self-centered, I guess, and she never figured out how to break through on her own. You're a different type of person, though. You're strong."

Oh yeah, right. Me. Miss Cosmo. Pass the barbells.

I feel like I'm in the middle of something important. But something important for everybody else. Georgia languishes in a coma. Uncle G, surely devoted to Georgia, seems to be mellowing into a new purpose, though I couldn't tell you what that is. And Sean's back, looking for his marriage.

So what am I doing here?

Braden called, trying to get back together, and oh my. I thought I would just scream, he annoyed me so much.

I'm going to bed.

Alone.

And I'm absolutely fine with that. I never enjoyed nighttime activities with him anyway. Sometimes I think nuns have nailed the secret to life.

I called my real estate agent in New York and told him to put the apartment up on the market, and I wrote a check for the down payment on the little house on Jefferson Street. The current occupants won't be moving out until the end of September, but that's all right. It gives me time to scout out the best contractors around here. And dream. Oh, that place will be just delicious someday.

After breakfast at Della-Faye's, three-bean-salad Gracen called my cell phone.

"Can you get to the hospital right away?"

"What's wrong?"

"Your cousin went into cardiac arrest."

One, two, buckle my shoe.

"Where's Uncle Geoffrey?"

"In the room."

So I left right away, slamming by Sean's to pick him up.

Three, four, shut the door.

And we made it out to Saint Joe's in seven minutes.

Five, six, pick up sticks.

Uncle Geoffrey sat on the floor outside the room, slumped against the wall.

Seven, eight, lay them straight.

"Uncle G!"

He looked up. "She's back. They got it started up again."

Nine, ten…

Sean exhaled with force. "Oh my. Oh my."

Uncle G pointed to Sean. "You might think about calling your folks, Sean. You probably could use the support."

"I can't."

"Are they out of the country?"

"No, they're dead too."

Good heavens. This is all there is? Really? Uncle Geoffrey, Sean, Georgia, and me?

"Is there anybody God doesn't take aim at?" I asked, feeling like I'd been kicked in the stomach.

And both Sean and Uncle Geoffrey looked at me with sad, grown-man eyes.

Georgia

Good night, that was a lot of fuss. I'm fine.

You really aren't, Georgia baby.

Mom?

Even undefined in the pink haze, I'd know that outline. And that voice. Husky and deep.

Yep, baby doll! It's me! I was so happy I was called to come. But oh, honey, you're in a coma.

Oh, Mom. Mom. Oh, Mom.

I thought of all the times I looked at blank sheets of paper and willed some cosmic force to draw her as she'd have looked at the age she would have been. Or sketch her and me together at all those places and events we should have been together. It could have been in charcoal, graphite, Crayolas, I wouldn't have cared. Sometimes I'd look in the mirror, praying that somehow it would turn into a magic mirror, and I'd chant, "Mirror, mirror on the wall, show me my mother—"

Warts and all? She finishes the line with her usual self-deprecating twist.

Oh no. You were always perfect.

The outline solidifies. And there she stands, wearing the dress she used to play jazz in. A sleeveless black number, hugging her curves. Even the pointy-toed shoes sit on her feet just like I remembered. The bone bumps of her delicate ankles protrude, her high arches peek above the sides, and even the backs of her heels are callused right above the shoe line, just like before. We stare at one another for...days? I don't know. But I just feel her and she feels me, down inside, down somewhere in that place we cannot see clearly or smell or hear, down in that place we just remember those senses.

And I rest.

How's Geoffrey, Georgia?

He's lonely.

I thought so.

He's busy.

That I've figured.

Why can't we touch here?

I don't know. The problem is you're not—

Dead yet. Yeah, Grandmom keeps telling me that. I went into cardiac arrest not long ago. That was weird. I kept thinking, with my heart stopped, I'd be moving out of the pink. But they brought me back around.

How'd that make you feel?

She sounds like a therapist!

So?

I have mixed emotions. Sad because Grandmom seems so happy. Mad, because Sean and Fairly know about the letters. Why did I leave them unopened?

You just couldn't face what was inside. It's sort of like not opening your bills. Unfortunately those letters, like the bills, still come due whether you choose to open them or not. Now, your father's letters. If you'd have opened them, Georgia, you'd be a different person today. Your music wouldn't have died completely with him.

That's another thing I don't understand. Why did that happen? I've tried and tried to figure it out. It's not like Dad and I were even close. He never encouraged my music. Whenever we were in the car it was always news channels and talk radio and stuff.

Mom suddenly sat down on a piano bench. Funny how seats appear at whim here in the pink.

Isn't it? Mom said. *Wouldn't you just love to be able to furnish your house like this back in the real world? Think of a sofa, and there it is. Think of a chair, and there you go.*

She sat with her legs crossed and her strong hands clasped about her knees, nails cut short like before, enabling her to play without impediment. *Here's my take on your father. You were trying to get him, just once, to say, "I love what you're doing. I'm proud of you, Georgia. You're really good at what you do." And when that opportunity was gone, it all went out the window.*

Really?

Like I said, it's only a theory.

Does God like jazz, Mom? Or is it all Handel's Messiah *around the throne?*

What do you think, Georgia?

I think He loves it all.

And you'd be right.

Outside of me I feel a pair of hands, one hand holding my hand, the other stroking my hair.

Sean. I still know his touch, after all these years.

I made a big mistake when I ignored him, Mom.

I'll say!

He couldn't have tried harder without literally moving in anyway, or somehow forcing the issue.

And Sean's not like that, Georgia.

No.

You took advantage of his ways. You held one thing against him, a squeaky thing, until it grew into a tyrant.

I know. I'm tired.

I know. Let's just be together. I'm so glad to simply see your face.

Oh, can you see me? I mean, I'm not dead. Isn't this all going on in my head?

It's a little complicated. It's in your head, yes, but then... well, heavenly physics are just different. I don't understand them. But yes, I can actually see you.

What do I look like?

Like you're twelve. It has to come from my memory. You'll always be twelve, I guess. Until you pass over, and then, maybe not.

Mom, this whole experience is throwing my theology into a tailspin.

She shrugs once, like a little girl. *For all you know, this really is just going on in your mind. This might not be real at all.*

Sure feels like it.

You'll just have to wait and see, won't you?

I'm weary.

Yes, it's hard work being in a coma. I won't leave yet. You can rest if you'd like.

Would you play something for me, Mom?

Yes. Rest in that.

And so I do. A piano appears as I close my eyes, and she begins, and oh, Lord, I think I really am in heaven.

I feel like I've been conscious for three days. Uncle Geoffrey's working quietly outside, papers flipping every so often. Peg visited earlier, and they talked about the true loves of their lives. I never knew Uncle Geoffrey was engaged once and that she ran off with a guy in his fraternity. And poor Peg. She was in love in tenth grade, but he used her, then dumped her, and she "kinda went off the deep end" after that. "No real guidance at home. My father was in love with his job, and my mother was in love with her psychiatrist."

On that note…

I succumb to whatever rest we find in places like this where we are neither here nor there, part nor whole, awake nor asleep.

Clarissa

The girl listens as the cousin slams into his bedroom. Drunk again. He's old enough to know better. She realizes this already. And when the mother gets home from work and checks to see if the rooms are clean, he's going to get it. And if he gets it, well, she'll be next.

So she sits on the couch and waits while crashes and curses explode from the crack underneath the door.

A horn honks from the curb.

"Reggie, Casey's here!" she yells as loud as she can.

He storms out of his room, throwing her a look of hatred.

She gathers her strength and a trash bag and heads into the room to clean up the mess.

Out by the kitchen door, she opens the lid to the trash can. The TV mom is crying on the garden bench. Clarissa doesn't know why, but she walks over, sits next to her, and holds her hand.

Fairly

Sean is now as frightfully addicted to Della-Faye's fried chicken as I am. I believe we've consumed it at least once a day for the past three days, and I'm going back tomorrow. A little something appears to be happening between Jonah and Della-Faye. A beautiful thing, love is.

I'm recognizing a sadness to Uncle G's house. In fact, the same sadness permeated his former apartment in New York. He's volunteering tonight, cooking dinner with Peg and Alex at the Catholic Action Center on Fifth Street. Pasta, garlic bread, and salad. I'm surprised he's not interested in Peg. She has this gorgeous hair, auburn with a bit of white near where her bangs would be if they were cut. She actually has tresses. But it's also plain to see she's set her sights on Blaine.

Which makes me think that years ago she might have been a princess in the making. Peg the almost prostitute, if born in the right neighborhood to the right family with the right attitude toward children—which means to me loving, kind, encouraging, industrious, and supportive like my own mom and dad—would have ended up healthy and whole. She wouldn't have been someone who walked the streets, someone who, one night, so down on her luck, nearly accepted the offer of "that greasy redneck" who asked her, "How much?"

"I had to think about it," she told me. "And that scared me as much as actually going through with it would scare others."

So she ended up checking herself into a home for drug addicts, and not long after that, she met Gracen, who wears his faith on his sleeve—that sleeve being broken in and highly comfortable.

Gracen likes Della-Faye's chicken too.

Gracen is the color of my mother's old mahogany jewelry box. Of all the cult people, I most want to be like Gracen. Gracen's so smart and kind and attuned to others. I'm so practiced at acting shallow, I don't know if I can project a different image.

My real estate agent called. With the market so sizzling, we received a full-price offer the first day. I'm sending Solo a list of the furniture I want to keep, to move down here to Lexington. The rest I'll sell.

I bought a bunch of chicken from Della-Faye, and she actually prayed over the pieces! "Lord, bless the folks that eat this chicken," and such. Isn't that a hoot? And honestly, it tasted better going down.

So when Uncle Geoffrey got back from the hospital, Sean came over, and Gracen, Peg, Jonah, and I set out Della-Faye's chicken. Also on the table were greens with egg and tomato, mashed potatoes with real gravy, and buttered carrots.

Uncle G ate and ate and ate.

"Whoa, Uncle G, you're going to have hardened arteries by tomorrow morning. Your system's not used to this stuff."

He pointed his fork at me. "Funny you should say that. I was sitting there by Georgia's bedside, and Peg came in."

"Mac'n'cheese Peg."

Peg smiled. "That's right, honey. Why die miserable?"

"I heard that!" Gracen agreed.

Uncle G nodded. "So I figured that there's something almost sacred about enjoying the food that others prepare and the way they, as creative beings, made it. To be choosy about others' gifts is like slapping Jesus in the face."

I laughed and laughed. "Uncle Geoffrey, you are way too much! You could make a theological statement about"—I picked up my greasy napkin—"this thing!"

Peg picked up the bowl of carrots. "That's what I love about the guy."

Blaine arrived for dessert and sat down right next to Peg.

And she blushed.

Blast.

I think my uncle is a much better catch.

He regathered his ponytail, shoved his feet in some old clogs, and headed out to the soup kitchen to make the meal. Why do people like him have to raise the bar for the rest of us?

Georgia

Wow, I blacked out for a while there. I didn't think you slept here in the pink, but apparently…well, something happened. Don't know what. But the last thing I remembered was a visit from Sean and Fairly, and do those two ever do anything apart these days? Good night!

And now I hear UG out there.

He's talking to me like he's sitting at my graveside or something. Oh great, thanks for the major creep-out. I mean, the baths are bad enough, being naked, turned over this way and that, limbs lifted and set down. I'm a total object. But UG's taking it to a new level.

He's slowing down. Or he needs to, I can tell you that. Talking about the need to simplify his life and saying, "Why do I have to be the big lawyer man, Georgia? I think of myself just serving in the neighborhood, driving Mrs. Stevens to her doctor appointments, making chicken casseroles, and I cringe. Is it because I don't think that's big enough or important enough? Or do I really feel it's wasting my gifts? I just can't tell."

He sighs, and then I hear papers rustling.

Oh, forget it all. UG has angst too? Now that's crazy. Shouldn't he at least have some peace?

It's a little lonely here in the coma zone. It's nice to be able to sit on a chair—sort of—when visitors come. But I'm just kind of floating right now, suspended in the foggy pink. I like the feeling of this, like floating on the Dead Sea, only the sky is pink. Pink is highly soothing. I just never realized it.

Someone begins to exchange pleasantries with UG. A doctor, the one I picture with blond curly hair and acne scars. The cardiologist. He tells my uncle that I should be all right as far as my heart goes. They've balanced me out with this medication and that, and dear heavens, this is too much to take when you're comatose.

"What about the brain damage?" UG asks.

"That's something you'll have to discuss with the neurologist. It's only been a week and a half, though. Too soon to tell much. I'd give her more time."

More time?

"Do you have power of attorney, Mr. Pfeiffer?"

"No, but Georgia's married. Her husband lives here in Lexington."

"Well then, I guess he's the one who can order the cessation of treatment if it comes to that."

Cessation of treatment?

CESSATION OF TREATMENT?

Gee, I guess I kind of liked it when it went dark for a while there.

Hello? Hello?!!!

Mom?

Come in, Mom. I need you. Over and out?

Nothing.

God? A little help?

Yeah, like I expected an answer to *that* one!

Oh man, now that the doctor left, UG's back to his mumbling. I love the man, but you know, *I'm* the one in the coma! Still…

"…and when I travel it's easier, Georgie. I don't think about the fact that I've slept in that same bed since I moved from the crib. Okay, different mattresses."

That is a little pathetic.

I want to ask him about his engagement.

Hey! Can you shoot subconscious vibes at people, sort of an ESP-psychic thing?

Okay. Here we go. Concentrate, Georgia.

Unnnnclllllle Geeeeeeeeeeoffreeeeeeeeeey. Listen up…

I focus my thoughts like a laser beam, a red line of will glowing with a slicing intensity.

Your fiancée…your fiancée…

Focus, focus, focus, focus.

Nothing. Rats.

And I was concentrating so hard, I don't know what he's talking about now. Something about having mosquitoes as his friends.

Oh, good night, UG, how weird is this?

"Well, at least they're more reliable than Jessica was."

Oooooh. Maybe my vibes worked.

"And tell me, Georgie, how in the world did I let that heartbreak go on for decades? I mean, you would know with the way you never got over your mother's death."

Hey!

"The way you pushed everything and everybody away, even yourself."

Hey! Hey!

"I'm wondering if I should blame myself so much for your turning off your jazz. I mean, you jumped on the classical bandwagon right away as if I was giving you an easy out. And the fact that you could switch so easily, that you were talented enough to do so, made it seem like the right thing. On the surface."

Hey! Hey! Hey!

"Still. Your mom would have been really disappointed in me for what I did. She knew, Georgie. She knew you were made to be something great. When I think about what she would have thought about your drinking…"

Hey, at least I was great at drinking.

"Man, I hope you come back around. I don't care what the doctors say about brain damage. I think you can will yourself back. Right? Can't you?"

He stops, coughs.

"Okay, this sounds very Hollywood, but if you're there, squeeze my hand. Give me some sign."

I will my hand to move. Come on! Come on!

Now!

Now! Now! Now!

So just shut up, Uncle Geoffrey. Please, just shut up. I can't handle this.

Clarissa

The young girl opened up her twelfth birthday present.

Underwear, socks, a chocolate bar.

She thought of Charlie Bucket. Well, but at least she got underwear too.

And when she didn't gasp with delight right away, the mother stood up from the sofa and stormed off.

White underwear too.

Down at the bottom of the bag…a training bra.

She reached in and held it in front of her. The cousin walked into the room, his face twisted into something she'd never seen before.

"If a boy ever takes that off of you, Clarissa, I'll kill him. After I kill you first."

The girl shoved it back into the bag, thinking that breasts weren't worth this. Growing up seemed like the biggest joke she'd ever heard.

She hurried next door. They were giving her a party. Thank goodness Leonard the Granddaddy Man was okay now. They were all scared while he was in the hospital. They prayed with a lot of people from the church and then he came home.

Fairly

Sean spread out a blanket in Duncan Park. We'd just been to see Georgia. No change. Sean's going to have to make a tough decision. I wouldn't slip on his shoes for a million dollars.

Life and death, life and death, life and death.

Believe it or not, we weren't eating! I've gained eight pounds since Georgia drank herself into a coma. My derrière looks like two balls of pizza dough. And I actually don't give a fig.

Well, not as much as I thought I would, anyway.

But I sipped on an Ale-8, and so did Sean.

The humidity of the late-July day made the breathing hard and my airy new Target clothes much appreciated.

I lay back, enjoying the sun on my face and the red veiny eyelids from behind. Was it true that people in comas hear what's going on around them? Was this crimson sheet of skin what Georgia was seeing? If she really could hear, she was going to have a fit upon coming to and finding out I organized those letters.

So be it.

It's amazing how glaring other people's hang-ups are.

"So tell me about that monastery business, Sean. Everybody wonders how you could go off like that and just pray and all."

He sighed. "That's the thing, Fair. It wasn't that kind of monastery. You all must think I'm some kind of monster with the way Georgia painted everything."

A blue jay bickered across the grass.

"This is a different kind of monastery. We were in the worst section of town. Still are, actually. Just served people, ran a soup kitchen and a tutoring center, and kept up the hours of prayer. I begged her to come with me."

"Why didn't she?"

"Can you see Georgia living communally?"

I snorted.

"Right."

I sat up, shielded my eyes against the sun. "Then why did you go?"

"I needed training."

"For what?"

He leaned back on his elbows, and the sun shone on his copper curls like a halo. "Fairly, have you ever felt like God was calling you to do something?"

"Never. It's why I'm in the mess I'm in."

"You're not in a mess."

"Go on. I don't want to talk about me."

"Okay. Well, it was like this: I knew I was supposed to be down in the rough sections, ministering to forgotten people in their forgotten places. You know. And Richmond is one of those places where the divide between rich and poor seems so decisive, so wide."

I sat up straighter, cross-legged. "Kind of like you were ministering at the bottom of the Grand Canyon?"

"Yes! And I felt like I was supposed to do that in Baltimore. So I went to train, to learn. For six months. That's all. I didn't leave with the intention of staying away completely all that time. I planned on visiting every other weekend."

"Why didn't you?"

"The first couple of times I was supposed to visit, Georgia had some excuse. And then when I'd show up anyway, she'd pretend she wasn't home and wouldn't answer the door. I used my key and she pretended she had been asleep. We had what I thought was a good weekend, but…two weeks later when I showed up, the locks were changed. Then she got a new phone number. Unlisted."

"She shut you out."

"Yeah."

"Why didn't you go after her more aggressively?"

"I'm not sure how I could have, unless there was some sort of legal thing I could have done. But how can you force someone to want to be with you?"

"You can't."

The wind that blew through the park began to dry the sweat on my forehead. I rubbed his shoulder. "For the life of me, Sean, I can't figure out why you're still in love with her."

"I'm not."

"Then why are you being so faithful?"

"I'm not *in* love with her, Fair, if you're talking those early days of love feelings. But I love her. I hope I'm not delusional in thinking that if we tried to make it work—if she got some help, if she wanted to repair our life—that the feelings would return."

"For your sake, then I wish that too."

"But what about you? Why haven't you married since Hort died?"

"Not ready to take the chance."

"At least you've figured that much out."

"Plus, nobody measures up. Well, maybe you do, Sean"—I tried to go for an impish smile—"but you're taken."

He nodded with a wide, close-lipped grin. He took my hand, squeezed it, and let it go. "I don't have a cousin, Fairly."

"Me either. Well, except for Georgia, and the jury's out on her."

He winced.

"Sean, I'm sorry."

"Don't worry about it. Listen, I'm hankering for some of Della-Faye's cobbler."

"Me too."

Hand in hand we walked across the park, up Limestone and down Sixth. And we sat on the stools, ate our peach cobbler, and chatted with the folks at the VIP Restaurant, and I thought how there's always a world of trouble wherever you go, and what's the sense in that? If you don't have much family, well, it stands to reason you must make some. And Sean needed family as much I did.

I spooned a bite of warm cobbler into my mouth and had to admit that somehow we all manage to find some sweetness somewhere.

"Della-Faye, I need a big helping to go."

"You got it, baby."

So I dropped Sean off at Georgia's apartment and headed up to the hospital. I wrapped my arm around Uncle G, who'd fallen asleep with his head on the end of Georgia's bed, and I whispered, "I've got something for you!"

He sat up with a start and thirty seconds later was eating the cobbler in large bites, savoring yet gobbling, and I willed the love to go down with it, straight to that corner of his heart that had grown cobwebs and hadn't seen the light of day for years and years and years.

Georgia

I'm tired of pink. So I'm wondering if I could order up some kind of change. Blue would be nice. It's awfully like a sky, but that might help me picture heaven or something.

A little elevator music might be nice. Cool Jazz 77.7FM. Playing all your celestial favorites. Coming up at the top the show, Empyrean, with their new hit "Supernaturally Sound."

Listen!

There it is. Oh, I think I can take the pink some more if this keeps up. Sounds a little like Vince Guaraldi's "Mass from Christ Church Cathedral." I expect to see him someday, I really do. And listen to the harp in there. Very Harp 46.

Care if I interrupt your concert?

Hi, Mom!

Pretty sounds. I can't tell you how relieved I was to find jazz up here.

It's hard to imagine anything free-form in heaven.

She laughs and a chair appears. This time it's a gorgeous chaise. White brocade with an ivory fringe circling the bottom. *I figured I'd bring something more comfortable today. I'll be here awhile.*

What's up?

We're going to watch a movie.

I love movies.

I know. By last count, you've spent about five thousand hours watching movies.

If I could get nauseated I would.

So I figure another stint in front of the silver screen wouldn't hurt you. Besides, you have the starring role.

Oh great. *Is this some big lesson?*

Bingo, baby doll. Movies really are a great way to get something across. She's sitting there with a big bowl of popcorn. *I'd offer you some, but...*

I'm not dead yet. Is that butter?

Tons. No calories after you pass on.

Okay, I'm convinced, she really is in heaven.

Told you.

The pink fades to dark, and from behind me a light beams and words appear upon the—screen?

No. God doesn't need screens.

Oh, of course.

Music rolls in—lots of brass and kettle drums thrumming into a crescendo until—

This Could Have Been Your Life

—dissolves onto a black background in white letters. And then—

with ears to hear and all

—bleeds in underneath.

Very smart—tony. The lowercase is nice there.

Thanks.

You did this yourself?

You don't honestly think we really sit around and play harps all day, do you? But I had a little help. And she crunches some popcorn, points at the screen. *Listen now. You won't want to miss this. Of course, I'm biased because it is you, and there's something moving about seeing your daughter as the star. Now pay attention, Georgia!*

I settle in as the story begins in a time and place I recognize.

Sean walks into our apartment. "Look, Georgie, I got a letter from Bart."

Movie-me jumped up from the couch and hugged him.

"What's up with Bart?"

"He's moved to downtown Richmond. To the slums, apparently. Crazy stuff, I'm telling you. Read this letter."

He hands me the note, and as my eyes trip over the lines, a voice layers into the experience, Bart's voice, raspy and deep. "Hey, guys, it's me."

Nice job, Mom.

Sh!

"Just when you thought I couldn't get any more whacked out, I decided to join up with this group of seminary students in Richmond. They moved into an old crackhouse, and you should see what they're doing on this block. Redemption city. Come down and visit, okay? Or send some money. Ha ha. Anyway, there's always a floor to sleep on, and we really do have fun. My cell phone's still working. It's about the only luxury I've got, and I'm determined to keep it. Keeps my mom from being too worried about me.

"So what's up with you guys…?"

The voice fades out.

Sean, by this time, is heating up a can of tomato soup in the kitchen and slicing cheddar for grilled cheese sandwiches. "What do you think? Want to take a drive down? It's only three hours. And man, wouldn't it be good to go have a beer with Bart?"

I shake my head. "Why don't you go though?"

Fade out.

Two weeks later.

And there I am again, kissing a very excited Sean good-bye. No sooner is our little Stanza around the corner than I pull out my bin of winter clothes and unearth a bottle of gin.

Oh man. Do I have to watch this?

Yes.

So there I sit on the floor by our bed, bottle in hand.

I remember that day so well. Something inside me said, "Call him. Call him. This could be your last chance." But of course, that's not in the movie. Even Mom isn't privy to that information, I guess.

No, I wasn't, Georgia, you're right. I'm not omniscient. Pay attention now, this is where it gets good.

Suddenly, I'm calling Sean on his mobile phone as I pour the contents down the sink. "Sean, come get me. I want to go. I need to go."

Fade to black.

Six weeks later.

Sean and I are laughing as we scoot our double sleeping bag away from the leak in the attic ceiling. You can tell we've done our best to make the room as cozy as possible. Some old yard-sale lamps with different-color light bulbs cast a warm, festive glow. Carpet remnants stapled to the walls remind me of a preschool room, and on a desk a study lamp casts its light on a supplies list in my handwriting. The camera pans down the list: turkeys, bread, potatoes, corn bread, sweet potatoes.

It must be a list I'm making up for a Thanksgiving or Christmas meal we'll be dishing up sometime in the future. Sean and I collapse on our sleeping bag, laugh at the drops in his wiry, puffy dreads. And I kiss him and he kisses me.

The screen goes dark.

Mom turns toward me. *There were other times after he left for the weekend that you turned away from it, weren't there?*

Many times.

She's sitting on one of the kitchen chairs now, and she's swiveled at the waist to rest her forearms on the back. *How many times did you expect God to come after you, Georgia?*

One more?

How many "one more's" did you need?

Apparently one more.

She laughs. *You always could be so funny. God put that in you to help you get through what He had planned. To help other people through too.* She leans forward. *I'll let you in on a heavenly secret.*

Okay, I whisper even though nobody is around for…what? miles? millennia?

God designed laughter as a sort of anesthetic.

Really?

So when Christians get all serious about stuff and act like some things are beyond a joke, guess what? It's like slapping God in the face! Did you know that?

I'm not tracking with you, Mom. Give me an example.

Okay, remember when you were little and we went to that baptism service of my bass player, and the minister tripped in the baptistery and went under?

Yeah.

Remember how nobody laughed, not even him?

Yeah.

See, that fall was supposed to ease up my friend Jack. It was designed to make his baptism a joyous occasion. Instead, it's something he looks back on with dread because he inadvertently tripped the minister!

Okay, I get it.

You didn't laugh enough. You could've, Georgia. Remember how we used to laugh together?

But you died.

And even that was funny.

Oh, good night, Mom, you're going way too far with this.

The way Aunt Drea played "Abide with Me" at the service? It was horrible!

You saw?

Sometimes we get a peek.

I'm tired again.

I don't blame you. I'll see you later, sweet girl. I'm going to go compose anyway. Got a big gig soon, and man, oh man, are we going to jam.

Will Coltrane be there?

But Mom just raises her brows.

Fairly

I'm not sure how I found myself in a church basement with ten five- to seven-year-olds, Sean, and the story of the rich young ruler, but it happened more quickly than Della-Faye can throw together a broccoli-and-cheese casserole.

Most of Uncle G's cult members were away visiting family, so Sean and I decided to go to Della-Faye's small cinder-block church. We walked in, and Della-Faye hurried over, her pink pumps with black clip-on bows echoing on the aged, golden wood of the entryway.

"I'm in a state. I'm in a state!" Her hands fluttered like ruddy moths, and the feathers on her pink-and-black straw hat did much the same. Della-Faye, in that pink, crisp linen suit with the polka-dot shirt and matching handkerchief peeking out of the pocket, somehow pulled it off.

Man, I wish I were black sometimes. African American women just have it, don't they?

"What's wrong, Miss Della?" Sean asked.

"I'm in charge of the Sunday school, and my primary class teachers didn't show up. Didn't bother to call me. Oh no! Della-Faye don't deserve no call! Didn't do nothin'! I can't sit with you chil'ren 'cause I got to go downstairs. But I brought you some cobbler."

Sean's eyes twinkled. "Hey, the class sounds like fun. Why don't we join you?"

Della-Faye bestowed her toothless grin. "Well, all right, then. Follow me."

As we clacked down the steps, I felt as if I was entering a place I never knew existed, much like when you walk down…well, a set of steps for the first time, like a set going down to a school friend's basement where video games and board games and who knew what else awaited. And then the smell was different, just like in your friend's basement. Nothing malodorous or anything, merely a collection of aromas you've never been around before because that family goes camping and your family doesn't, or they do decoupage and your family doesn't, or maybe they raise exotic birds, and of course, your family definitely does not.

I was the only white face in the basement, and I marveled at all the luscious brown skin, the shades varied and warm, and the brightly colored dresses and shirts; the way the children ran around laughing and playing; the way Della-Faye, swatting them on their behinds as they passed by her, caused them to laugh even harder.

She opened a door off the main room and showed us into a spare little room with a short-legged table and short-legged benches. "Now let me get my flannelgraph set up."

"I haven't seen one of those in years," I whispered to Sean.

"Me either!"

Della-Faye set her hands on her hips. "Now what's wrong with flannelgraphs?"

I pointed to the Jesus. "Oh, look. Jesus is black!"

"Of course He's black. He's our Savior too."

Sean grinned and shook his head.

"Don't you be laughin' at me, young man! The Savior said He 'come to seek and to save that which was lost.' There ain't no black sheep that's going to follow some white shepherd to safety. At least not in North Lexington."

"Ahh. There you go then." Sean.

"There I go where?" But Della-Faye laughed, her great chest bouncing with ha-ha-ha's. Then she laid a hand on Sean's arm. "You poor lamb. You neither black nor white."

I put my arm around him. "Then Jesus is that color too."

"I heard that!"

Soon the children filed in, boys in shorts and bow ties, girls in sherbet-colored dresses, their feet shuffling in shiny church shoes. They sat on the benches, wiggling like worms, poking one another, until Della-Faye said, "Chil'ren!"

Zip-zip—zip.

"Good morning, Mrs. Monroe!" Like a chorus of singing stars shining in a brilliant sky of silky blue.

"Now let's pray. Fold your hands, and bow your heads. And I don't want to hear one peep."

They did. Still wriggling, but not daring to breathe heavily.

"Our Father..."

They joined in. "Who art in heaven..."

Something about the singsong sweetness caught my heart in a glossy net, and I remembered the little church my parents attended before we moved to the house in Essex. No, it wasn't perfect, really. There was a grumpy man who yelled at the kids when we ran around on the lawn after church. "You're wearin' a path in my turf!" This one lady always grabbed my arm too tightly if I got in the front of the buffet line without thinking. "The old people should go first!" she'd hiss, looking like a skinny dragon with a lace collar. And my, could she squeeze those talons into little-kid flesh.

But we prayed this prayer.

I'd forgotten this prayer, really. It had stopped being a breathing poem, a communication, at some point in time. When, I couldn't say. I guess I just never really owned it. It all seemed to belong to my parents.

I closed my eyes and allowed myself to mouth the words. I didn't feel I deserved to say them out loud, but something inside me longed to play a part here in this undemanding scene, a scene that seemed to be written with me in mind in a small way.

Dad would have joined in. And he would have arranged that black flannelgraph Jesus on that background so He would have come alive, winnowing fork in His hand.

Winnowing fork in His hand?

Where did that come from, and what did it even mean?

"...for Thine is the kingdom, and the power, and the glory, for ever and ever..."

"And ever!" a little boy in striped shorts said.

"Amen!"

"Now then." Della-Faye laid her hands atop her Bible.

A light rapping vibrated the hollow plywood door, and upon hearing "Come on in!" from Della-Faye, Jonah's head appeared through the crack.

"Sorry to disturb you, Ms. Monroe, but your niece Marjorie is outside on the church steps. She says she won't leave until you come out."

Della-Faye heaved her wide shoulders in a sigh, and in that moment I saw past the food, and somehow even past the faith to that burdened part that I don't guess humans ever rid themselves of until, as my mother always said, "The Lord comes again."

"Tell her I'll be right there, Mr. Jonah." She turned to us. "I'll find a substitute, just hang on."

"We'll take the class, Miss Della." Sean.

She closed her eyes briefly. "All right then." And opened them. "If it wasn't Marjorie..."

As she gathered up her cellophane-covered Bible, she told Sean, "It's the rich young ruler today," and she aged like time-lapse photography as she walked to the door and followed Jonah up the steps.

I got up and closed the door. Turned around and clapped my hands. "Okay guys, it's time to learn about Jesus!"

"What's you doin' here, lady?" a little boy with brown eyes the size of serving spoons asked.

A girl obviously older than her years jerked a thumb at Sean. "Now him I can figure on."

Sean and I laughed. "Sean is my friend. And so is Miss Della-Faye."

And they shrugged, and Sean got to teaching, and I chimed in with some timely historical facts and read an Arch Book about the rich young ruler, and boy, could I relate. I poured the juice, spread out the cookies, and honestly, I hadn't felt that alive since death began to call.

And then yet another Arch Book. This one on Jonah, who, it appeared, had nothing in common with my friend Jonah.

My friend Jonah.

Well, yes. I suppose he is my friend.

Soon the children were fighting over who could sit in my lap. I'd never felt so blessed in all my life. Perhaps Jonah felt like this after being coughed up on dry land. I don't know. Maybe I need to read about it.

I called Solo on the walk home. My friend Solo. And my friend Sean walked beside me.

And here you think you've done well at fogging yourself in for the long haul, reachable only by fog bells and the sharpest beam from a faraway lighthouse, and you find you've got three men, all different shades of brown no less, and each is your friend. And you wonder. How in the world did that happen?

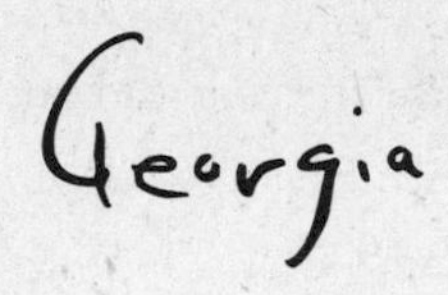

Sean and Fairly are telling UG about Sunday school. My cousin also talked about how my hands are starting to curl in a little bit.

Good night.

"Will you be coming back for dinner, Uncle G?" Fairly asks.

"She's actually making pasta, Geoffrey." Sean adds. "The rest of the group is coming for the meal."

"God knows I need to be with everyone."

Fairly making dinner?

"And besides, I'm wondering if I just need a break altogether. Even Christ took time away."

Sean chuckles. "That's the truth."

"You know, Uncle G, I think you just need to pour juice and give out butter cookies. That's what I think."

"I'm not following you, Fair."

"Like today at Sunday school. You want to save the world. I don't know if you can."

UG sighs, and I hate Fairly as much as I can from in here.

"I know what you mean, Fair."

What?!

"I've been all over the map, literally, and I have our group to serve here, but what do I really do for the people on East Third?"

A chair scrapes, and Fairly says, "I think you need to come with me to Della-Faye's VIP Restaurant."

"Why?"

"Because it's a great place to gather your strength. Right, Sean?"

"I'm not going to argue with that." And Sean uses his smiley voice.

So there they all are, doing God things, and here I sit, listening from the sidelines. The sidelines? I'm not even in the stadium. I may not even be in the neighborhood of the stadium.

I used to be on the sidelines. I'd love to be on the sidelines now. Well, sort of.

Oh rats!

Grandmom sits next to me.

Stop feeling sorry for yourself.

How did you suddenly appear?

I'm not sure, Georgia. I'm just here to tell you to stop going back to your old self-pity. It's what got you here in the first place.

Oh yeah, there is that.

All right, I'm gone. I don't like having to appear in these pantyhose all the time. Would you mind if, next time I came back, I didn't look exactly like you remembered?

Not one bit.

And Grandmom disappeared.

Fairly

I lifted the basil bunch up to my nose and inhaled as deeply as Uncle G does on one of his cigarettes. Some smells you can practically eat. I held it up to Sean's nose. "Take a whiff."

"Man, that's wonderful."

"So pull off the leaves and tear them up just a smidge while I put the pasta on."

"You're doing well at this kitchen stuff."

I searched the pantry for the bottle of olive oil Uncle G always uses. Cold-pressed, all-natural, la-di-da-di-da. "Oh please, Sean. This is one step above ramen in the dorms." Except maybe for the cold-pressed, all-natural olive oil, of course.

"Girl, I don't know how much ramen I've eaten over the past ten years in Richmond. This right here is a feast! Do you have any idea how rich we actually are?"

I spilled a dollop of the rich green oil into the simmering water. "So you called this a monastery, but it's not Catholic."

"No, but it is scheduled, and we have certain things we adhere to. Chastity—"

"Chastity? You're married."

"Abstinence for the singles, faithfulness in marriage for the marrieds. Also poverty and obedience. The usuals."

"I like the idea of serving down there like that."

The basil loosed more aroma as he wounded the leaves. "Never thought I'd hear anything like that coming from you."

"Me either. Crazy, isn't it? And don't think I'm picturing myself in one, because I'm not."

"Hey, I'm the last person to assume anything."

"True. I just like the freedom of simplicity. It's what modern design is all about. This is just living it. Sort of."

We worked in silence for a while, and even though he's married to my fruity cousin, I have to admit we were quite the team. But something very different bound us, something more universal than romance. Besides, I couldn't imagine myself with Sean in *that* way. He's gorgeous, sexy, built, talented. But, well, yuck, for some reason. Don't ask why.

I handed him a cellophane bag of pine nuts. "Just chop these up. Not much."

"You were so much fun to watch this morning, Fair."

"Really?"

"Yeah. You were a natural with those kids."

"I love kids."

He stepped back from the counter. "Well, you sure never let on before this."

"There are a lot of things I never let on, believe me."

He picked his task back up. "Well, spill it then, girl."

So I did. I told him about Braden, all the parties and the *dahling* people in my circles, and how it really made me feel good for a very long time and how shallow was that? His eyes got bigger and bigger and when I finished he laughed and laughed.

"What?"

"That's a whole lot of extra work to go through to grieve a good man."

"True. I mean, how ridiculous can somebody be? I can't begin to imagine Hort approving of such behavior. Especially in his honor! But don't forget, all those people made me money. They were my insurance against not only loneliness, but the Box N Save."

"God forbid you have to go back to the Box N Save, Fairly!"

And I joined in his laughter.

Uncle G walked in, set his backpack on the floor. "What's so funny?"

I set the pasta like pick-up sticks into the rolling water. "Oh, just the lengths people will go through to keep from being real."

Later on, as we passed the Italian bread to one another and shared the wine, I looked around me and thought, I am part of this. I bought this bread and poured this wine. And in the taking I was given something I can't explain now and don't think I'll ever be able to. But I understood something in the midst of these people that I'd never seen before. I finally understood something about Jesus's death that nobody ever told me with all the talk of eternal punishment, hellfire, and brimstone.

He didn't just die to save me from something. He died to *give* me something too, and when Peg proposed a toast and said, "To life abundant, to life in Christ," I knew just exactly what that something was, and if I had been standing on the dusty roads of Galilee and heard it from the lips of Christ Himself, it wouldn't have been plainer or any more profound.

I saw my own hardheartedness and my pride, my jutting lip and growled words of "I'll do it myself, thanks," when all the while, as Peg testified at the previous gathering, "Jesus was telling me to cast all my burdens on Him. That He would give me rest."

I got it. Like my parents before me.

And Blaine held the plate of bread, the cup of wine, and said, "The blood of Christ, shed for you," and I took and ate saying, "Thanks be to God."

The flannelgraph Jesus took on three dimensions. Perhaps four. I was all too glad to rest, to cast away my cares. Lord knew, I needed that.

Georgia

It's really weird to see UG so vulnerable. He's totally obsessed with his direction in life these days. As in, "How can God be calling me to step back when so many people are in need?"

Well, gee, UG, I don't know. I guess God can do whatever He wants, pretty much, right? I mean, here I am in the pink, so who's to say?

He takes my hand and opens up the fingery curl and massages my palm. "This is the thing, Georgie. It hasn't all been one great big success. I've lost lots of people along the way. Regina Marzollo, the abused woman I was trying to help—her scumbag husband killed her."

At least you tried, UG. I mean, come on.

"And the Maguire children. Did I ever tell you about them?"

Wouldn't he absolutely freak if I actually answered?

"I don't remember anymore how I got in the middle of that one, but they were taken from a neglectful set of parents, and they did fine in foster care. I went away for a couple of years to Mexico, and when I got back I made it to the foster parents' house to visit the kids.

"There were three of them. Paul, Vickie, and Stubby, who was always stubbing his toe on everything.

"Their foster mom answered the door and said the children had been returned to their parents."

Uncle Geoffrey stops talking. I can't hear anything, but the bed is shaking, and he's lying across me.

He sniffs a great sniff. "When I talked to the social worker, she said they fell through the cracks. That Paul, at sixteen, was fifty pounds when they finally got him out. Vicky, at twelve, weighed thirty pounds, and Stubby had already died. It was the smell of his corpse that alerted the neighbors."

And then a great gulping sob shook his body and therefore mine.

He's crying. My uncle is crying and crying and crying.

And I can't put my arms around him, I can't tell him it's all right, he did what he could. I can't tell him anything.

And I realize this is nothing new. I can't blame the coma for this. It's been this way for years and years.

And I cry too, the pink suffocating me, my own tears drowning me, and the light fades as I descend into a world of regret so deep I wonder if it is possible to ever see my way back through. I wonder if I really desire to at all.

Fairly

Nope, couldn't imagine being with Sean. Definitely couldn't, considering every time I looked at him I realized that Georgia probably wouldn't be in the coma if not for my vindictiveness. I should never have brought him around to Uncle G's without preparing her.

I'd like to say I didn't know what came over me. But I certainly did. Georgia's comment about my clothes filled me with an icy rage. Who wants to be found out like that? And for such a creepy thing? I mean, being an alcoholic is one thing. Scads of people are alcoholics. But how many people wear their dead mother's clothes?

My solitary comfort regarding my cousin remains the fact that if she hadn't drunk herself into a coma last month, surely this month, or the next or the next, would have seen her lying on the floor in a pool of her own vomit, right? Did she ever picture herself like that? I can't imagine she did and continued to pour Jimmy Beam down her throat like that.

Clarissa

The girl's training bras don't really fit anymore, but she doesn't want to ask the mother for new ones. She's been saving up a little here, a little there, from the grocery money. If she had time for friends, maybe they'd pass a few along.

Oh well.

The cousin stomps into her room.

"Kurt said you were flirting with him at school today."

"No, Reggie, I wasn't. I swear, I just said hi in the hallway. That's all."

"No relative of mine is going to be an easy mark. Do you understand?"

She smells a little beer on his breath. Just a little.

"Yes. But I didn't think—"

"Shut up! Just shut up and make me a sandwich."

The night before, the girl heard the mother yelling at the boy she calls her son, calling him a no-good lowlife just like her ex-husband.

But at least the mother didn't tie them up and lock them in closets. At least the mother didn't beat them with belts and spoons. At least the mother didn't go off and leave them alone in a world that brings nothing but pain.

No idea how bad things could really be. No idea.

She makes him a sandwich: chopped ham on white with American cheese, mayo, and mustard. A crisp lettuce leaf. Some Doritos on the side. And then she's off, next door.

And there's a cake with her name on it and mint chocolate chip ice cream and presents. A collectible doll, with pink cheeks, red lips, and a dress as blue and innocent as a summer sky at noon; a necklace with a cross in silver hanging at the bottom; a bright pink T-shirt with flowers scattered like windswept petals over the chest.

Leonard the Granddaddy Man and TV Mom hug her and tell her she's growing into quite the beautiful young lady.

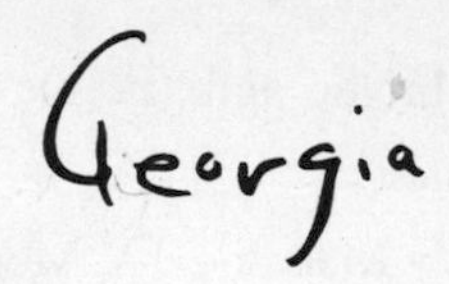

Tears and sadness feel different here in the pink. More crystallized, magnified because you can see exactly why it is you're crying. None of that intermittent, smeared grief and frustration; feeling worthless and without recourse and you don't really know why, but hey, it deserves a good cry, right?

I wish I could lend some of this clarity to UG right now.

He's back, of course, and I can't understand why he sits here all day. He shuffles his papers less and less and makes fewer phone calls. I honestly don't mind listening to his business. Gives me something to do when the ghost ladies fail to show.

But today he's rambling on about theology.

So here's the thing. I have faith. I can't say I made good use of it, that's for sure, but nevertheless I always knew Christ had me in mind up there on the cross. Other than that, I kept it shoved aside. It's actually good of God to give me this coma chance. I hope He does stuff like this for other people, stuff we'll never know about.

I don't think I'm going to make it. The doctors' buzz offers neither a vignette nor a vista. I'm in a persistent vegetative state. Good night. The chances of me resurfacing are about as great as the Loch Ness monster's. I should be the one crying, not UG!

Nevertheless, he rambles.

"So, God, I just don't get this. How could You have given someone so much potential, so much to live for, and she couldn't work her way around the bad things in life? She's not the first person to have lost her mother as a child, and most of them don't flounder for the rest of their lives.

"Couldn't You have stepped in with a heavier hand? Snapped her out of this? Given her cancer or paralyzed her or something to make her stop?"

Cancer? Paralysis? Uh, thanks, UG! Although his prayer does make me see why God would actually choose to cause someone to suffer if it actually gets them to stop pickling their liver, to stop urinating their life away.

"I just don't get it, Lord. I just don't."

I feel for Uncle Geoffrey. Here he's given his entire life to helping people, and he did it for God's sake even if he didn't have a Bible in his hand or a WWJD bracelet on his wrist. And now he sits day after day in his niece's hospital room asking all sorts of questions. Wouldn't you think he'd feel more peace?

And yet, who am I to judge? Does the fact that he asks questions mean he's not at peace? Are the two mutually exclusive? If so, then I warrant peace cannot be found, for a human that asks no questions is (1) dead or (2) brainwashed.

The wispy rustles of onionskin paper tell me of the little pocket testament UG owns, pages worn to a breath, and I wonder what he's reading. Psalms, maybe? Soon enough, he falls asleep, and I pray to God no one disturbs him for a good long time.

Clarissa

The girl examines herself from the front in the mirror. Yes, the new bra from Fashion World fits just right. She turns to the side. It's a little mature, with pretty lace inlays and satin bows. She glides her fingertips across the smooth bows. Yes, very alluring. But it was also the most inexpensive one she could find in her size—34C.

A naughty thought about her music teacher surfaces, and she blushes, then looks at the doorway to see if her brother is watching.

She throws on a sweatshirt, tosses in a load of laundry, and begins her homework—earphones glued to the sides of her head, keeping out everything but her new favorite singer, Carole King. She's kind of an old lady now, but the girl likes that about her. She kind of reminds her of TV Mom next door, all that wavy hair flying all over the place.

Georgia

Mom and I discuss the old days, like when we took tap-dancing lessons together and she sprained her ankle. Since it's back-to-school time, we're remembering how she always packed me the best lunches in the class, sometimes even shrimp salad when my dad, who was also a photographer, sold an important photo. I brought up our yearly trip to downtown York, Pennsylvania, and the Bon-Ton department store to buy school clothes because goodness knows Baltimore didn't have stores.

It wasn't about the selection in York, Georgia; it was about the small adventure, about the tradition. To be honest, I doubt the Bon-Ton had as good a selection as Hutzler's.

Remember that place we used to stop for lunch, Mom? What was it again?

The Lincoln Woods Inn.

I can barely remember what it looked like inside, but it had the best Reuben sandwiches. Remember?

Mom nods. *Oh yes, open-faced and bigger than the plate!*

All that melted swiss. Piles of corned beef.

Wonder if there's food like that in heaven?

Of course there is. Jesus was Jewish when He was incarnated.

Ha, ha. It's always scared me that food won't be as good.

Oh, Georgia, cast those fears aside! I can't even begin to explain what food tastes like up here. First of all, it's not fallen food.

Fallen food?

All of creation fell, even our food. As good as you think a drippy hamburger is—

I love drippy hamburgers.

As good as you think they are, the food here is even more glorious.

Kind of like the difference between a fast-food burger and a steakburger on Texas toast with melted provolone, grilled onions, mayo, and horseradish sauce?

You're on the right track there. Only the steakburger is the wimpy little burger-joint burger.

You know, Mom, I kind of miss food. I haven't tasted anything in weeks. How long has it been? I've lost count.

Almost eight weeks.

Weren't they going to take me off the machines by now?

Yes, but Geoffrey can't do it yet, and Sean's being kind to him. God's got Geoff thinking about things.

Well, at least this is doing somebody some good.

Oh, make no mistake about that. God's not going to waste an opportunity like this. Really, Georgia, your ultimate act of stupidity on earth, no offense, may end up doing some real good.

Wouldn't it be nice if we could see that ahead of time?

Maybe it would be possible if people learned their lessons, learned from history, or at the very least learned to say "I'm sorry" or "I was wrong."

Well, it never seems so clear and concise. Was all the pain worth it, Mom? I mean, you wasted away in pain. You never got the acclaim you deserved. You were married to Mr. I'm-Consumed-with-Myself. You had some tough pills to swallow. So was it worth it? Is a yes answer to that the answer we're all searching for?

Mom laughs and laughs and laughs. Some great big cosmic chuckle echoes around me and drives away some of the pink angel hair.

Okay, Mom, good night.

I'm sorry, dear. I was just remembering a time when I thought there'd be one great big answer that would make everything better, like a nausea shot or something. Or plastic surgery. Or butter. Butter makes everything better too.

She keeps on laughing.

Let me know when you're done with the hilarity. I'll check on Uncle Geoffrey.

So I tune her out and realize he's not there, but a tech is.

This one comes in during the weekdays, and I'm sure she's wearing blue scrubs and a ponytail, but I can't help it, I picture her in a leopard-print velour sweat suit, with curly red hair caught in a turban, cat glasses, and long earrings with glitzy, pavé diamond balls. Sort of like that Laverne character Cher used to do on *Sonny & Cher* reruns, but without smacking the gum, and with an extra fifty pounds and a softer voice.

This tech, she'd take me out for ice cream if I were little, and get me a Coke, too, and on the way out give me a quarter for some SweeTarts in the machine by the door. She'd hold up her hand and say, "Wait. Listen. I used to love this song," when "Close to You" came on the jukebox.

"On the day that you were born, the angels got together and decided to create a dream come true."

Yes, she'd sing that to me.

She's clicking her tongue, tenderly moving my hair away from my face so she can clean it with a warm, soapy washcloth. "Poor, poor little baby. You poor baby girl."

Her tone is soft and truly sorry. You see, Georgia, I'm just a tech passing through on my daily rounds, but I'm noticing you, I'm seeing that your life is sad and painful, and I'm recognizing the suffering, you poor baby girl. You poor baby girl.

I see you crying inside there somewhere.

I really do.

"You poor baby girl."

Oh, God, and that was all I wanted, you see. It's all I ever wanted after Polly Bishop left the world.

Dad only said, "You'll get through this somehow."

Uncle Geoffrey only said, "God will help you."

Aunt Bette said, "You're strong and you'll do fine. We're here for you."

Grandmom made me bratwurst.

I just wanted someone to say, "You poor baby girl."

The words wash over me, filling cracks, smoothing the dried-on sand with its cool flow. Tears inside her. Tears inside me.

Yes.

The touch ceases.

More, lady, please. Just a little more.

"She's flatlining! Somebody come quick!"

The anemic whine of the heart monitor fills a bigger space than it deserves. She's right! The thin, single tone underpins all else as I hear nurses running into the room, shoes squeaking on the linoleum tile.

"Georgia! Georgia!" Another voice.

Blip-blip. Blip-blip. Blip-blip.

The tech sighs with relief. "She's back."

"Odd." The other nurse walks to the foot of the bed. "Very odd."

I'm sure she's just checking once again the state of my brain damage. So how does a person in my state respond to a shout?

I laugh here in the pink.

Mystify them, Georgia. You've always been good at that.

Nicely done, baby doll!

Oh, Mom.

I'm sorry. I'm sorry I couldn't have given you the comfort you needed when I died.

Uncle Geoffrey tried, though, Mom. He just, well, he's Uncle Geoffrey, you know?

A heart of gold, but sometimes he gives people too much space.

Exactly!

Sometimes he needs to turn over the tables in the temple, so to speak.

Is that what he's learning here?

Perhaps. I can't say what God's trying to teach Geoff. It might be something as simple as the need for rest. He may have a big job for Geoff to do and knows he needs to gather strength. I'm sorry I laughed so hard.

That's okay.

Let me answer your question. I don't know if this is the answer you person-

ally are looking for, Georgia. I think everybody has "the answer" they need from God. But I don't think everybody has the same question.

Huh?

It's like this: you need to know if the trials are worth the glory prepared, right? I needed to know if what I did had any great sort of meaning. Other people need to know if God is knowable. Some people's questions include things like creation and evolution, the end times, the problem of evil coexisting with a holy God of love, or why God created the world in the first place if He knew there'd be pain. One of the biggest foul-ups, I think, is when one person expects everyone else to also have that particular all-consuming question. We all have one, make no mistake about that, but if we think we all have the same one, we're vastly mistaken.

Okay, yeah, got it. So I'll take my answer now, Mom.

She laughs. *Yes, Georgia, it was worth it. It was worth every disappointment, every trial, every circumstance that was beyond my control. It was worth every needle, every IV, every enema, every stabbing pain, every tear shed. I'm privy to glories I couldn't have imagined, love so filling and gorgeous you never feel sad, and even the pain that once filled my heart is now a part of something more complete and redeeming than a simple solution, a simple "Poof, it's gone!" could ever be. It's not so much that you forget about your past suffering, but somehow, you fulfill it, or rather, it becomes fulfilled in you. I'm doing a poor job in the explaining.*

No, Mom, I doubt it can be explained to me because I'm…

Not dead yet! We both say it together.

She taps her chin. *Here's a good way to think of it. It's like cutting through a deep, dark, sweltering jungle. You trip, you gash open your leg, scrape your palms, cut your forehead. And bug bites? You're positively covered! You haven't slept for days, you're thirstier than an old washrag left in the sun, and food, what's that? And suddenly, you're in a paradise resort. The drinks are fabulous, the water's clear and blue and just the right temperature, and there are all sorts of interesting things to do and people to talk to. Would you sit there and do nothing but complain about the journey?*

No.

Exactly.

But why does it have to be like that?

That's Geoff's question, not yours, Georgie.

I think I'm tired again. I died earlier, you know.

Mom scrunches her eyes into a smile and caresses me with their warmth.

UG breathes softly, holding my hand. I didn't realize he'd come in. He doesn't move, and I wish I knew what he was thinking. It could go one of two ways: too bad she didn't pass away earlier so Sean doesn't have to make such a horrible decision, or don't go, Georgia, I'm not ready to lose you yet.

Fairly

I've never really thought of my scribblings as much, but Sean found my little sketchpad journal when he was vacuuming the bedrooms earlier. We're trying to help keep the place neat while Uncle G keeps the Georgia vigil.

He came out of my bedroom and held it up. "Now I didn't read a word! But I saw your drawings!"

"They're just simple little sketches."

"I know, but there's something really nice about them. What's up with the little dolls?"

I took the journal and flipped it open, staring at the drawing I'd sketched the night before. "I was just remembering what I used to do when I was little. Other girls played tea party. I always gave them a five-course meal."

"Uh-huh!"

"Yeah, uh-huh. What are you getting at?" I set the book on the couch.

"Well, someone once told me the way to find out who you were made to be is to look back to what you loved to do when you were a child."

"Oh yeah, right, Sean! I played dolls. That's encouraging. Hey, grab that duster and swipe the blinds, would you?"

"Sure. It's what you did with your dolls, Fair. And look at how much you enjoyed that Sunday school class." He ran Uncle G's obnoxious, hot-pink feather duster along a set of miniblinds on the front window.

Those kids, their round faces just ready for juice, cookies, and a story—how much cuter could they have been? "And how easy was that? Please! They were happy to be there. And who doesn't like a good butter cookie?"

Kids naturally understand what's important in life, don't they?

"I'm just saying you had a real knack there and I don't think you even realized it."

"Who was your favorite teacher, Sean?"

He moved on to the side window. "Oh man, I haven't thought about that in forever, but the answer would still be the same. Mr. Herring."

"Mr. Herring? Like the fish?"

"Yep. Eleventh-grade business math. He made balancing a spreadsheet seem like child's play! I swear I could have learned rocket science from that man. What about you?"

I root through Uncle G's rag bin. "Mrs. Walston. Second grade. Roundish, sweet—one of those appley-shaped ladies, red headed, really darling. She always let me help get out the snacks."

"See? You're born to feed people. Or something to do with kids. Maybe you're born to feed kids."

"I could throw tea parties for all the kids I meet. That sounds practical." I began to dust the coffee table. "I don't know, Sean. My business supports me well. I can't imagine going back to the days of my childhood, clipping coupons, shopping at the Box N Save."

"I'm living testimony to having little and actually still being happy. Come on, girl. You're a natural."

"Well, money aside, I really love my work."

"But how often do you get to be with kids?"

"Rarely. It does seem a shame."

"Maybe you should start volunteering or something. To me it's very obvious. Mrs. Walston would approve."

"You know, I should probably look Mrs. Walston up."

Sean tipped his head. "Be careful now. She's probably dead too."

And for some reason, I actually found Sean's remark funny.

Feed people? Sean is a strange bird.

"What do you think of volcanoes, Sean?"

He shrugs. "I haven't given them a whole lot of thought. But they sure are beautiful, don't you think?"

"I love them."

"Now why is that?"

Of course, I had an answer. "Because there's so much more going on under the surface than you could ever see."

"Kinda like an iceberg."

I snorted. "Hardly!"

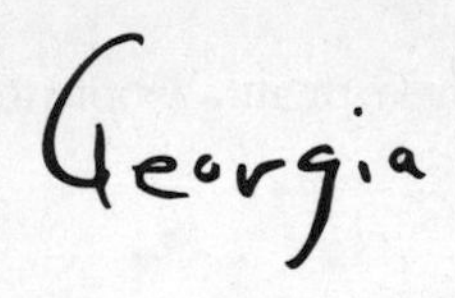

Mom? Is that you? A shape approaches, but it doesn't look exactly like her. Just the gait seems right.

Hi, honey!

Oh hi, Mom! It is you.

And another materializes next to her.

Grandmom? That you too?

Hello, Georgia! Grandmom raises her hand and waves.

How come you guys are dressed in those…gowns? Is that what you're wearing? Mom, you look like somebody from Queen Elizabeth's time. And, Grandmom, what is that you've got on?

Oh my, it's a replica of a Marie Antoinette gown.

What's this for?

Mom looks absolutely gorgeous. She looks like a nonfreaky Elizabethan, if you know what I mean.

Thanks for the compliment. We've got some more This Is Your Life *to show you.*

Oh man.

Grandmom fans herself. *Now, now. It'll be fun. We're going to watch a play this time.*

Who are the actors?

Who were the people in the film, Georgia? Mom asks.

Good point. I guess it's best not to try to understand this stuff right now.

Smart cookie. Grandmom.

From behind me an unseen orchestra begins a showy musical opening—flutes and violins and triangles and trombones. And the pink goes black and a spotlight punches out a crisp white spot in front of…curtains? Yes, burgundy curtains.

A woman appears, looking familiar. Not extremely so. I actually think I'm recognizing her because she was eccentric when I came in contact with her, and she's still somewhat eccentric.

"Good evening!" She steps forward as applause erupts.

What?

Mom and Grandmom look at each other with pretty tilts of their heads and clap little classy-philanthropist-at-a-fundraising-gala handclaps. Oh, my dear, what a delightful performance lies in store for the likes of us!

Hush, Georgia!

Sorry, Grandmom.

"I'm Janet Burn, your host and narrator for tonight's performance, *This Would Have Been Your Life.*"

A kettle drum starts rolling.

"Sans the Bottle."

More applause.

Applause?

Oh, if you must know, Mom looks back, *it's just for effect. Now stop questioning all the details and pay attention. Honestly! Georgia, you're acting like a third grader.*

Whatever.

Georgia Ella! Grandmom chastises.

You know it's totally not fair that you can hear my thoughts but I can't hear yours.

Simultaneously they hold index fingers up to their mouths. *Sh!*

The narrator spread her arms wide, benevolently and with invitation. "Join me, if you will, on a journey of what might have been. Georgia Ella Bishop was born to one of the world's jazz greats, not that the world ever knew it. Georgia was blessed with a potential so great that even I couldn't believe it."

How melodramatic can you get?

The circle fades to nothing, and the curtain rises.

Is that me? You chose that woman to play me? Mo-o-om!

Good night, I'll bet she weighs twenty-five pounds more than I do.

She looks fabulous, Georgie. Just right.

Nevertheless, I watch in fascination as she sits down at the piano at the Ten O'Clock Club. Behind her, banners hail it her high-school graduation day.

A group sits at the round tables, tea candles flickering in their red, crinkled-glass jars like votives at church. "Play us some music, Georgia!"

She smiles and waves.

Hey, this really happened. I thought—

Sh!

And the notes flow in a stream of butter and honey, and I'd forgotten my fingers flowed like that at one time.

You really were something. Now watch closely! Mom.

A woman enters the club—Janet Burn—and quietly assumes a seat near the door. I play brilliantly, I have to admit. I'm in a coma, grant me a little self-flattery.

Janet nods, writes like mad, and sits there the rest of the evening, entranced. She's overacting a bit, really, but who am I to criticize? The stage goes dark.

I didn't realize she was anybody important that night.

No, honey, you didn't.

Who was she?

Just watch! Good night.

Hmm. I knew I got that phrase from somewhere.

Janet appears once again in the circle of light. "I'd never before heard playing like that in one so young! Eighteen years old and the maturity of the playing astounded me. Perhaps she would bring jazz alive again to a large audience of young people."

Oh brother.

"I immediately called my boss at the record company. He told me he'd fly down the next morning and we could see her play that night."

How did she know I'd be there?

"I knew she'd be there because I asked the man at the bar. I think his name was Jesse."

If I were able to roll my eyes, I would.

The circle fades again as the music slips in, and the rising curtain reveals a new scene. It's a setting for an awards show. A man stands at a Lucite podium.

Is that Wynton Marsalis? Dang, he looks old!

Music fades and a huge Grammy award lowers on invisible strings. Well, I guess there are strings. Of course, here in the pink they may not need strings.

Mom bats her fan at me.

Okay, okay.

"It gives me a world of pleasure to present this Lifetime Achievement Award to a woman to whom, happily, I presented her first Grammy twenty-five years ago when she was only twenty. She's been entertaining us for well over two decades, has worked extensively in bringing music to the disadvantaged, and has broken ground in a new jazz style she dubbed Polyfunk for her mother, the late, great jazz pianist, Polly Bishop, whose priceless recordings became known to us through her daughter."

Mom turns. *See? You would have made me famous!*

Okay, so that makes me feel like refuse.

"Georgia Bishop has done more to further jazz piano performance and composition than any woman preceding her, and tonight we celebrate her contribution to the world of jazz music."

A large screen drops, and a film segment begins, a typical awards-show montage. Just the right amount of cheese too.

There I am in my first recording session, smiling and young and pretty. My marriage to Sean, various performances, trips, sweet shots of me with inner-city children as we play "Chopsticks" or do some hopscotch.

Enough, Mom. Grandmom, please. Enough.

Mom turns and rests her forearms on the back of her seat. *This was the original plan. Record your first album, marry Sean, do all the things Wynton said, travel all around the world doing amazing things. He's going to go on after the film and talk about how you and Sean made ten albums together, him singing and you playing, and how you set up several foundations. But you didn't show up to play at the club the next night when Janet and her producer were there. And guess why?*

Are you deliberately trying to be cruel? What can I do about this now?

Nothing really. You're not supposed to. You're simply getting the opportunity to give up all the perceived wrongs you think God's done to you.

I feel like someone has thrown me into a mud puddle, so thick I'm unable to feel, see, hear. But wait!

What about the monastery, inner-city ministry, and all that? Wasn't I supposed to end up there with Sean?

Plan B. That was your second chance, Georgia. And I have to admit, I've seen the movie already, and it was a plan every bit as wonderful as the first.

So did I do anything worthwhile?

You loved me, purely and truly.

Is that enough?

Only you can be the judge of that, Georgie.

Fairly

I don't know why we didn't think of it sooner, and it's not like the rector had any way to contact us. Georgia's cell phone died weeks ago. The poor man must have been wondering why she never showed up and why he couldn't contact her.

Sean's new job at Subway consumes the bulk of his day, which if that doesn't break your heart—a beautiful man with heavenly pipes making sandwiches all day—I sincerely can't imagine what will. So that left me to carry out the task. I could have called on the phone, but Della-Faye's VIP isn't far from the church, and I figured some ribs and cobbler afterward would suit me like Chanel on Audrey Hepburn.

Pretty church, even in the dimness with a storm brewing outside. Loved the stonework, the old-time craftsmanship, the screaming red doors.

"May I see the vicar?" I asked the secretary, a woman who'd obviously tanned so much and thinned down so much at some point that she reminded me of one of those freeze-dried ice men they uncover in the tundra every so often.

She showed me into a study with two lit hurricane sconces by the window and a general hurricane theme, if scattered books and papers, old coffee with a thick skin on top, wild rug fringe, and blowing curtains constitute a theme. The rector's white hair was consistent with the overall motif, and he ran his red British hands through it before shaking hands with me.

Okay, so he seemed a tad awkward, but I liked him right away. "Ah yes, Miss, ah…"

"Fairly Godfrey."

"What can I do for you today?"

"I just came to tell you about Georgia Bishop."

The invisible string of surprise drew his brows up like window shades toward his hairline. "I've wondered what happened to her. I called her cell phone repeatedly."

"So I gathered. May I sit down?"

He threw his hands up. "Oh dear me, what poor manners I have. Sit down, and we'll have a cup of tea. Ms. Sparks!"

The beef-jerky face appeared. "Yes, Reverend?"

"Tea if you would, please?"

She shook her head and made a tsk sound.

"My new assistant. Work release. What have you."

"Good of you, then." I tried to broadcast as warm a smile as I could.

"Work release or not, my old secretary put her to shame."

Beaten down by the women of the parish, I supposed.

"Anyway, Reverend, Georgia is my cousin. Two months ago she had…an accident."

"Oh my! Is she all right?"

"Not really. She's been in a coma. I'm sorry I didn't think sooner to come and tell you."

The past month had been a blur, really. Three short buying trips, helping Della-Faye and Jonah with Sunday school, the cult, and the vigil. And thank my lucky stars, Braden finally got it through his head that we were over, and thank the good Lord, Solo thinks maybe a fresh start in Lexington is exactly what he and his boys might need now that he's finished his MDiv. I practically burst his eardrum I hollered so loudly into the phone. He laughed his great, loud laugh that always fills my soul with warm tapioca pudding.

Reverend Smithers sat down behind his desk. "Terrible news. Is there anything All Souls can do to help?"

"No, thank you. We're fine."

Ms. Sparks entered with two mugs of very weak, barely warm tea as if to say, "That'll teach him to ask me to make tea."

She disappeared without a sound, almost daring him to thank her.

He peered into the cup and set it down. "Oh my. Sorry."

"I have an idea, Reverend. Have you been to Della-Faye's VIP Restaurant?"

"Not yet. I've only been in town for a year and have been meaning to get there."

"Can I interest you in partaking of the most delectable, the most delicious, the most..." I searched for the perfect word.

"Diabolical?"

"Yes! If you're talking calories. The most diabolical fried chicken you've ever tasted?"

"We may get the vestry talking. I am single, you know."

We chuckled together. It felt nice to chuckle. "Let's go then. I'm new in town too. Actually, I haven't even moved in yet. But I will soon. Down on Jefferson Street."

"Welcome to Lexington then, Fairly."

He reminds me of Hort, somewhat. Just a little.

Two blocks from the VIP, the clouds cracked open, spilling their contents right on top of our heads. Reverend Smithers resembled an English sheepdog and I some waterlogged rat terrier when we huffed and puffed ourselves, him growling and me yipping, into the restaurant.

Della-Faye laughed until she finally had to sit down at the only table and wipe her eyes with her apron. "Oh, you two made my day. If you're the only business the storm blows my way, it'll be worth it."

"Just hand over some chicken and a piece of fried corn bread, and we'll call it even. This is Reverend Smithers, by the way, from over at the Episcopal church."

"An Episcopalian, huh? Well, we don't discriminate here at the VIP!"

"Thank God for that," the reverend said.

Della-Faye squinted her eyes. "You're not from Kentucky, are you?"

And we all laughed, the sound of it filling the tiny place.

"Be kind to him," I said. "He's from England. He's not used to good food."

She made her way behind the counter. "Then he's definitely not used to some good soul food."

"No ma'am, he's not."

Meanwhile, Reverend Smithers examined the menu, wire half-eyes resting down his nose. "Are you ladies finished discussing my disadvantaged palate?"

"Never!" I said. "Right, Della-Faye?"

The level of wonder rose inside me. I belonged somewhere, a place where I not only felt at home, but a place I wanted to share with an almost-perfect stranger.

I should have gone and visited Georgia. But I didn't. I stayed there at the VIP with Reverend Smithers and Della-Faye, and her strung-out niece tumbled in and asked for money, ten men ordered lunch, and we talked about everything, nothing, and maybe something of import in between. We didn't solve the world's problems or figure out how to end sickness, loneliness, and poverty. We just waited out the storm, sheltered from the rain, together. And somehow that was all we were called to do on that gray afternoon.

Jonah walked in, served himself up a heaping measure of banana pudding, and joined us at the counter.

Sean met me at Third Street Coffee later that evening. He'd been to see Georgia, and he looked as though he'd been scraped off a shoe.

I set down a mug of decaf onto a hand-painted table. Sean went off caffeine years ago in Richmond. "So spill it. What happened? You look horrible."

"We've got to make up our minds about the respirator and the feeding tube."

"She's not coming back, is she, Sean? Is there any hope?"

He shook his head. "Not really. She's totally gone."

And he set his face in his hands and sobbed and sobbed.

What seems like a lifetime ago, I would have felt a little embarrassed there in a coffeehouse seated next to a large bronze man with copper hair who was crying in anguish. Honestly, nobody looks good when they're crying gale force.

I simply held his hand, squeezing every so often, smiling at the passersby with an "I know this isn't really the place for this, but if you're a big person like I am you'll understand" apology. And I sipped my latte, hoping he didn't notice, and I remembered once again it was somewhat my fault he was weeping at this round table, that I'd set the gears in motion with my sense of revenge, and that maybe I wasn't only acting out against Georgia, but against God, too, who seemed to think it was okay to take away the only people who ever really cared about me.

We come to these realizations in the strangest places, don't we?

But I realized something else, foam atop my lip. That faith can be full of doubt, too. As long as the doubt recognizes that it is the intruder and not the landlord.

"You need to be singing again," I told Sean after the crying jag. We sipped on our second round of coffee. He'd pretty much cried himself out and didn't really want to talk about everything, which was fine by me because I'm a dreadful consoler. "I mean, you can talk all you want about me working with children, but, Sean, you're working at Subway."

"I just can't focus with Georgia like she is."

True. "Did you do much singing in Richmond?"

"Oh yes. Quite a bit. Nothing like I would have done had Georgia and I been together, though."

Georgia, Georgia, Georgia.

"Does she have any idea what she cost others?"

"She's in a coma, Fairly. I doubt it."

"Before that."

"Probably not."

"What was your favorite song to do together?"

He smiled. "You're going to laugh."

"Oh, I doubt it. Not after that crying jag."

"'You Are My Sunshine.'"

"Really?"

"Yep. That's it. Just that."

Lovely. And that made me sad, as sad as I should have been a long time before this.

"Yeah, we really had a special groove."

I heard that.

Clarissa

The girl feels the simple pleasure that new makeup in a drugstore bag dispatches. She swings it as she walks down the warm sidewalk. Fourteen years old! The mother said she could wear a little blush, some mascara, and pink lip gloss now. Just pink, though.

She leaps up the front steps onto the wooden porch, shoves her key in the lock knowing she should have a couple of hours to herself to experiment.

After emptying the bag into the spotless sink in the bathroom, she breathes deeply, splays her fingers on the edge of the porcelain, leans forward, and looks herself in the eyes. "Okay."

And she begins.

First a bit of blush. Not bright pink, for she's more peachy in tone. The contours of her cheeks are new as she brushes on the color. Not too bad for a first try.

Okay, not the actual first try. She did go to a slumber party once. The mother grounded her for a month when she found out.

Then the mascara. Very tricky. And she keeps blinking, dotting her lower lids with the inky blackness. She reaches for the roll of toilet paper.

"Clarissa!"

A fist pounds the door.

Oh! He shouldn't be home yet. Think, think.

Calm yourself. Remember how fun that party was, though?

"Reggie? You're home early."

Say it nice and bright and sweet. And young. Remember how young you are. Oh, Megan's mother thought you were so nice, didn't she?

She begins to put the makeup back in the bag.

The way you helped set out the food when all the other girls were listening to CDs.

"What are you doing in there, 'Rissa?"

"Going to the bathroom!"

They'd done their nails and their hair, too.

"What's that noise?"

"Just...girl stuff, Reggie."

"Let me in."

The door shakes as he yanks it again and again. It's an old house. An old door. Her hands shake as she throws the mascara into the bag.

The door opens with a loud bang. Fiery eyes below the blond curls send her stomach into tumbles.

"I knew you were lying to me! Give me that."

The cousin has been drinking.

The girl hands him the bag. He upends it, the items crashing to the black-and-white tile floor.

"Makeup! What do you need makeup for?"

"Mom said—"

"Don't lie to me. You want to party, don't you? I see how the guys look you up and down. You've been sneaking out at night, haven't you?"

"No," she says. "No, no, no. Nothing like that."

He grabs her arm, grimy nails digging into her bicep, and why wasn't he working at the garage? Did he get fired again?

"If you want to party, you can get it right here."

"Reggie! No! Get away!"

And she tries to beat him off, but he grabs her other arm and smashes it against the wall. She cries out as he presses his mouth against hers, crushing her lips into her teeth and his. She kicks, but he leaps clear.

"You'll get it when I say! And when I want to give it to you."

She cries out again as he pulls her hair and forces her into his bedroom. But as she falls onto the bed, the girl sees the small dumbbell on the nightstand. The cousin falls on top of her, and the weight, held tightly in her fist, crashes down on his head.

Just once.

Timed like a pro.

She runs from the house and longs to scream out for somebody to help her. TV Mom and Granddaddy Man are on a winter vacation in the Poconos. And nobody else is home these days, and if they are, they've turned up the afternoon running of *Friends* just a tad too loud.

Georgia

I'm scared of dying, to be honest. I know they're going to have to take me off of the machines eventually, when they're ready. And that's okay. I mean really, I made UG's and Sean's lives miserable. I can at least give them the time they need.

The ladies are coming for another show. I told them I liked the movie better than the play, and both Mom and Grandmom agreed, but, *Hey, it's always worth a shot, right, Georgia?*

And I said, *You said it,* as expected. Family dialogue, you know. So we agreed the next display would be a movie.

According to Mom, I still haven't let go of my offenses against God, which is why I'm subject to yet another display. Yes, Mom's doing fine, and that comforts me somewhat, but something sticks in my soul like a big piece of roast beef in my esophagus that just won't go down all the way no matter how hard I swallow.

And isn't that what it's all about? Trying to do more than accept the hardships and pain of life; to see the purpose, the grand design; to know there's a happy ending *before* we find ourselves walking the streets of gold? I mean, if all there is here on earth is heartache, what's the point? Why does God continue the game? If it was all about salvation and our eternal destiny, why didn't God just let Herod kill Jesus as a baby and be done with it?

But Jesus grew and loved and gave and showed us the way God would be if He were human.

Is that what I've missed, the imitation of Christ?

Is that what Sean always understood and I failed to recognize, even resented, and finally rejected? Is that why he gave me that book so long ago, because he knew?

They should be here any moment, I guess, but until then I close whatever eyes I have that feel like they're closing. The rest here in the pink feels like none other. Certainly not like a drunken stupor, I can tell you that! Can you imagine what it's like to be on a soft bed with lots of covers and pillows and down quilts, a bed as big as a king-size bed is to a baby, with bedding every bit as thick as it would be to a small child?

Well, there you have it.

Do we get to rest once we've passed on? Another question for Mom, I guess.

Yes, dear, we do. At least I do. But then I've always loved to sleep. Not like your father.

Oh good, you've come. Dad didn't like to sleep?

No! In fact, he still held on to those funny little-kid ways of bedtime feeling like a punishment. He didn't even like for me to go to bed early!

I never knew that about him.

He was a bit of a mystery to almost everyone.

But you?

Yes. I sometimes found it hard to believe he let go even around me. He didn't have an easy time of things, you know.

Dad? Oh please. He was the most confident person I ever saw. What do you mean?

It's his story to tell.

Mo-o-om!

Really. But let's just say you might try giving him the benefit of the doubt. Something you never did before.

Was that really my job? I was his daughter, for pity's sake.

Fair enough. He had a very hard time talking about his life before we met.

His childhood?

Primarily.

Oh, come on! Tell me, Mom. At least a little clue, okay?

He was a terrible stutterer.

Daddy? Really?

Yes. And he lisped too.

But he spoke beautifully.

He trained himself. Practiced for years and years. Got tired of being beaten up and called a fag. In junior high he was beaten to within an inch of his life.

So he only spoke when he absolutely had to?

Mom nods.

Those letters, Georgia. They revealed his heart. They said what he didn't trust his tongue to divulge.

Oh man.

Yeah. Not facing things never does anybody any good.

Why now, Mom?! Why am I learning all this now when it's too late?

Because you wouldn't learn it when you had the chance.

Let's just get to the movie. This is a load of jive.

All right, and I can't say I appreciate your tone. I'm still your mother.

Where's Grandmom?

I don't know, honey. I'm not omniscient.

The zone darkens, and once again the words appear on the screen, letting me know I'm in for yet another time of regret. The subtitle today: had you forgiven God.

A cute little musical number begins.

Is this a musical*?*

Yes! Mom turns, eyes glowing. *Isn't this exciting?*

Chorus girls holding big golden coins whirl and tap onto the screen.

The Gold Diggers? Oh, for pity's sake, Mom!

Well, I love it.

Can you imagine a group of dancing women being called the Gold Diggers these days?

She frowns. *Well, no. But aren't they cute? Now please, don't make this about nothing but me shushing you, all right?*

They sing in cutesy little "Santa Baby" voices, kicking their cute, dimpled Ziegfeld legs.

Here we go, pack your bags

Richmond calling, wearing rags

People hungry, people scared

You've got to be kidding me.

Sh!

Lonely, blue, and feeling bad

You can help them

Don't be sad.

Mom! This is the most ridiculous thing I've ever seen!

Oh, all right. You're a party pooper, you know that? She stands up. *Okay, girls, go on back. Miss Artsy-Fartsy doesn't like musicals.*

It's not that. It's just the inappropriate juxtaposition of—

Please. I was thinking of it as hybrid entertainment.

What's with the gold coins?

Treasures in heaven.

Oh. My. Word.

Don't judge it so hastily. You didn't give it a chance. And you should know better.

She twists back around in her chair, this one a pretty little French salon chair with gold upholstery. Matches her gorgeous Oriental-cut sheath dress nicely.

Why thank you! I like this one myself. Okay, how about Smell-o-vision?

Smell-o-vision?

Yep.

A remote appears in her hand and she clicks a button. A television appears in front of us, a space-age fifties TV. She clicks it again, and we start right in on the episode. Thank goodness I didn't have to sit through the title again!

Sean and I are pulling costumes over little heads as we laugh and dance to "The Monster Mash."

It was a graveyard smash.

A little creepy considering the circumstances, Mom.

I know. But do you smell the stew you made? And the bread the wino—or used-to-be wino who lives in the third bedroom down the hall—baked just an hour ago? Do you smell that?

Yes. Nice touch. I admit it.

The house is pretty, old and in need of a few updates here and there, but large and once grand, it definitely looks habitable. From where we stood in the entryway, bright colors bled in from the downstairs rooms: red, gold, green, a dusty purple. And the stairwell was painted sunshine yellow.

Downtown Richmond, still?

Nope. Baltimore. You all decided to move back home once the first year was up. You're near Patterson Park.

Nice place for Patterson Park!

Oh yes. You put in hundreds and hundreds of hours on that place.

Did I choose the colors?

Yes. You actually had a lot of artistic talent built in, but the music eclipsed it. You're a great cook, too.

No kidding?

You'd be surprised at what's locked inside people. Everybody's multigifted. Once I saw this film of what the world would be like if we all used our talents even fifty percent. It was electrifying.

The feel-good film of the year?

She shrugs. *Guess you have to see it to believe it.*

Are those my children?

See the two with the olive skin and dark-brown curls? They're yours and

Sean's. The other four are from various places. Two from Baltimore—the ones dressed as ghosts—brother and sister you adopted when they were only tots. He's seven and she's nine. The little pirate is from Bulgaria. And well, that tiny little cow—she came only the week before from South America.

Wow. Six kids!

Aren't they cute?

When was this supposed to be?

This month.

Oh, God. Really. Why?

Did I have children in the other scenario? The number-one scenario?

You sure did. These kids actually.

Sean hands out old pillowcases and says, "Head 'em on out. Hup-two-three-four. Hup-two-three-four!" He kisses me with an economical passion and opens the door. I grab a big mixing bowl full of popcorn balls wrapped in wax paper made earlier in the afternoon, sit on the porch on a swing badly needing a coat of paint. I'm thinking lime green.

That's exactly what you would have done.

I can feel my own happiness. And a little stress. Somehow I know that one of the residents, a young runaway, is lying to us about where she goes each night. It isn't work, I can tell you that.

Please tell me there were more chances, Mom.

Every letter Sean sent was a new chance, Georgia.

You can weep here in the pink. You can weep though you have no eyes. And you can feel tears of a sadness deeper than an ocean trench and wider than the sea itself.

Those children. Sean's and mine. Where are they?

They're not, of course, Georgia.

And the others?

I can't say I know, honey.

A piano version of "My Way" erupts.

Thanks, Mom.

On the television screen the children begin to argue about who gets to hold Sean's hand.

Mom laughs and clicks the remote, the set going dark. *Well, nothing's perfect.*

What about my music?

You're about to record your fifth album, and your fourth is up for a Grammy. Sean has been touring with Harry Connick Jr.

Really?!

Incredible, isn't it? Their voices were made to go together.

You know, I think George Bailey got a much better deal from Clarence than I'm getting from you, Mom.

Maybe George deserved better. Look at all the sacrifices he made for people early on.

So what you're saying is I got what I deserved? Is that what God is really all about?

Mom crosses her arms and looks very momlike. *Are you honestly saying you'd have taken one more chance, Georgia?*

The load settles for good upon my shoulders.

I can't go back, I whisper.

I know, baby doll.

Clarissa

The girl pulls up great chunks of her hair, hacks them off with the scissors, wincing as the blades pull and bite. Big chunks. Pretty curls. Pretty hair.

She smashes the blush and squeezes out the lip gloss, flushing them both down the toilet. Pulling the wand from the mascara, she breathes heavily through her nose, then writes one word on the mirror in turgid black streaks.

NO!

Into the bag she slips the containers. She ties a bandana over her butchered locks, walks down the steps to the trash can at the side of the house.

Now. Supper. What should she make?

Fairly

It was one of those superb days I couldn't have dreamed up. Reverend Smithers agreed to come over for dinner when I invited him after church. I decided to be Episcopal that Sunday. He said he'd love to meet the cult. I really should stop calling them—well, us, actually—the cult, shouldn't I?

He helped me slice up onions for the burgers that Sean was grilling outside. "I'm so very glad we met last week, Fairly. However, the fact that you introduced me to the lovely Della-Faye has been a horrifying experience for my waistline!"

"Five pounds in one week?"

"Yes."

"Me too." I handed him a tomato Uncle G brought back from the Saturday farmers' market the day before. "And still on the rise."

"The apple cobbler is something you can't quite get out of your mind, isn't it?"

"Yes. It's torture to wake up in the middle of the night with a hankering for Della-Faye's cobbler."

"Oh, quite right! That happened to me last night."

Sean walked into the kitchen from the back door, a delightful puff of grill smoke following him. "Ten minutes. Tops."

"We'll be ready. Do you like blue cheese?" I asked Smithers.

"On a burger?"

"Where else?"

I realized then that food is something we all have in common. The love of it, the care in the preparation, the joy in the eating, the communion of the gathering. "Do you view eating as a spiritual experience?" I asked him.

"Highly."

"Would you lead us in communion tonight?"

"I'd be quite honored."

So the bunch of us gathered, Peg and Blaine, Gracen, Uncle G, Sean, and me; Old Al, who had fallen off the wagon but was back on; Alex and Melissa the cabbies showed up too, a nice surprise. We passed around a seven-grain hamburger bun and a goblet of merlot. And we feasted not only on the One we belonged to, but on all the possibilities of life in God, an abundance found in the bread and in the cup and in the way of Jesus.

We remembered the Savior, His death, and His life.

And Gracen said, "Thanks be to God," when he dipped his bread in the wine.

The body and blood of Christ.

The reverend raised his glass at the end and said, *"Le chaim!"*

And I thought, yes, that's it exactly. To life.

We only have so much time on this earth. I decided it would be a shame to waste even a day.

And I decided, after many years of deliberation, truly, that my favorite kind of volcano was not the kind that exploded up into the air, but the steady flow that meandered slowly in heated purpose toward the cooling waters of the sea, creating new ground.

Sean had left about an hour earlier, the house was quiet, and Uncle G and I rested on his sofa with mugs of chai. I read another cozy mystery while he tip-tapped a few e-mails. His tip-taps comforted me.

"It's all set, Fairly. My sabbatical officially starts tomorrow."

"What are you going to do?"

"I'm going to get up early and pray right off the bat. I've always wanted to do that."

"You don't now?"

"No. I've never been much of a prayer type. Not that I'm proud of that."

"Wow. You seem like that type."

He shut his laptop. "And then I'm going to run, shower, read, read, and read. At the hospital, of course."

"Sounds good."

"For about a week."

"Then what?"

"I don't know. We'll see where God takes me."

I sipped my tea. "You know, God does some crazy stuff."

"Yeah. Who'd have ever thought you'd be here?"

"Not me."

"Me either, to tell you the truth."

I tucked my feet up beneath me. "So why didn't I see it before now?"

"I'm not following you."

"I went to church all of my growing-up years. My parents were pretty progressive people, you know that. An artist and a social worker? Why do you think it took me so long to *get* God?"

"Who knows, Fairly? That's probably a bad question. Nobody *gets* God. He's a little beyond our imaginings."

"So what's the better one?"

He looked up. "How about something like, 'What's God got up ahead for me that coming to Him before this would have made impossible?' "

"I've got to tell you, it never really felt like I was running from God. More like, well, trying to get Him in some kind of focus. He always felt like such a blur."

"So maybe now was the season He revealed Himself to you in the way you could finally grasp."

"Exactly!"

"Good of Him to do that."

"I suspect He'll keep on going with it."

"I suspect so."

We sat in silence for a while longer, and I thought about Mom and Dad and how they were most likely delighted about my change of heart. But honestly, it feels so different from how it was described in my church growing up. I never felt like I made some big intellectual decision, or some conscious giving up of my will. I felt more like I'd come to a realization, an understanding, and, well, the rest just followed along. Sort of like realizing you like mayonnaise after years of turning it down. Well, of *course* you're going to keep using mayonnaise, you love it so much! Who makes that an intellectual decision?

Maybe for some people faith is a choice, but for me, faith was a happening, a simple lifting of a fog, and once confronted with something so beautiful and gracious, I couldn't look away. And when I felt this touch of Christ, the thought of letting go of Him would be like deciding not to breathe.

Maybe I'm lucky that way.

"So, Uncle G, I've got this idea."

"You look pretty serious."

"Yeah, but it's fabulous. You met the reverend. And you've met Della-Faye. What if we get churches like that together somehow?"

"Stuffy Episcopalians and African Baptists."

"Yes. We could do a lot for the city, for so many things. People like Reverend Smithers and Della-Faye need to be together. And me. Me too, Uncle G. I need to be with them."

"Where will you go to church?"

"I'm fine here with the cult."

He leaned forward. "The *cult*?" Then he laughed and threw himself back against the cushions of the sofa. "Oh, Fairly. That's fantastic!"

"You have to admit I'm onto something, though. Reverend Smithers fit right in."

"I'd still like to know what you have in mind that will get everybody in such a lovefest. People have tried it for years and years. Nothing seems to work for long."

I did have an idea actually. And it was big. "A citywide communion service, right in Duncan Park."

"It'll never work."

I bopped him on the leg. "Get thee behind me! You were always the one with vision."

"Maybe I'm just tired, Fairly."

"Go to bed then. I'll finish up in the kitchen."

He patted my knee. "Let's talk about this tomorrow. It really does sound rather interesting."

He took his mug to the kitchen, then appeared back before me. "You know, your cousin is weighing heavily on me. I just don't know what to do." And he left.

At the sink I washed the goblet from communion and I thought about it. Really now, what was the one thing all Christians had in common, the one practice we do over and over again?

"Do this to remember Me."

Maybe we'd just forgotten what we were here for.

Maybe everything we do is a communion of sorts, remembering Christ by being like Him.

Georgia

I've been off the respirator for a while now. It's just IVs and a feeding tube. I can't imagine what I look like with that thing running out of my nose. At least they refused to have the stomach tube inserted. Kind of lets me know I won't be attached to this stuff for years.

Mom? Mom?

Yes, baby doll?

Oh good. I have a favor to ask you. I need to know something.

What is that, dear?

I'd like to know what my life would be like if I went back down. If I woke up.

Mom's lips pursed.

You know something, don't you?

Yes.

You know whether or not I'm going to live, don't you?

Yes.

And you still have that great poker face. You're not going to let on, are you?

I'm doing my best not to. I can't drum up a movie at a whim, but how about if I play a little music and you sleep awhile?

The zone darkens. Her beautiful fingers caress the hidden piano.

I am gone.

I'm playing organ at All Souls Episcopal. Sean is standing in the balcony singing, leading the congregation. The music from the congregation, the singing, the parts, the community of song, fills the sanctuary. Sean looks back at me and smiles.

I feel his love for me.

We go back to the apartment I almost lived in, and we take a Sunday roast out of the oven, watch a movie as we eat. We kiss each other asleep before napping.

"What a nice life we have," I tell him.

When I awaken, who knows how long afterward, Mom sits quietly nearby. I tell her the dream.

Mom, that was nice. But do you know what else happens?

She looks up, then nods, listens to something I obviously can't hear, and says, *That's about it.*

Really? Just playing the organ in a church?

I'm afraid so.

So in other words, I had my chances to do something big and I blew it?

Pretty much, yes, I guess. But I don't see what the fuss is. Look, you and Sean are happy. The congregation is singing, everything sounds so lovely.

What about jazz? Do I get to play jazz again?

I don't think so, Georgia. At least it doesn't seem that way to me if your dream is any indication.

Why not?

Because—I'm not positive about this now—I think that if you go back, you won't remember any of this. Not really.

But why don't I play jazz?

There's rent to pay, bills due, and you don't want to take that kind of chance again is my guess.

I won't want to slip up. At least I'm not drinking. Maybe going into the clubs and playing is too much of a temptation. Do you think that could be it?

Maybe. I know it would be hard for anyone to do.

Sometimes you just can't start over, can you?

Not really. We only can work with what we've got, with who we are.

Surely there's something more than this later on!

I can't say, Georgie. I'm not God.

No! I want to know more! I want to see what's going to happen.

I'm sorry, Georgia. I guess it's just not allowed.

Well, that stinks! That really stinks.

Oh, baby doll…

Just go away! Leave me alone.

Mom's face melts. *I'm sorry, Georgia.*

And she fades away.

What about Sean? Doesn't he deserve better? He was the innocent bystander in all of this. How could I have done something like this to someone I loved so much? Why does he have to bear the brunt of my sin?

Sin always leads to sorrow. My Sunday-school teacher, Mrs. Barker, told me that years ago.

Every time I tipped that bottle, I knew. Oh, I know all the old stories. I was wounded psychologically; I couldn't help it.

But I always knew I needed help. I always knew it, and I never cried out.

UG seems very peaceful this morning. I had a hard time breathing on my own last night, so they intubated me again. I think that sabbatical he was talking about began today. A page flips occasionally, and he does that little nose-breathing thing every so often. The chair squeaks sometimes.

What I don't hear is the cell phone ringing.

The nurse named Robin asked him about it earlier, and he said he wasn't going to be carrying it around anymore. "I'm becoming a sort of urban hermit."

"Like a monk?" she asked.

"Yes, I think."

"So are you going to start making cheese and fudge to sell?"

"Who knows?" His voice held a smile. I think he kind of likes her, which means…so much for being a monk!

I can amuse myself even in here.

I wonder what he's reading?

Oh good, nurse shoes squeak in that particular timbre, which means my leopard lady returns. Her shoes have a certain throatiness to their squeak.

"Good morning again, Mr. Pfeiffer!"

"Hi, Joanne."

Joanne. I don't think I've ever heard him use her name before. Joanne. I like that. Of course, something like Mercedes would have fit my mental picture a little better.

"How's she doing this morning?" Joanne asks.

"Same."

"Oh, sweet girl. Let's get her cleaned up then."

The chair scrapes away from my bed. "Time for a cup of tea for me. Would you like one?"

"No thanks. Got my travel mug filled to the brim."

He leaves, and the soothing touch of Joanne begins.

Why is it I can feel the nice touches but nothing painful?

Hmm.

She purrs. I cuddle into the warmth.

Clarissa

Leonard the Granddaddy Man pulls her close and hugs her with the little strength he has left these days. "I can hardly believe it's been nine years since I moved in and saw you at that kitchen window, young lady."

"I don't want to go."

"Oh, you'll be fine. I'm only a phone call away." He turns his face toward his daughter. "Isn't that right, Dianne?"

"Anytime, Clarissa. Call collect too."

Leonard reaches behind him and lifts a box off the kitchen counter. "Here's a little present from the two of us."

Clarissa receives it, smooth fingers skating over the gnarled bumps of the hands holding the brightly colored package. She opens the paper carefully.

"A memory book!"

Each page tells a story of grace and kindness: the trip to Six Flags, the Fourth of July picnic at their church, Christmas Eve caroling, the jack-o'-lanterns they carved each year, the box of dress-ups Dianne had kept in the spare bedroom for Clarissa to use. The overnights. Leonard's famous waffle breakfasts.

As Clarissa's family drives away, her friends stand out on their porch, tears baptizing their faces, and wave until the van turns the corner for good.

She can't believe they've moved away from that old house. And she thinks about the new place. It's old too. Lots of cleaning to do.

The mother pulls into a gas station somewhere in West Virginia. "I thought sure we'd make it farther on that tank. Figures."

The girl pulls on the door latch and hops out. The cousin does the same from the back of the minivan.

"Clarissa! Go get us a couple of Cokes. Reggie, don't forget to make a pit stop."

Reggie pushes the girl forward.

"Hey!" she cries. "Stop that."

"Stupid."

"Whatever."

She hurries toward the store. In the reflection of the plate-glass window, she sees the mother striking up a conversation with a dark-haired woman pumping gas in front of their van.

Seems like a nice lady.

The brother pounds on the restroom door. She wants to relieve herself, but she can't seem to let go.

"Let me in, Clarissa. Right now. Or I'll tell Mom how you really are. I'll tell her about Nick."

And who knows what the mother will do? Probably freak. Commit suicide like she's been on the brink of doing since the father left.

"I mean it!" he hisses.

"No."

"Then I'll kill her. And then where will you be?"

With Leonard the Granddaddy Man?

The girl opens the door and lets him in, but as he reaches for her she slips out. Not this time. In fact, probably not ever again. She doesn't know how she'll keep him away, but somehow she will.

Fairly

I wasn't sure why I was called into the room, but apparently Uncle G and Sean thought it was the right thing. We sat down at my uncle's kitchen table. No tea. Just clean linoleum, shining chrome, the smell of pine cleaner, and the gentle tones of Vince Guaraldi's "Cast Your Fate to the Wind" floating in from the living room.

Sean laid his hands flat on the surface of the table. "It's time, Geoffrey. We can't just let her rot. You've seen the CT scans. We need to take her off. It was one thing when she was breathing on her own, but not now."

Uncle G. "I don't know if I can handle watching her die like that."

"But that's about you, Geoffrey. Not Georgia."

"What do you think, Fairly?" my uncle asked.

"First of all, it's not my decision to make."

"But if it was?" Sean asked.

"Well, if you think about it, she's already died twice. The only thing that brought her back was technology."

"That's true," Uncle G said. "But are we playing God to let her go?"

"Maybe we're playing God to keep intervening in something that's inevitable. Think of what we're keeping her from."

We just stared at our hands for I don't know how long. I didn't really care. Sometimes time isn't our problem at all.

Uncle G finally looked up. "Two more weeks. That's all I ask."

And Sean nodded.

So I stopped by Reverend Smither's church, and he brewed me a cup of tea himself. "You are simply a breath of fresh air, Fairly, my dear."

"Why, thank you!" I took a sip. "Good tea!"

"Thank you. Right. So what did you get last time you went to Della-Faye's?"

"The breaded pork chops in gravy."

"Oh my, yes! Aren't they delightful? And greens. Who knew?"

"Precisely. So, let's finish our tea, and I'll take you there for lunch. I have something to run by you and Della-Faye, and I might as well save my breath and tell you together."

He sipped. "Sounds intriguing. But then you do seem to be a rather intriguing person."

"Thank you."

"So while we drink our tea, tell me a little about yourself, your past, your plans. If you don't mind, that is."

As we sip, I tell him about Mom and Dad, about college and high school and my life. I tell him about Hort, and he raises his brows. And even with that quirky love affair in the mix, I realize I haven't done a whole lot of living yet, that there's so much in front of me if I decide to take it.

This is a matter of will and choice, and now, with faith rolled into the mix, I draw a sense of breathless expectation into myself, look up, and think, *I'm ready for this.*

Georgia

Okay, I really didn't mean to send Mom away like that. There's just so much a woman can handle, even in this state, without falling apart.

It's all right, baby doll, I understand.

Mom?

She spreads her arms as she appears. Then she holds a hand up to her mouth and laughs. *I was going to say, "In the flesh," but that wouldn't apply, would it?*

Have a seat. I could use the company.

I know last time was difficult for you.

If I could've made myself die, I would have.

I know. She sits in a La-Z-Boy, cranks up the footrest, and swivels around to face me. *I'll tell you something more encouraging if you're interested.*

I don't know if I can handle any more.

I think it'll give you a little peace if that's what you want.

Okay.

I hear a strange sort of music—ethereal really. And a familiar voice lies over the top.

Sean?

Uh-huh.

Tribal voices join in.

Is he in Africa?

He is! Mom's eyes dance. *He and Fairly have literally saved a village. It started with a well Fairly paid for, uh, next year, actually.*

Fairly?! Don't tell me they end up together.

The music is so haunting, yet joyful.

Well, no. Fairly and Sean? Honestly, Georgia.

Does he end up with anybody? I really do not want to know the answer.

Yes.

Who?!

Mom reaches into her pocket and pulls out a photo. *This is eight years from now.*

Fairly holds hands with an African child. My cousin's hair falls in dreadlocks, making her a cross between the Crocodile Hunter and Mama Cass. She's plump! Her T-shirt reads Lexington Faith Community Partnership. On it, in stylized artwork, are a loaf of bread and a goblet, a grail.

She's a doll.

I know. Isn't she cute?

Fairly looks so grounded! Did she draw that logo?

Probably, Georgia.

Another child, blacker than soot, has thrown his arms around Fairly's legs. It's obvious she's laughing and reaching into her pocket for something.

What's she reaching for?

A butter cookie.

I never thought I'd see my cousin like this. Does she do this in between flights to auctions?

No, she'll do auctions in between these trips. She's become quite the humanitarian.

So she still loves her crazy furniture?

Not as much. But those forays will keep her in the house on Jefferson Street and help finance her trips. Not to mention the wealthy clients adding their bits to help. She still helps out in the neighborhood too. Just out of frame, her next-door neighbor, who just graduated from college at this point, is giving out food. She was at risk, to say the least, when Fairly met her. Here's another photo.

In a pathway between two tents, a dark-headed girl about nine years old leaps into Sean's waiting arms. He captures her midair.

The baby from South America? The little baby dressed up like a cow?

Uh-huh. She'll become the love of his life. Mom nods. *Some things just can't be changed.*

But she wasn't in the picture in yesterday's movie.

No.

But you said she and Sean were meant to be together.

Yes, I sure did.

So that means…I have to go, don't I? I can't go back down?

Honey, that choice was never yours to begin with.

I understood. I don't know how or why it became so clear. Why I didn't just die and go on, why I had to reside in the pink zone. I wasn't really ready to face God. Somewhere along the way I'd hardened my heart, stiffened my neck, become my own worst enemy. And maybe God wanted me to enter in under the best, the brightest of terms. Maybe He wanted me to see that my death was the final chance He was giving me to shine, to sacrifice myself not to the bottle but for the good of those who loved me, and I needed to take that with all the joy I'd been allotted but never used.

Fairly seems utterly wonderful, Mom!

I know.

I doubt she'll have to spend time in a coma to come to grips.

I think you're right. Your coma did her a world of good.

What's the little girl's name, Mom?

Ella. After you. He'll name her after you.

I wonder if Ella will go on to do all the things I was made to do but never did. I wonder if Sean will be the father she needs to succeed?

Of course he will, baby doll. Sean will show her the world, and he'll lay the possibilities before her feet like a magic carpet. Living with a love like that demands it.

And she'll step on and ride it, won't she, Mom?

That, Georgia Ella, will be up to her, won't it?

I thumb through the stack of snapshots. Fairly and Sean dishing out meals, Fairly surrounded by excited kids. They pump out fresh water in another shot, and my favorite picture of all is an evening scene, a riotous sunset the backdrop as they sit in camp chairs around a great fire spitting sparks like a volcano. Fairly plays on her old flute, and Sean sings. Reverend Smithers is frozen in midclap. So he's somehow in the picture. And what? I hear a guitar.

In fact, I hear the music clearly again. So beautiful.

UG's guitar! In the next picture there sits my uncle, strumming away, eyes closed. He's never looked so peaceful.

Mom?

Yes, Georgia?

What would it look like if everybody nurtured everybody else with their talents?

Mom touches my chin, and this time, I feel it. I feel her touch, her warmth. And I am twelve again, and I am whole. *It would look like heaven, Georgia. It would look like heaven.*

I want Dad to come too, when it's time.

He'd like that. He's very different now, you know.

So am I.

Yes, so are we all.

I'll never get to read those letters, will I?

No.

But it won't matter, will it?

Not one bit, Georgia.

Dad?

His form accumulated in the atmosphere as the light changed from pink to a blinding yellow. *Ready, Georgie?*

Yes.

And the three of us walked away, hand in hand.

Fairly

Georgia lived only a minute after they removed her from the respirator this time. Sean held one hand, Uncle G the other, and I stood by the foot of the bed watching them, as if my beholding them somehow captured the moment for its importance. I grasped the warmth of her ankle.

Naturally it was a small funeral. Just the cult, Uncle G, Sean, Jesse, Drea from the Ten O'Clock Club, and me. We didn't bother with viewings or a service. We stood at the graveside and did a lot of crying, though, and I wore that old dress my mom wore at Aunt Polly's funeral. Seemed only fitting. If a little snug.

We kept saying, "She's happier now and in a much better place," like people always mutter at funerals, but this time, we really believed it completely.

As it turned out, the interment took place on the same day I moved into my house on Jefferson Street. I threw on some jeans and buzzed over to direct the movers.

And I thought I'd gotten rid of a lot of stuff!

That little house is practically filled to the ceiling.

What a rushed day. Tonight, Solo and his boys move into a small rental house down the street. He'll be teaching religion at Lexington Catholic High. We're all meeting at Della-Faye's for supper.

After I watched the truck pull away, I met my new next-door neighbor, a young teenage girl. She stood on her porch looking at me, gave me a shy kind of wave, so I called, "Come on over! I'm Fairly, your new neighbor."

She hopped down her walkway, opened up the iron gate in the fence surrounding her yard, swept up her hair in one of those giant clips, and in several graceful bounds met me on my porch.

"We just moved in a little while ago too."

"What grade are you in?"

"Ninth."

Her eyes told me she was really ninety. She shoved her hands into the pockets of her jeans.

"Well, come on over anytime. Maybe we can figure out this town together."

"I'd really like that."

"Want a Coke?"

"Yeah."

"Come on in."

And so she did. And we sat on the old counter in the kitchen and drank our sodas straight from the cans.

"What are your hobbies?" I asked.

"I love fashion. I'd like to be a model or a designer someday."

"I'm a designer. Interior designer. Not fashion."

"Really?" Her eyes, a vague color I really couldn't put my finger on, widened.

"Yep."

She picked up a thermometer that somehow made its way out of one of the boxes.

I set down my drink. "I used to break those things on purpose and play with the little balls of mercury."

"Me too!"

"I'll bet that worries your mom as much as it did mine."

She just shook her head. "Nah, not really. My mom's under a lot of pressure."

"What's your name, by the way?"

"Clarissa."

"Wanna come with me to dinner tonight? A bunch of us are meeting over at the VIP."

"Sure."

"Let me warn you. We're a crazy bunch. But everybody's really nice."

She nods. "I had the nicest neighbors back in Chicago."

"I'll try to live up to their standards."

She takes a sip of her drink. "You're off to a pretty good start."

It's a wonderful thing when you start to live.

About the Author

Lisa Samson, author of eighteen books and winner of the Christy Award, recently moved to urban Lexington, Kentucky, with her husband, Will, and their three children. They live in a drafty house that's older than all five of them put together, and they have the sky-high electric bills to prove it. Find out more by visiting her Web site, www.lisasamson.com.